You first met Annie in
The Comeback of Con MacNeill!

* * *

**Her life was complicated
enough without her taking on
a big, tough cop with his own
emotional baggage.**

She sighed. "I'm sorry."

His face was still carefully blank. "I don't want
your apologies. I don't want your pity. And I
don't want your damn gratitude, either."

Annie put up her chin. "Maddox…I'm a
convicted felon on probation. A witness in an
attempted murder case. Before you get mixed up
with me, maybe you should think about what
you *do* want."

The memory of his words whispered between
them, roughening her nerve endings. *You are
what I want, Annie. You've always been what I
want.*

"Is that an offer?" he asked quietly.

Her heart skipped. W[h]
said yes?

Dear Reader,

The year is ending, and as a special holiday gift to you, we're starting off with a 3-in-1 volume that will have you on the edge of your seat. *Special Report,* by Merline Lovelace, Maggie Price and Debra Cowan, features three connected stories about a plane hijacking and the three couples who find love in such decidedly unusual circumstances. Read it—you won't be sorry.

A YEAR OF LOVING DANGEROUSLY continues with Carla Cassidy's *Strangers When We Married,* a reunion romance with an irresistible baby and a couple who, I know you'll agree, truly do belong together. Then spend 36 HOURS with Doreen Roberts and *A Very...Pregnant New Year's.* This is one family feud that's about to end...at the altar!

Virginia Kantra's back with *Mad Dog and Annie,* a book that's every bit as fascinating as its title—which just happens to be one of my all-time favorite titles. I guarantee you'll enjoy reading about this perfect (though they don't know it yet) pair. Linda Randall Wisdom is back with *Mirror, Mirror,* a good twin/bad twin story with some truly unexpected twists—and a fabulous hero. Finally, read about a woman who has *Everything But a Husband* in Karen Templeton's newest—and keep the tissue box nearby, because your emotions will really be engaged.

And, of course, be sure to come back next month for six more of the most exciting romances around—right here in Silhouette Intimate Moments.

Enjoy!

Leslie Wainger

Leslie J. Wainger
Executive Senior Editor

Please address questions and book requests to:
Silhouette Reader Service
U.S.: 3010 Walden Ave., P.O. Box 1325, Buffalo, NY 14269
Canadian: P.O. Box 609, Fort Erie, Ont. L2A 5X3

Mad Dog and Annie

VIRGINIA KANTRA

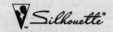

INTIMATE MOMENTS™

Published by Silhouette Books

America's Publisher of Contemporary Romance

For my mother, Phyllis Kantra,
who always found time to drive to the library;

and my mother-in-law, Therese Ritchey, my Ohio sales force.

Special thanks to Joan Cunningham, for her continuing
patience with my legal questions; to John Aldridge,
for explaining guns and fireworks; to Nancy Northcott,
for sharing her courtroom experience and to Pam Baustian and
Judith Stanton, for the usual reasons.

SILHOUETTE BOOKS

ISBN 0-373-27118-2

MAD DOG AND ANNIE

Copyright © 2000 by Virginia Kantra Ritchey

This edition published by arrangement with Harlequin Books S.A.

Visit Silhouette at www.eHarlequin.com

Printed in U.S.A.

Books by Virginia Kantra

VIRGINIA KANTRA

credits her enthusiasm for strong heroes and courageous heroines to a childhood spent devouring fairy tales. After graduating from Northwestern University with honors in English, she shared her love of books as a children's storyteller. She still visits classrooms on Valentine's Day dressed as the Queen of Hearts.

When her youngest child started school, Virginia fulfilled her dream of writing full-time. Her first book, *The Reforming of Matthew Dunn,* won Romance Writers of America's Golden Heart Award for Best Romantic Suspense, received the Holt Medallion and was nominated by *Romantic Times Magazine* as Best First Series Romance in 1998. Her second book, *The Passion of Patrick MacNeill,* was a Golden Heart finalist and Maggie Award winner, a *Romantic Times Magazine* Top Pick and the winner of a W.I.S.H. Award.

Virginia is married to her college sweetheart, a musician disguised as an executive. They live in Raleigh, North Carolina, with three children, two cats, a dog and various blue-tailed lizards that live under the siding of their home. Her favorite thing to make for dinner is reservations.

Desire

 #1333 Irresistible You
Barbara Boswell

#1334 Slow Fever
Cait London

 #1335 A Season for Love
BJ James

#1336 Groom of Fortune
Peggy Moreland

#1337 Monahan's Gamble
Elizabeth Bevarly

 #1338 Expecting the Boss's Baby
Leanne Banks

Romance

 #1486 Sky's Pride and Joy
Sandra Steffen

#1487 Hunter's Vow
Susan Meier

 #1488 Montana's Feisty Cowgirl
Carolyn Zane

 #1489 Rachel and the M.D.
Donna Clayton

#1490 Mixing Business...with Baby
Diana Whitney

#1491 His Special Delivery
Belinda Barnes

Special Edition

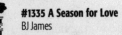 **#1363 The Delacourt Scandal**
Sherryl Woods

#1364 The McCaffertys: Thorne
Lisa Jackson

#1365 The Cowboy's Gift-Wrapped Bride
Victoria Pade

Rumor Has It... **#1366 Lara's Lover**
Penny Richards

#1367 Mother in a Moment
Allison Leigh

Here Come the Brides **#1368 Expectant Bride-To-Be**
Nikki Benjamin

Intimate Moments

#1045 Special Report
Merline Lovelace/Maggie Price/
Debra Cowan

A Year of Loving Dangerously **#1046 Strangers When We Married**
Carla Cassidy

#1047 A Very...Pregnant New Year's
Doreen Roberts

#1048 Mad Dog and Annie
Virginia Kantra

#1049 Mirror, Mirror
Linda Randall Wisdom

#1050 Everything But a Husband
Karen Templeton

Chapter 1

"**I** heard he shot that boy, and the department fired him."

The comment ricocheted under the normal lunch crowd noises, shocking as a gunshot in the cheerful dining room. Ann Cross, topping drinks one table over, flinched and slopped iced tea onto the varnished wood.

She swiped at the spill with a towel. She was getting to be some kind of expert at cleaning up her own messes, she thought wryly. "Sorry." She smiled at the offended patron. She couldn't afford to lose her tip or, worse, cost her friend Val a customer. "Can I get you anything else?"

"N-o-o-o, I guess not."

Resolutely, Ann disregarded the woman's disgruntled tone. "Well, you just let me know if you change your mind."

She picked up her pitcher. A positive attitude, that's what she needed. But over at the next table, the voice continued, low with scandal and sharp with relish. "...saw it on the Atlanta evening news. His father must be mortified."

Her companion shook her head. "But the newspaper said

he was a hero. My cousin sent me a column right out of the *Journal-Constitution.*''

Ann didn't want to listen. She shouldn't want to listen. She knew from firsthand experience how hurtful the town gossips could be, and how wrong. But as the first woman—it was Gladys Baggett, the receptionist over at First Baptist—spoke again, Ann stopped, snared by a name. Trapped by a memory.

''I don't see how you can defend him. I always said that Maddox Palmer would come to no good.''

Maddox. Ann's hand tightened on the pitcher. Another one of her Life Mistakes.

Oh, Lord. And now he'd *shot* somebody?

''Maybe not as long as he stayed in this town,'' the other woman agreed dryly.

''Well, he's back. Mackenzie Ward saw him at the bank. Shameless as sin and handsomer than ever, she said.'' The church secretary broke off to glance at Ann, her steel-rimmed glasses glinting with reproach.

Ann cleared her throat. ''More tea?''

''I believe I will.'' Gladys sat back and patted her mouth, smudging the napkin with Carnal Carnation. ''And how are dear little Mitchell and that handsome husband of yours?''

Ann stiffened. Her son was fine. Her divorce would be final in just a few weeks. And neither the health of her son nor the state of her marriage was anybody's business but her own. ''They're fine, thank you. Enjoy your meal.''

Gladys's whisper pursued her across the dining room. ''It was so…trusting of the MacNeills to hire her, don't you think? Do you suppose Val counts the silverware every night?''

Ann quailed inside. Biddies. Returning to the hostess station, she pulled on the social mask she'd learned to wear as Rob's wife, determined not to show that she heard or cared what the town of Cutler thought.

It never thought much of Annie Barclay Cross, that was

for sure. Nobody expected any of the Barclays to amount to much. It was as if the smell of her parents' farm clung to them even in town, a betraying mix of chickens and drunkenness and defeat. The only thing Ann had ever accomplished in her mother's eyes or the town's mind was to turn one night of fumbled sex with the local football hero into marriage and an upscale house on Stonewall Drive. Oh, they'd all whispered enough at the wedding, Ann remembered, but they'd approved.

Nobody approved of her now.

Except Val, she thought with a squeeze of gratitude.

The kitchen door swung open and Val bumped through in a soiled cook's apron, her blond gypsy curls in a neat French braid and a row of silver hoops dangling from one ear.

She surveyed her crowded restaurant with pride. "You doing all right out here?"

Ann smiled. "Checking up on me?"

"No, of course not. Well, maybe I am, a little. Looking out for you, I mean. There's a difference."

Ann had learned the hard way not to expect anyone to look out for her, ever.

"Everything's fine," she said.

"Okay." Val tossed her head, making the silver hoops dance. "Hey, did you hear? Mad Dog Palmer's back in town."

Despite her gratitude at the change of subject, Ann felt her stomach drop. "I heard something. How did you know?"

"Oh, Mother called last night. She had it from Betty Lou Prickett who had it from Mackenzie—"

"—Ward at the bank," Ann finished for her.

Val chuckled. "That's it. The Cutler grapevine. It never fails, and it never forgets."

Never. Sudden frustration closed Ann's throat. She could change her name, change her life, earn a salary and support her son, and in Cutler she would always be the Barclay girl who tricked poor Rob Cross into marriage and then mixed him up in that trouble over at the bank.

Seven months ago, Ann had pleaded guilty to helping her husband steal twenty thousand dollars from her best friend. He'd been convicted on the strength of her testimony. But when the theft was first uncovered, Rob had also attacked Val and set fire to her restaurant. Charged with both crimes, he was still awaiting a second trial for arson and attempted murder. Town opinion remained stubbornly on his side. But in Ann's heart, she knew her husband was guilty.

And so was she, for somehow allowing it to happen.

At her sudden silence, Val's face turned a deeper shade of pink. "Oh, shoot, honey, I didn't mean— I don't want you to ever think Con and I—"

They were the same age, but there were times Ann felt years older. "It's all right," she said gently. "I'm the one who can't forget what I owe both of you."

Val rolled her eyes. "Oh, please. You don't owe us anything."

Ann set her jaw. "Not according to the court."

"I've told you we can work something out. You don't need to repay—"

Ann stopped her, more tempted by the offer than Val could know. Money was tight. Mitchell needed shoes for basketball and a dresser that wasn't constructed of cardboard. But then, her son needed lots of things she couldn't give him. Like a father who cared about them.

"My probation officer says I do. And I want to, Val. I need to. Anyway, aren't you supposed to be in the kitchen nagging your other staff now?"

Val laughed reluctantly. "Remind me to resent that remark later when I have time," she said, and went back to marshal her kitchen forces.

Ann went to work, too, seating a mother and daughter out shopping, busing a neglected table, making sure the dining room ran smoothly. She enjoyed her job, despite the occasional whispers. It wasn't just that she was unfit for anything else or unlikely to be offered any other position in town. She took pleasure in the cleanliness and order, took pride in being responsible for the fresh flowers on the tables and the changing displays of wicker and North Carolina pottery on the walls.

Snatching a couple of dirty glasses, she got busy, got moving, got her mind off Rob's latest threats and Mitchell's outgrown sneakers and the things she did and should have done with Maddox Palmer back in high school.

No regrets, she reminded herself. Figure out what has to be done now, and do it. After nine years of having the spunk and the tar whaled out of her, initiative still came hard. But she was learning, she thought with satisfaction. In the past year, she'd had to learn.

The cheery little bell over the door summoned her back to the hostess station. She grabbed a menu and a smile to welcome the new customer and then stopped dead and let both of them slide.

It was him. Maddox Palmer, in the flesh. In jeans, she corrected herself, and a tan T-shirt that almost matched the color of his skin. She squeezed the menu tighter. This time the Cutler grapevine was right. He *was* handsomer than ever.

He had to be over thirty now, big and broad and somehow harder. Solid. His face had a lot more lines. Well, he was three years older than her, though only two years ahead in school. He'd been kept back in first grade, she remembered, the year his mama died. He had thick brown hair that his new short cut couldn't tame and hooded eyes that still saw right through her, and a juvenile-delinquent slouch that made him look tough and ready to react to whatever punch life threw at him. He dangled a cigarette between two fingers of his right hand, and he still had that not-a-dimple in his chin that tempted every good girl to press a finger to it.

Ann damned the way her heart speeded up just at the sight

of him. She'd given up Big, Bad and Dangerous to Know almost a year ago.

He smiled crookedly. "Hey, Annie," he said.

Like they were just passing in the hall in high school. Like he'd never shared gum or secrets with her on the school bus or filched cookies from her mother's kitchen or stood up for her on the playground.

Like he'd never grappled with her in the back seat of his father's unmarked police car and then walked right past her locker the next day.

Well, he could take his "hey" and…and… Her racing brain stumbled. Nice Southern girls simply did not think that way. Take his hay and stack it, she amended silently.

"No smoking in the restaurant," she said.

He looked at her, wrinkling his brow in the way that used to make her go soft inside. "What?"

She flapped her hand at the printed sign by the cash register. "No smoking. Sorry."

"Just like high school, huh?"

It was so close to what she'd actually been thinking that she goggled.

He looked at her like she was mentally defective. "No smoking in the halls," he explained.

"Oh. Yes. Right."

He stubbed out his cigarette in the clay pot provided and grinned. "So, who died and made you hall monitor?"

She flushed with annoyance. His grin spread. "Val doesn't like smoking," she said.

"Val Cutler? This her place?"

She nodded, put on guard by his quick, assessing questions. He was a cop, she remembered, like his father. Assuming he was still employed. *I heard he shot that boy and the department fired him.*

She shivered. The last thing she needed back in her life was another large, violent male. "It's Val MacNeill now."

"She married?"

"Eight months ago."

"Anybody I know?"

"No one from around here. Con's a financial consultant from Boston." An incisive giant of a man with a lean, clever face who adored his wife. Val's happiness in her new marriage was a source of wonder and joy and envy to Ann. But then Val had never hesitated to go after what she wanted.

Unlike Ann.

A smile ghosted across Maddox's mouth. "You gonna let me sit down or do I have to go put on a tie or something?"

"Oh." She flushed and fumbled with the menu. "Sorry. Just one of you for lunch?"

The sandy eyebrows lifted again. "Unless you maybe want to join me."

"I can't."

"That's what I figured."

"I'm working."

"Yeah, I saw you. Through the window."

Was that why he'd come in? The notion disturbed her. She bolted for one of the small side tables, her hands smoothing her shapeless apron. Foolish, she scolded. What did it matter that she looked like last week's laundry?

She turned, tucking her hair nervously behind one ear. "Is this all right?"

He looked over the room and then sat on the bench with his back to the wall. "Fine. Thanks."

"Doralee will be your server. Enjoy your meal."

"What do you recommend?"

His quick question stopped her getaway. She still wasn't used to having her opinion consulted, even in the smallest things. "I, um…"

"Come on. There's got to be something decent to eat in this place. How are the hamburgers?"

She lifted her chin. "No hamburgers. Wild Thymes doesn't serve red meat of any kind."

"Why not?"

"Val's a vegetarian."

"Hell." He scanned the seasonal menu, looking genuinely perplexed.

Against her will, Ann felt a smile forming. "You might like the catfish sandwich. Today's special is a smoked salmon salad, but—"

He laid the menu aside. "The sandwich will be fine. So, what's a chicken farmer's daughter like you doing in a place like this?"

Her smile died. "I told you. I work here."

He tilted his head back, regarding her from beneath his lids. "Old Rob doesn't mind?"

Rob hated her working at the restaurant. Hated anything that took her out of his house and his control. But Ann had clung stubbornly to her friendship with Val, never dreaming her husband would find a way to use it against them.

She forced the thought away. *You are not responsible for his actions,* the therapist intoned inside her head. *Not responsible.*

Another voice broke across the first, brutal as a slap. *Irresponsible bitch.*

She blinked. "Rob has nothing to do with it," she said carefully. "We're separated now."

"Separated?"

She winced at his heavy disbelief. But then, how would he have heard? It was common knowledge around town he hadn't even come home for Christmas the last few years.

Still, it wasn't Ann's responsibility to bring him up-to-date on the town's biggest scandal. She could not, she really could not, bear to pick the scabs off her marriage again. Not in the restaurant with Gladys Baggett and half of Cutler's lunching ladies looking on.

And not, dear Lord, with Maddox.

Let him find out the rest on his own. He was a cop. There were plenty of folks who would be only too happy to fill him in on the whole sordid story. No one was interested in her side, anyway.

"Yes. I need to get back to work. Enjoy your meal," she said again, and hurried back to her station.

Maddox watched Ann walk away from him—Annie, with her grave, sweet eyes and her small, serious smile and her skin so fine a look could bruise it—feeling like he'd just been socked in the chest. Enjoy his meal? He'd be lucky if he could even taste it.

Hell. He'd stayed away for twelve lousy years, and she was separated.

He slid out from behind the table, overtaking her before she reached the hostess station.

"How long?" he demanded.

She slapped a receipt on the spindle by the cash register, her movements quick and agitated. "What are you talking about?"

He caught her elbow. "How long since you and Rob broke up?"

Broke up. Swell. Now he even sounded like some high school moron.

She turned, her face white. "Let go of my arm."

He loosened his grip. "Just tell me how long."

"A year. Let go of me."

Her eyes were dark and enormous, the pupils nearly swallowing the green. Damn. He was thirty-one years old, a veteran cop, a sergeant, and the sight of the woman could still reduce him to a raging lump of testosterone. He released her abruptly.

Beneath her neat white blouse, her breasts rose and fell with her breath. "I have work to do," she said clearly. "Customers. Would you please leave me alone?"

Customers. Right. He glanced around the dining room. People were staring. Bag lady Baggett had practically fallen into her plate in her eagerness to eavesdrop. And over by the kitchen door, the Misses Minniton were glaring at him as if he'd firebombed their garage sixteen years ago instead of merely throwing up into their rosebushes after drinking too much beer one hot August night.

"Sure thing, darlin'. You don't have to ask me twice."

Oh, now, that was cool. He sauntered back to his table, feeling like an idiot, and sat with his back to the wall so he could keep an eye on the room and on Annie. Gladys Baggett met his gaze and smiled, very tentatively. He stared back until she reddened beneath her makeup and looked away.

"Catfish sandwich," the waitress said, sliding it expertly in front of him. "Will there be anything else?"

Her smile, wide and white against her honey-gold skin, suggested there could be. Not everybody in Cutler remembered him as the town screw-up. Of course, the waitress probably didn't remember him at all. She must have been skipping rope on the playground when he'd left home.

"No. Thanks."

He picked up the sandwich, looking over the thick sliced bread at Annie seating guests on the other side of the room. From a distance, she looked sixteen again, too skinny and so pretty with her quick, neat movements and shy smile. Her smooth light brown hair still brushed her shoulders when she walked, and she still had the nervous habit of tucking it behind one ear. From a distance, he couldn't see the faint lines bracketing her mouth or the wariness in her eyes.

She didn't come near his table again. Well, she wouldn't. She wouldn't want anything to do with him, any more than she had in high school. His fault, he acknowledged, coming on to her like a gorilla on Viagra. Again.

The catfish tasted like paste in his mouth. He needed a cigarette. Dropping a couple bills on the table, he made his way to the cash register, choosing a moment when Ann was ringing up another customer and couldn't avoid him.

"Annie."

She took his receipt and busily punched some buttons on the register. "How was your lunch?"

"Fine. Look, I—"

"I'll tell Val. She'll be glad you enjoyed it." She handed him his change, not quite meeting his gaze.

He was suddenly, unreasonably ticked off. Maybe once upon a time, in a dumb effort to win his father's notice, he had run wild. But he'd never done anything to make Ann afraid of him. Only that one October night... And he'd stayed away from her after that, hadn't he?

"Maybe I'll be back for dinner," he said.

She looked at him directly then, and her eyes that he remembered as the color of spring grass were cool and sharp as a broken beer bottle. There was a bump in the bridge of her nose he didn't remember at all.

"We're closed for dinner Monday through Thursday," she said. "But I can make a reservation for the weekend if you like."

"Never mind. I might not be around then."

Just for a second, her pretty lips parted, and his heart revved in his chest like a dirt-track race car. And then she hit him with her fake, hostessy smile, and he knew he'd been imagining that brief moment of regret.

"That's too bad," she said.

"I'll get over it," he drawled.

So, they both were lying. He wasn't about to admit his breath still backed up in his lungs every time he looked at her.

"Goodbye, Maddox."

She didn't have to tell him twice.

Chapter 2

Maddox heard the familiar blip of a police siren behind him. He glanced over his shoulder just as the squad car coasted to the curb and stopped, blue lights flashing. Well, damn. He turned slowly, resisting the impulse to put his hands up.

The door opened. A big, dark, uniformed cop got out and walked toward him with a wide smile.

"Cut me a break," Maddox said.

Patrol Officer Tom Creech, former third-string fullback for the Cutler Cougars, grinned all over his broad face. "Hey, Mad Dog. Heard you were back. Can I give you a lift?"

Maddox caught himself angling to leave his gun arm free and forced himself to relax. He wasn't jumpy. He did not feel vulnerable, whatever the department shrink said. He was fine.

"Hey, Creepy. Nope. I'm just going for a walk."

"Actually…" The patrolman shifted his weight from foot

to foot. "I thought maybe I could give you a ride to the station house. Your old man wants to see you."

"The chief? Hell, he can talk to me at home."

"He wants to talk to you now."

Maddox raised both eyebrows. "And he sent you to bring me in?"

Tom rolled his shoulder uncomfortably.

Maddox swore.

His high school teammate grinned, friendly as the Newfoundland dog he resembled. "Hey, come on, Mad Dog, it'll be like old times. Remember when we stuck potatoes up Reverend Dean's tailpipe, and your father had us picked up on eight counts of criminal mischief?"

"The good old days," Maddox said dryly.

"That's right."

He clamped his jaw. Hell, it wasn't Creepy's fault the chief's idea of a cozy father-son chat was to drag his butt down to the station house in a squad car. "Fine. I'll go quietly."

"Great." Tom beamed. Maddox reached for the passenger side door. "Um…you got to get in the back, old buddy."

The patrolman's smile faded under Maddox's hard stare.

"Sorry," Tom said. "Department regulations."

"Screw department regulations. It's been twelve years since I've ridden in back."

"Right," Tom said hastily. "Front seat it is."

He eased his bulk behind the wheel and waited until Maddox slid in beside him before starting the patrol car. "Guess you're kind of a celebrity now."

Maddox clenched his jaw. "That's one way to look at it."

"Saved those kids' lives, the paper said."

At the cost of one of their own. Maddox stared through the windshield at the gold and green bars of sunlight sliding across the hood. "Drop it, Creepy."

Tom sent him a surprised look. "Sure. Say... You hear the Cougars took the division title again last year?"

Maddox roused himself to a show of interest. "Big deal around here, huh?"

"I'll say. Your father damn near closed the town for a day. 'Course, it's not like when you and Rob won that state championship."

Maddox knew what was expected of him. Not to deliver would have been like kicking his hound dog. He'd been accused of many things, but cruelty to animals wasn't one of them. "It was a team effort, Creepy. You all did a good job."

Tom's grin spread from one big ear to the other. "Yeah, I guess we did. Remember that party afterward at Betty Lou Burton's when you and Robbo spiked the punch and I spent the whole night throwing up in the bathroom? Man, those were the days. Remember that night?"

He remembered. The vision of Ann's hurt face rose up to haunt him. He'd come to Cutler to escape his demons. He'd forgotten the power of old ghosts.

His father's office hadn't changed in twelve years. Hell, neither had his father. The cinder-block walls were still painted dingy white. The North Carolina Agriculture calendar still hung beside a photo of the chief standing with the governor and a yellowed newspaper headline proclaiming Cutler Cougars Roar. Files crammed the tops of the cabinets. A dying vine—presumably not the same one—still decorated the windowsill.

Chief Wallace Palmer stood behind his desk, straight and imposing as the Confederate soldier in front of the county courthouse, a big-shouldered, red-faced, gray-haired old son of the South.

"I still think you made a mistake, leaving Atlanta under suspicion."

Maddox slouched in the brown vinyl monstrosity that was

some bureaucrat's idea of an office chair. "The investigation is closed," he said evenly. "It was a clean shoot. My job isn't compromised."

"But your name is."

He had no answer for that. His father was right.

"You ought to get back to work," the chief stated definitively.

Right again. Unfortunately, the department didn't see it that way.

Maddox studied the burning tip of his cigarette. "Yeah, well, I've got six more weeks before I can go back on the street. Department policy."

The chief clasped his hands behind his back. "Don't you have somebody waiting for you back in Atlanta? What about that girl you were seeing?"

"Sandra?"

"Was that her name?"

Maddox drew in a long, slow drag of his cigarette and released it carefully. "That's over."

"She didn't like the publicity?"

"No. She liked it too much. I didn't like reading the details of my private life in the *Journal-Constitution.*"

The chief snorted. "I saw that one. 'Smolders with suppressed energy on and off the job,' wasn't that it? Some damn fool sent me a clipping."

Father and son exchanged a brief, rare look of shared disgust.

And then the chief shifted his stance. "Well, you're too old to loaf around the house for the next six weeks. What are you planning to do with yourself?"

Maddox released another breath, watching the curling smoke, surprised that the old man could still get to him. What the hell had he been thinking, running home to lick his wounds? The chief had always been able to smell blood. "Get drunk?"

The chief glared. "It's not funny, MD."

"I'm not laughing."

"As long as you're here you can make yourself useful. Put some time in for me."

"You're joking," Maddox said flatly.

The chief's red face turned redder. Just his luck high blood pressure ran in the family. "No. Bud Williams's wife got a teaching job over in Wake County, and they're moving. I need somebody to take his place."

"Not me. I told you, I'm on leave."

"And I'm a detective short."

More than anything else, Maddox wanted to forget the events of the last two months in the reassuring routine of the street. He was a cop, damn it. A good one. He wanted to get back to it. But not in Cutler, where every second citizen remembered him as a seventeen-year-old juvenile delinquent. And not for his father.

"Leaving you with a force of—what? Five? You'll manage. This town is hardly a major crime center."

"Listen, Mr. Big City Cop, we have a situation here. We've got a big felony trial in a few weeks, and I'm not satisfied with the direction the D.A.'s office is taking."

"What kind of situation?"

"Case came up last year. I thought I told you."

Oh, right. He'd had maybe two phone calls from his father in the past nine months, and a card at Christmas. Maddox had always figured the lack of contact was one of the advantages of working for the Atlanta PD. Maybe he'd been wrong.

He shook out another cigarette and lipped it from the pack. "Why don't you remind me?"

The chief hesitated. "It's a stupid thing."

He looked up from lighting his smoke, his attention caught by his father's unusual indecision.

"It's all on account of that outsider getting involved, that Boston fellow who married Val Cutler. He got Ed Cutler over at the bank all stirred up, and now we've got a bunch of bleeding hearts targeting a man for something he didn't do." The chief stared at him fixedly. "You should know what that's like."

Oh, no. He'd had enough experts poking around in his feelings, trying to stir up some big confession of resentment toward the shooter, the department, the media. He wasn't going there again. Especially not with the old man.

He pocketed his lighter. "Not really," he said coolly. "I never denied I shot that boy. So, who's the target?"

"Rob Cross."

That was a kicker. Rob Cross was the John Kennedy of Cutler, North Carolina. One of the good guys, one of the golden boys, with a "just folks" smile and a steady job at the bank. His people knew your people and your people wished you were him.

Maddox swallowed an old resentment. "I saw Ann Cross at Val's place," he said slowly. "She told me they were separated."

The chief smiled without warmth or humor. "Really? And did she also mention she's helping frame her husband for attempted murder?"

"What the hell are you talking about?"

The chief tapped together a stack of papers, straightening the edges of an already squared file.

"Ann Cross stole deposit money from that restaurant where she works. Rob accepted the deposits at the bank, but he says he didn't know what she was doing. She claims he was behind the whole thing. Whatever, they both got felony convictions—him for embezzlement, her for larceny."

It was like hearing the Tooth Fairy was wanted for breaking and entering. Maddox scowled. For years, he'd squashed the temptation to ask after Annie. He'd cut off conversations at the mention of her name. This was a hell of a way to catch up.

He wasn't surprised anymore by the stupid, criminal things people did. But Annie... He didn't want her to be guilty. Of course, the way things had been running for him lately, that alone was cause enough to believe she could be.

"You're still talking theft, not murder," he said.

"Well, now, the restaurant owner alleges Rob did more than steal from her. They have a history, you know, Rob and Val MacNeill. She says that during their latest…disagreement, he knocked her out and set fire to the place."

"Damn. Did he?"

"Look, everybody knows Rob has a problem with his temper. He admits to hitting the MacNeill girl. But arson? What did he have to gain?"

The thought of the big blond athlete using his fists on any woman burned in Maddox's gut. But he kept his voice cool. "He still at the bank?"

"No," the chief said. Reluctantly, Maddox thought. "The bank president is Val's father. Of course he couldn't keep Rob on after he was charged."

"So, where does Ann come into the picture?"

"Witness for the prosecution."

Maddox froze. "She was there?"

"No, she's some kind of character witness. Trying to pin all the blame on Rob. *Rob,*" the chief repeated, shaking his head in disbelief.

The whole thing stunk like three-day-old roadkill. "Why would she do that?"

"Who knows why those Barclays do anything? She and Rob are getting divorced. She's mad at him, is my guess."

"The D.A. still wouldn't go forward with the case without proof."

"You defending her, MD?"

He grabbed for his patience. "No. I'm just saying—"

His father looked him over scornfully. "I always thought you were sweet on her."

"Bit late for you to be taking an interest in my love life, Dad. Besides, what's that got to do with anything?"

"Nothing. It should have nothing to do with it. You've got your problems, son, but I always hoped you were a good-enough cop not to let personal feelings interfere with the job."

There was just enough truth laced in the accusation for it to sting. Maddox blew smoke deliberately. "You mean, like you do?"

"Don't get cute with me, MD. I've been doing my job since before you were born. Rob Cross has been arrested and charged. But as I see it, I have a duty to use my judgment in this or any other investigation."

"And your judgment tells you Rob didn't do it?"

"That's what I want you to find out."

"No."

"You could help Rob," his father insisted. "He needs you."

That appeal had worked in high school when Maddox was a center and his biggest goal in life had been protecting Rob's quarterback butt. He wasn't in high school any longer.

He raised his eyebrows. "'Go, Cougars'? I don't think so."

"Damn it, boy, you were teammates. State champions, thanks to him."

"That always meant more to you than me."

The chief leaned both hands flat on his desk. "It still counts for something."

"Not to me, it doesn't."

"Don't you feel any loyalty? What kind of man are you?"

Sharpshooter Hero. Kid-Killer Cop. The headlines still burned.

Maddox regarded the smoldering eye of his cigarette before he dropped it, grinding the butt into the floor. "I'm a cop on suspension. And I left my badge back in Atlanta."

Before he was out of the building, he lit up another cigarette. He'd picked a hell of a time to play at coming home. He wasn't about to give up smoking.

* * *

"Cool. It's a new *Droid Zone* book," nine-year-old Mitchell said with unusual enthusiasm. He plucked the paperback from the rack as they stood in the checkout line. "Can I get it?"

Ann wanted to say no. The unexpected meeting with Maddox had upset her. There were too many years and too great a distance between her old dreams and her new reality. She could barely afford toilet paper this week.

She brushed her son's fine, straight hair out of his eyes. He needed a haircut too. They couldn't afford that either. "How much?"

He consulted the cover. "Three ninety-nine," he said hopefully. "Please?"

Ann sighed. The long summer stretched before them. Once the empty days had been filled with the wide, flat waters of the club swimming pool, and the corner room with its computer and its bunk for a friend to sleep over when Rob was away, and the big-screen TV in a long room chilled to movie-theater cool.

There had been no swimming pool this summer, no computer and only one trip to the movies. Mitchell had spent the two weeks since school let out alternating between the hot public day camp in a dusty park and their cramped two-bedroom bungalow.

Oh, God, what if she'd been wrong? She'd wanted so many things for her son, and now she was balking at the cost of a book.

"Dad could get it for me," Mitchell suggested.

Of course he could. But he wouldn't. Rob didn't encourage his son's flights of imagination. Ann straightened her spine. "No, we'll get it today. Your dad is taking you to basketball practice on Thursday."

Mitchell lowered *Droid Zone 11: The Resurgence.* "Do I have to go?"

Rob insisted that his skinny, bookish son participate in at

least one team sport. Ann wasn't interested in raising this
generation's Golden Boy Cross. But she accepted that
Mitchell needed some masculine bond with his father. Besides, she couldn't afford to violate their custody agreement.

"Well, your daddy and I agreed he could see you one
night a week. Don't you have fun there?"

"It's all right," Mitchell said.

Meaning, Ann guessed, it's-awful-but-I-don't-want-to-
worry-you. Guilt squeezed her heart.

"Mitchell, honey…"

He ducked his head. "Come on, Mom. The cashier's waiting."

Sighing, she nudged her cart along the narrow aisle. A
front wheel jammed against the magazine rack, and when
she jostled the cart to free it, her purse swung from her
shoulder and knocked a candy display off the counter.

"Mo-om!" Mitchell wailed, embarrassed.

"Got it," a rough male voice said behind her.

She turned, her face already hot. Maddox Palmer stood in
line behind her, his hands steadying the box of candy dis-
pensers and his hooded eyes amused.

Her mouth dried. Oh, no, she thought. She didn't want to
recognize the speeding of her heart or the flutter in her stomach. Feelings like that could turn on you. *Men* could turn on
you.

"I'm sorry," she blurted.

"No problem," he said.

Mitchell was watching, his green eyes guarded. Growing
up with the echoes and bumps-in-the-night that marked his
parents' marriage had made him sensitive to undertones.

She touched his forearm, hiding her own misgivings to
reassure him. "My son, Mitchell. Mitchell, this is Mr. Palmer. He…I…" *He shot that boy and the department fired
him.* "We went to school together," she finished weakly.

Maddox nodded. "Hey."

"Nice to meet you," Mitchell mumbled politely.

Ann lifted a plastic gallon of milk onto the moving belt. "What are you doing here?"

Maddox grinned at her, that rare, invitation-to-trouble grin he'd turned on her in seventh grade, and she almost forgot to be afraid. "In the grocery store? Buying groceries."

She glanced back at his cart. Beer, bread and cigarettes humped together with a roll of paper towels and a carton of orange juice. "You don't eat much," she observed.

"I can't cook much."

She smiled faintly. "That would explain the cereal and peanut butter."

"I eat out a lot," he said defensively.

"I imagine you have to."

He shrugged. "Don't you? Working in a restaurant and all."

Val encouraged Ann to take her meals at Wild Thymes, but she resisted accepting charity. And she couldn't afford anything else. She shook her head, letting her hair veil her expression. "I don't work dinners very often. And I like to cook."

"Yeah? What does she make?" he asked Mitchell.

Put on the spot, Mitchell shuffled. "Well…"

Rob would have snapped at her son to speak up. Maddox just waited, like one of those Catholic priests. Or a cop.

"Tacos," Mitchell managed to say at last. "She makes good tacos. And spaghetti and hot dogs and stuff like that."

Cheap meals. A far cry from the beef and three sides Rob had expected on the table every night. She waited for Maddox to make some disparaging comment.

"Sounds good. Maybe I should come to your house for dinner."

Was he angling for an invitation? Was he—Ann stumbled over the thought—could he be lonely? She had a sudden memory of him at ten, his cool pose a front for his desperate longing to be noticed. She remembered his quick flush of gratification when she'd offered him a stick of gum, and the time he'd beat up Billy Ward for calling her "Chicken Legs."

She concentrated on unloading her squashables from the cart, aware that the checkout girl had stopped snapping her gum to listen. What was a nice person supposed to do? "Oh, my dinners are nothing fancy. Nothing you would want."

"Try me," Maddox said softly.

His eyes met hers, hot and hooded and intense, and her insides constricted like they did when she was afraid, only this time it wasn't with fear.

Dear Lord. She hadn't felt this way in... She couldn't remember the last time she had felt this way. She couldn't want him, she thought in near panic. She couldn't want any man ever again, not that way, whatever the counselor had said, whatever Val had promised.

"I'm getting pretty tired of peanut butter," Maddox added, deadpan. Teasing, the way he had the first time she'd boarded the school bus for kindergarten and stared hopelessly at the crowded seats. "I don't know if you'll fit," he'd told her solemnly, sliding over to make room beside him. "You're awfully big."

Remembered gratitude pricked her. A nice woman would invite the poor man to dinner. Her heart beat high and wild in her throat.

Forget nice. Nice had gotten her pregnant at eighteen and married four months later. Nice had made her smile and lie to her mother, to her best friend, to her son and to herself.

She couldn't afford nice anymore.

"Frozen dinners are in aisle four," she said. "You should check it out. They have a good selection."

The cashier's mouth gaped so far open Ann could see the color of her gum. And Maddox...

He stuck his thumbs in his front pockets, regarding her with those deep-set eyes. "Frozen dinners, huh? Don't you think that's a little...cold?"

Her stomach jumped. Pushing her hair behind her ear, she

gave him a quick, nervous smile. "I'm afraid that's the best I can offer."

"Right. I remember."

She wasn't the one who'd walked by in the hall the next morning without a word. She swallowed the hot answer that rose in her throat, but there was nothing she could do about the heat in her cheeks.

He continued to watch her as she paid the cashier, as she put her purse on her shoulder and loaded her bags and pushed the cart. His intense, unsmiling regard shook her. She did not want to be reduced in his eyes to what the years had made her, what marriage to Rob had made her.

It didn't matter, she reassured herself, as she crossed the baking parking lot with Mitchell. Nothing mattered anymore but Mitchell.

"Who was that guy?"

Ann glanced over at her son's blond head, almost level with her shoulder. "Mr. Palmer. I introduced you."

"Yeah, but how well do you know him?"

Love filled her at his protective tone. "Oh, sweetheart. It's okay. We were on the same bus route when we were your age."

"People change," Mitchell insisted.

She unlocked the trunk of her rusting compact, a far cry from the fully outfitted SUV she'd driven a year ago. "Yes, they do."

"He looks like trouble to me," Mitchell muttered darkly.

Ann remembered how in high school Maddox had skirted the edges of Rob's crowd, silent and sexy and usually on his way to detention.

Trouble, her mother had warned her.

Trouble, the town agreed.

Trouble was the last thing she was looking for.

She thumped a milk jug into the trunk. "Don't worry about it. I don't think we'll see him again."

"Well, that's good. Dad wouldn't like it."

No, he wouldn't. "Your father doesn't really have anything to do with it," Ann said bravely.

Mitchell handed her the last bag of groceries. "Aren't you…are you guys getting back together again?"

She wasn't sure what put the hesitation in his voice, the tension in his shoulders. Hope? Or fear? But she answered him as gently as she could. "No."

"Because he hit you?"

Even now, eleven months after she'd left the big house on Stonewall Drive, it was hard to talk about it. Harder to admit to her child that his father, the father he saw one evening a week and on alternate weekends, was a wife-beater. But that was part of the healing, learning not to lie. "Because he hurt me, yes."

"Not because of me?"

How could she answer him? She'd stayed for his sake, to give him the advantages she'd never had. And she'd left—at last—for his sake, too, because she didn't want her boy to grow up in the circle of violence, to be abused or learn to use his size or his words or his fists against someone smaller or slower or weaker.

He was only nine, she reminded herself. Really, really smart and middling tall, but only nine. She wouldn't add to whatever childish guilt he carried.

"No, sweetheart, no. We talked about this, remember? Nothing that happened was because of anything you did or didn't do."

He still looked unsatisfied. Ann sighed and dug into one of the plastic grocery bags. "Want a cookie?"

"Mo-om. I'm not a baby." But there was a glimmer of interest in his eyes, a suggestion of a smile around his mouth. "What kind?"

"Chocolate chip?"

"Okay." He took his hands out of his pockets to accept the cookie.

They got into the car together, and Ann loved him so much she thought her heart would burst with it. Whatever other mistakes she'd made, she couldn't regret Mitchell. She would never do anything—*anything*—to risk losing him.

Chapter 3

Temporary insanity, Maddox decided. That was the only excuse for his recent behavior. Something in his hometown—the air, maybe, or the drinking water—had obviously shorted his brain cells.

He drove his made-in-America sedan under budding crepe myrtle through the wide wrought-iron gates of the South Hills Country Club.

He'd told the chief he didn't want anything to do with this damned investigation, and he'd meant it. Forget that he'd almost made it with Ann once and still wanted her now. Putting the moves on a suspect was not his MO. Never mind that Rob's invitation had broken into another intolerable day of stewing boredom. Golf was not his game. Cutler was not his jurisdiction.

And the country club had never been his style.

Growing up, Maddox had preferred fishing with the Burrell boys down at Oakley's Pond to lounging poolside. His teenage drinking had been six packs behind the sawmill, not Scotch and bourbon smuggled from parental liquor cabinets.

He parked between freshly painted lines beside a blue-and-white-striped canopy and got out of the car. He didn't lock the doors. Nobody was going to choose his junker for a joyride in this parking lot.

His footsteps echoed in the cool tiled foyer of the club-house. Ceiling fans stirred the flower arrangements on the polished glass tables. A barbered young man in white shorts and the blue club polo shirt looked up at his entrance.

"Can I help you?"

Despite his smile, the words weren't meant to welcome.

Maddox made eye contact until the "Aryan youth" poster boy reddened and looked away. "Maybe. I'm here to meet Rob Cross."

"It's all right, Peter, Mr. Palmer is my guest." Tanned, distinguished, with an extra six inches of belt dangling to emphasize his still-flat stomach, Rob Cross walked across the foyer with his hand extended. "MD! It's good to see you."

"Rob. Been a long time."

"Too long," Rob said, his smile flashing.

Almost against his will, Maddox felt the tug of that concentrated friendliness. Well, that was Rob. Everybody's pal, everybody's prince. He remembered your birthday and your favorite beer, the ailments of all the regulars who loitered at the service station and the names of all his clients' kids.

It made the guy occasionally tough to take, especially when your own father held him up as a model. Or if, say, you'd recently been both hailed as a hero and pilloried as a child murderer in the local media. Maddox retrieved his hand.

Rob didn't appear to notice. "I'm glad you could get away," he said easily. "We're teeing off at two."

"You're teeing off," Maddox corrected him. "I told you, I don't golf."

"You sure? I could loan you a set of clubs."

Maddox's mouth twisted in a smile. "And watch me

stumble behind you chopping chunks out of the golf course? No, thanks."

Rob laughed, leading the way through tall French doors to a manicured patio out back. "Whatever you say. You'll drive, at least, I hope?"

He eyed the jaunty cart with its bright blue canopy. "Sure. You gonna give me a tip?"

"How about, 'Diversify your holdings'?"

Maddox levered his body into the toy car and looked for the controls. "That's right. I heard you were a financial advisor now or something. Left the bank?"

That earned him a quick, suspicious look, and then Rob smiled again. "Why do you ask? Interested in putting together a portfolio now you can't count on that police pension any longer?"

Screw you, thought Maddox. He hadn't been fired. But Rob had always had this nasty edge on his tongue. You couldn't let it get to you. At least, you couldn't let it show.

"Could be," he said calmly. Steering the golf cart up a slight rise, he jerked to a stop in front of the tee.

Rob glanced at him sideways and then climbed down, pulling a club from the back. "Sorry about that. I guess I'm a little touchy on the job thing. The chief must have filled you in on my recent spot of trouble with the law."

"He mentioned something, yeah."

"You know it was all a mistake."

Maddox pulled his cigarettes from his breast pocket. He was not getting involved. Besides, he heard that one all the time. "Your mistake? Or the department's?"

"Look, I'm not faulting the chief. He really had no choice, given the information he had to work with. And I can see that a jury—even knowing me, even knowing what this community means to me—could believe I knew about Ann taking money from the restaurant. But this other thing... Hell, there's just no way I set fire to Val's place. I mean, what was in it for me?'' Rob tugged an outside zipper on his golf bag and tossed Maddox a book of matches.

He caught it neatly. ''I didn't know you smoked.''

''I don't. But I like to be prepared. I have enough clients who do.''

Maddox nodded acknowledgement and lit his cigarette, watching as Rob sent the little white ball sailing over the sunlit hills to the green. It was none of his business, he reminded himself. He inhaled deeply. ''You want to tell me what happened?''

Rob climbed back into the cart. ''Well, now, there are two sides to every story.''

He'd heard that one before, too. Generally, he figured one side was the truth and the other was whatever excuse the perpetrator could come up with. He started the golf cart after the ball, asking, almost from habit, ''So, what's your side?''

''Not the same as Ann's, that's for sure.''

''You think she's lying.''

Rob drew himself up in his seat, the perfect Southern gentleman. ''That's not something a man wants to say about his wife.''

His wife. Right. The reminder hit Maddox like a fist in the gut. Like a slap upside the head. He wasn't involved. Not with the woman and not in the case.

And then he opened his big mouth and said, ''I heard you two were separated.''

''Only temporarily.'' Rob lowered his voice confidingly. ''She's a little upset with me right now.''

''How come?''

''The usual thing. There was someone at work…I let myself be tempted. I told Ann I was sorry and it wouldn't happen again. The girl left town, actually. But you know how women are.''

Maddox couldn't see how any man married to Annie Barclay could be tempted to stray, but he did indeed know how women were. Domestic disputes led to a lot of police tips.

Unfortunately, resentful informants couldn't always be trusted.

"So, your wife testified against you because she was mad you had a bit on the side?"

Rob shrugged. "That's about it."

"What about Val MacNeill? You want me to believe she was jealous, too?"

Rob approached his ball and squatted to inspect the line to the hole. "Who knows? But she could be after me because of what happened before the fire."

Tom Creech had filled him in. Hell, the whole town had taken sides on that one. "Because you beat her up, you mean."

"I hit her."

"Enough to get her admitted to the hospital."

Rob straightened, meeting his gaze in rueful acknowledgment. "What can I say? You know I've always had a temper. And hell, MD, she was interfering between me and my wife. But I never wanted her dead. I never set fire to her restaurant."

It wasn't his investigation, Maddox thought, almost desperately. It wasn't his business. He was on leave. Department policy, his captain told him, never quite meeting his eyes. *To regain objectivity,* the shrink explained, with a frank and friendly look.

He sure as hell wasn't doing his objectivity any good getting mixed up in this mess.

But the habits of the interview room died hard. And what actually came out of his mouth was "Hey, I've got temper troubles myself. But these D.A.s, they need somebody to be guilty. Who else could have done it?"

"Who knows? I was long gone. Ann admits she wasn't even there. Val *says* she was knocked out." Rob selected another club. "You want my honest opinion, I think she did it herself. Her or that new husband of hers."

"That MacNeill guy? The Yankee? Why would you say that?"

"Her business wasn't doing that well, you know. That insurance money must have come in mighty handy."

It was plausible. It fit with what his father had said. And if, deep in his heart, he didn't want to accept that the girl he remembered stole and lied to pay back her cheating husband, well, hadn't he learned by now that believing the worst of somebody generally meant you weren't disappointed?

Rob turned on his all-American smile. "You could really help me out here, MD."

"You want me to take the flag out of the hole?"

"I want you to look into this for me. Prove I didn't do it."

"Did the chief tell you to ask me?"

Rob twinkled disarmingly. "See, there, you figured that one right out. I knew you could help. You're good, MD."

Once, maybe. Maddox took a short, vicious drag of smoke. "Not everybody would agree with you."

"Prove them wrong," Rob suggested. "Show the hometown boys how it's done."

He was tempted. He'd been going crazy with inactivity since the shooting. Investigating this case from the sidelines would keep his hand in and his brain sharp. At the very least, looking at Ann and her gal pal Val would get his father off his back for the duration of his stay in Cutler. Why not? He wasn't committing to anything, he wasn't drawing his gun, and he for damn sure wasn't going near any middle school. How far wrong could he go, asking a few questions?

It didn't matter that he'd never been a member of the Rob Cross Fan Club. Poking around might uncover something that would help Ann. And if it didn't… Well, if it didn't, maybe proving her guilty of perjury and obstruction of justice would cure him of his schoolboy crush for good.

Right. And maybe he was just kidding himself. Maybe he

was nuts enough to grab at any excuse to see her again. Felon or not.

He pitched his cigarette to the turf, ignoring a splinter of doubt.

"I'll think about it," he said.

Ann's doorbell clunked two broken notes, and she froze like a rabbit on the lawn.

Coward, she scolded. Move. Breathe.

Her gaze darted to the clock on the stove. Six-thirty. Rob wasn't supposed to pick up Mitchell for another half hour.

Wiping her hands on a dishcloth, she forced herself to the door. She checked through the peephole, her breath congealing at the sight of a big, fair man waiting in the shadows of the porch. Rob.

And then he shifted, and she recognized the slouched posture, the sandy hair. She shot back the bolt and opened the door.

"Hello, Annie," Maddox said in his whiskey-and-cigarettes voice.

She crossed her arms protectively over her stomach, standing in the narrow opening. That one distorted glimpse hadn't prepared her for the impact of his broad, hard body and intense, unsmiling face on her doorstep. Even shaved and dressed in rumpled khakis and a collared sports shirt, he looked disconcertingly like the boy her mother had warned her against.

"What are you doing here?"

"Can I come in?"

"I guess so." She knew she sounded grudging, and the nice Southern girl who still lurked inside her protested softly. "How did you get my address?"

"How do you think?"

He was a policeman, she reminded herself. He could probably get whatever he wanted. Just like Rob. The thought made her shiver.

Maddox stopped inside the threshold, and she watched as he did a quick check of the hall and living room. Was that a police thing, too? Or was he as curious as the rest of Cutler to see how she lived now?

As his hooded gaze roamed from the battered banister to the stained carpet and secondhand chairs, she resisted the urge either to straighten or explain. This was her home, hers and Mitchell's, and she was stubbornly proud of it. Maybe it was on the poor side of town. Maybe it was small and shabby compared to the house on Stonewall Drive, but she'd decorated it herself. Paid the rent herself.

His gaze returned to her face. "When did you decide to take up slumming?"

Her stomach knotted. "I grew up slumming, remember? On a chicken farm."

"I remember you married off it."

She had no retort for that one. No defense, because it was true. "What are you doing here, MD?"

Feet pounded the stairs. "Mom! I saw a car. Are you o— Oh." Mitchell stopped as he rounded the wall and saw the man beside her.

She didn't want to worry him with their adult hostilities. She reached for the reassurance of good manners. "Mitchell, you remember Mr. Palmer."

"What's he here for?"

That's what she wanted to know. But the same question from her nine-year-old son was plain bad manners. "He just stopped by. You want to say hello?"

He scowled. "Hi," he said to Maddox's shoes.

Maddox nodded. "How's it going?"

He didn't offer to shake hands. He knew better. The kid had "get away from my mom" written all over his face.

Maddox couldn't blame him. Since Ann had opened the door for him, slender and graceful and wary, he'd been fighting a swarm of thoughts, most of them lustful and all of them out of line. He felt fourteen and stupid again as she inspected him with eyes that were just as green and much cooler than he remembered.

She wasn't what he remembered.

Did that make her a criminal?

"Mitchell," she prompted gently.

"It's going okay," the kid mumbled.

She touched the back of her son's hand where it rested on the banister, and the light, casual touch shot a shaft of longing through Maddox, devastating in its suddenness. He sucked in his breath. Maybe this visit hadn't been such a good idea. Maybe it was one more bad idea in a long string of them.

"Why don't you go change for basketball," she suggested. "I'll call you when it's time, okay?" She waited until the kid shuffled upstairs before turning to Maddox, her face closed and her voice resigned. "You might as well come back to the kitchen. I'm doing dishes."

Which put him way down on her list of things to deal with, he thought. He followed as she led the way briskly down the narrow hall, her long straight skirt pulling with her stride. The house might be slumming, but that khaki skirt and buttoned blouse were pure suburban chic, obviously chosen with an eye to her friends' tastes and her husband's wallet.

"Your boy was none too happy to see me," he observed.

"We don't get much company."

He pulled his attention from the graceful sway of her hips. *Company.* Did she mean men?

"Besides," she added, "he was expecting his father tonight."

"Yeah?" He watched her back carefully for a response. "Rob told me the two of you were getting back together."

Bingo. She straightened and turned, her face flushed, her eyes defiant. Her sudden passion quickened the beat of his blood.

Don't go there, boy, he cautioned himself. You are not

involved. You are not getting involved. You're here to ask a few questions, that's all. Easy in, easy out.

And then he had to battle another inappropriate image conjured by the thought.

"No," she said.

"No?"

"Not a chance. The marriage is over." Her chin set, but her face was flaming. "That doesn't mean, though, that I...I don't know what you've heard since you've been home, but I am not in the market for a white knight or a meal ticket."

He raised an eyebrow at her directness. She *had* changed.

"Fine by me. I've got enough on my plate right now without a road trip down memory lane."

"Then...what do you want from me?"

He leaned against a counter. "How about a drink?"

She stared. He counted his breaths until her tentative smile flickered. "Should I ask to see your ID first?"

Her unexpected humor slid into his heart as easily as a knife. Damn. He didn't want to like her so much. "Iced tea is fine. Or water. Although I'll remind you, darlin', I've been drinking longer than you've been wearing lipstick."

She rounded her eyes teasingly as she reached for a glass. "You were thirteen?"

"Thirteen when I started smoking. Fourteen for drinking." Fifteen for sex, but he wasn't telling her that. Not when she was almost qualified to remember how very bad he'd been at it. He'd improved since, but there was no way to tell her that, either.

He sat at her kitchen table, still set with dirty dinner dishes and flowered place mats and some lacy weed sticking from a jar, as she moved efficiently around her tidy kitchen. It felt weird to have her wait on him. Weird, but good. She filled a glass with ice and pulled a brown plastic jug from the refrigerator. He watched her pour, her slender, capable hands, her gentle, serious face, and his mouth parched.

"There you go." She stepped back after she'd served him, as if he would bite.

Hell, he might.

"What did you mean by you have enough on your plate?" she asked.

"What did you hear?"

"Do you always answer a question with another question?"

He grinned, surprising them both. "Pretty nearly. Occupational hazard."

"I *heard*—" she stressed the word "—that you'd been fired."

For a little bit of a thing, she was implacable. "On leave," he said briefly, and reached for his cigarettes.

She turned from the sink, where she was rinsing pans. "Not in the house," she said.

He stopped. "Sorry. You didn't used to mind."

"I didn't used to mind a lot of things. But Mitchell has asthma. I have to look out for him."

"Sure. I've been meaning to quit anyway."

He respected the way she did a mother's job. Not that he had much experience with mothers. His own died when he was six, and the domestic disputes he saw on the job tended to skew a guy's perceptions. Annie, though, seemed to be doing a good job. Too bad he wanted that cigarette.

Her eyes were sympathetic. "Was it hard?"

"Quitting smoking?"

"Leaving your job."

It was the hardest thing he'd ever done. Being ordered off the streets had stripped him of the credentials and identity he'd worked twelve years to acquire. Routine, the department insisted. But it felt like punishment.

He shrugged. "It's not like I had a choice." Damn, he wanted that smoke.

"Was it an accident?" she asked.

He narrowed his eyes. "Was what an accident?"

Her hands twisted in a tea towel, but she drew herself up to her full five-feet-not-very-many-inches. "I heard you shot somebody. A boy. I heard you shot a boy in Atlanta."

Hell. The doubt in her eyes hurt worse than any accusation. "Yeah, well, you heard right."

"Who was it?"

"Does it matter?"

"It might." She tilted her head. "You're doing that question thing again."

"Maybe I just don't want you to throw me out before I finish my drink."

She squirted soap into the sink and turned on the tap. "Then, tell me. How old was he? Was he armed?"

He'd faced the same questions before. From himself, from his peers, from the press. A clean shoot, the inquiry had concluded. But the judgments didn't stop.

The nightmares didn't, either.

"Fourteen," he told her roughly. "He was fourteen. And yeah, he had a gun. But it was my job to get him to lay it down, and I didn't."

Ann watched the bubbles rising in the sink. His admission should frighten her. *He* should frighten her. She glanced sideways at his guarded face, his passionate mouth, and a shiver ran down the backs of her arms.

He did.

She shut off the water. At least he took responsibility for his action. No excuses. No fixing the blame on someone else. The counselor at the women's shelter would have approved. Healthy adults, she liked to say, did not insist that the people they hurt were "asking for it."

But then, Mad Dog had never had a problem accepting the consequences of his actions. He'd been too proud to plead off trouble or deny his crimes. He'd spent a lot of lunch periods in detention.

"Let me give you a hand." He stood, picking up a dirty plate.

"You don't need to do that."

He shrugged. "Might as well."

Confusion washed her face. She wasn't used to men taking on the tasks she accepted as a matter of course. Oh, Val's husband, Con, was quick enough to lend a hand around the restaurant. But it felt different, Ann discovered, when it was her own kitchen.

When it was Maddox.

He was so big, for one thing, and so, well, male, she supposed. Those muscled forearms and strong hands didn't look right carrying her dirty dishes. He prowled from table to sink, clearing as she washed.

So big, she thought, and so close. She could smell the soap that he used and the faint tang of his cigarettes. Not unpleasant smells, she decided, hiding her shaking hands in the soapy water. But unfamiliar, and very masculine. Still, she had to admit the work went quicker with two.

He came up unexpectedly behind her, and she yelped.

"You all right?"

"Fine," she croaked.

His strong hands closed on her shoulders and turned her. "Sure?"

Her breath stopped at his nearness, his intensity. But it wasn't hurting. It wasn't awful, though her heart pounded and her knees quaked and his hands were really big and close to her face.

She ordered herself not to squeak. "Sure. You startled me, that's all."

"Sorry about that." His hooded gaze searched her face. His hands still lingered at the tops of her arms, his thumbs absently smoothing her blouse. "Okay now?"

She nodded, speechless. There was a dip in his upper lip where the razor had missed and a tiny white scar by his left eyebrow.

His eyes darkened. His thumbs stopped.

And the doorbell thunked in broken warning.

She jumped.

Maddox's big hands tightened protectively on her shoulders. "Will the kid get it?"

"No."

He frowned. "You want me to—"

"No!"

Breaking free, she hurried down the hall, her flat shoes slapping in rhythm with her heart. The two sour notes clanked again.

"Mom?" Mitchell quavered down the stairs.

"I've got it, honey."

She stopped before she looked through the peephole, her hands pressed to the cool flat wall and the sturdy door.

I am a worthwhile human being. The therapist's mantra sang in her head. *I do have power over my own life.*

"Ann?" Her ex-husband's voice penetrated the door clearly. The tarnished knob jiggled as he shook it from the outside. "I know you're home. I can see your car."

I can use my power to take good care of myself and my child.

"Ann!"

She took a deep breath and opened the door.

Rob scowled at her, handsome even in displeasure. "What took you so long?"

"I was in the kitchen." She was proud of her steady voice. She did not apologize for keeping him waiting. "Please come in. Mitchell will be right down."

He stepped over the threshold, jingling his keys in the pocket of his pressed khaki shorts. His knit shirt cost more than her week's groceries.

"MD!" She watched his surprise give way to suspicion and then the bland social face he used to cover it all. "Great to see you. You looking into that little matter we discussed?"

Maddox stalked up the short hallway to stand at her back. She stepped away. She wanted to see his face.

What little matter?

"Just stopped by to say hello, Rob."

"Stopped by, huh? Yeah, why not?" He leaned closer, speaking man to man. "I always felt a little chat with Ann would make this whole thing go away. You straighten her out?"

A chill crawled up her back. She hugged her arms, but it didn't make her warm.

Maddox's face blanked. "The subject didn't come up."

Rob frowned. "Oh, I get it. Well…"

Well, at least she had the answer to her question. It was pretty clear now what Maddox wanted of her, and it was her own stupid fault if the answer made her as miserable at twenty-eight as it had at fifteen.

She moved to the bottom of the stairs, shrinking to avoid brushing against either one of them, her ex-husband or his friend. "Mitchell! Your father's here."

Rob grinned amiably at Maddox. "Kind of like old times, all of us together. Remember third quarter, the big state game? You threw that great block, and I ran a touchdown to win. I would have made it into the end zone either way, but it was good to know I could count on you. Remember that?"

"I remember."

"Do you remember, Ann?"

She twisted her hands together to hide their trembling. "I don't pay much attention to football, Rob."

"You used to. Bet you remember that night, anyway."

That night in Maddox's car, out on the river road. Oh, she remembered. Rob had seen them leaving the party together. He'd reminded her of that often enough in the last twelve years.

The cold was deep inside her now. Dinner—meat loaf—congealed like cold lard in her stomach.

Mitchell trailed down the stairs in mesh shorts and a UNC T-shirt, his face pinched, his eyes watchful.

She brushed his hair back from his forehead, seeking and giving comfort. "Do you have your water bottle?"

He nodded.

"Guess it's time for us to go, then," Rob said. He clapped his hand on his son's shoulder. Mitchell leaned away from the touch. Rob turned on his way out the door to wink at Maddox.

"Remember, Mad Dog, your first job is to protect the quarterback. 'Night, all."

The door closed behind them.

"Annie..." Maddox reached for her. She shrank.

He was a liar.

And she was a fool.

She reached inside and found her anger, used it to warm the icy lump inside her and thaw her frozen voice. "I think it's time for you to go, too."

He took a step toward her. "Look, it's not like what you're thinking."

She folded her arms over her stomach—*in an attack, protect your head and middle*—letting the anger out in a welcome geyser of heat. "You have no idea what I'm thinking. You have no clue what I'm feeling right now. Just leave. Please."

He stopped, his hooded gaze intent on her face, and then he nodded slowly. "All right. I'm going. But I'll be back."

Chapter 4

The more things changed, the more they stayed the same. Maddox grimaced through the windshield at the town's main drag. That was a song or something. And Cutler, North Carolina, could have been the set of the music video.

The video store had obviously replaced the record aisle at Woolworth's as the teen hangout of choice. A new bench supported the old regulars in front of the hardware store. The model head in the window of Barb's Beauty Salon— now Unicuts—still sported a honey-colored perm.

Annie Barclay was thinner, tougher, jumpier than he remembered, but he still had a major jones for her.

Maddox shook his head. So, he was still an idiot. And she was still all wrong for him.

But she was free now, a sly whisper teased inside his head. Separated. *The marriage is over,* she'd insisted, her voice flat and hard.

Maddox rummaged on the seat beside him for his cigarettes. Yeah, and she thought he was somewhere below troglodytes on the evolutionary scale.

What had happened to the slim, shy girl with hopeful eyes and an elusive laugh? Something. Was it the trial? The separation? Rob?

Maddox scowled as he headed toward the outskirts of town and an end-of-shift beer with Tom Creech. He didn't like the way Golden Boy had finessed things last night to make it appear that Maddox was acting as his personal junior deputy. No, he didn't like that at all. He ought to throw this whole damn investigation back in the chief's lap and haul ass to Atlanta.

Only in Atlanta, he had the same old problems to think about and even less to do. He didn't like the picture he got of an innocent Annie up against his father and Rob. And innocent or guilty, he didn't want her thinking he'd shown up on her doorstep last night just to pump her for answers.

He drew on his cigarette. Even if he'd told himself that's what he was there to do.

He expelled smoke in a moody cloud. Maybe especially because he'd told himself that's what he was there to do.

On the road ahead, an old black Toyota was pulled up on the shoulder, its raised hood a warning to motorists.

Not his jurisdiction, Maddox reminded himself as he switched lanes. A sheriff's patrol would be by any minute. Or a state trooper. Somebody. But he slowed as he passed, checking in the rearview mirror, anyway, making sure everything was all right. A lone woman in a long skirt bent over the engine.

And then he identified that slim back, that smooth brown hair.

Annie.

His heart beat faster. He pulled onto the verge in front of her car.

Ann stared into the black bowels of her wounded car. She'd opened the hood without the slightest idea what she was doing, but the problem was depressingly easy to see. Right there, smack in the middle of the greasy, confusing tangle, a thick black hose sputtered and steamed. She had a hole in her...well, she didn't know what to call it, but it definitely had a hole.

Oh...drat. Could she drive with it? She didn't think so. Determined to pick up Mitchell when his camp day ended at four-thirty, she had ignored the temperature gauge's stubborn climb to red. She'd pulled over only when steam started gusting over the hood. She eyed the hissing, spitting hose. She was going to be late for sure.

She pressed her lips together, fighting the too-familiar demons of helplessness and frustration. *I do have power over my own life,* she recited silently, invoking one of her therapist's favorite mantras. *I can use my power to take care of myself.*

A thin stream of green fluid puddled by her shoes. It was just too bad she didn't have any power over her car.

She barely registered the dark blue sedan that swept by until she heard it stop behind her.

Tension coiled her stomach. She thought of the horrible things that could happen, monsters who preyed on stranded motorists, before giving herself a mental shake. Her car had broken down in broad daylight on a well-trafficked road. Probably someone had stopped to offer help.

She turned to thank her well-intentioned rescuer. The driver's door opened. A man got out. And a different kind of tension gripped her.

Maddox.

She recognized the shape of his broad shoulders, the rough silhouette of his head, before she saw his face. His eyes were unreadable behind dark glasses. He cast a long shadow in the late afternoon sun. Something about the way he moved toward her, the contained awareness of his body, his unthinking masculine competence in the face of her mini-disaster, triggered a rush of feelings: Gladness. Attraction. Relief. And a deep, residual anger.

She squared her shoulders. "Rob send you to 'straighten me out'?"

The sharp words surprised them both. Maddox halted a yard away. "No."

"So, why did you stop? To gloat?"

He pitched his cigarette to the ground. "To help."

Shame squiggled inside her. She knew that. Of course she knew it. He had a man's tendency to meddle, a cop's training. He probably would have stopped for anyone. But she was still stinging over the way she'd nearly fallen for his show of concern last night. "And what will this help cost me?"

She winced at the provocation in her voice. But Maddox stood very still. Solid. As if she could batter him with her anger and he'd never hit her back.

"I don't know yet," he said. "Why don't you show me the problem first?"

She drew a shaky breath. "I have a hole in my…" She still didn't know what to call it.

He took a step closer. She flinched. He froze. And then he leaned in casually, taking off his sunglasses to look over her shoulder. "Radiator hose."

"Radiator hose," she repeated, committing it to memory. "Can you—can it be repaired?"

"I can rig it. But it needs to be replaced. Both of them need to be replaced. The lower one's ready to crack. See?"

She looked, but it didn't matter. She didn't have the money to replace things on her car. And she had other, more urgent concerns. "I need to pick up Mitchell."

"Where is he?"

"Jaycee Park."

He considered the distance. Considered the hose. "I can probably get you that far."

"And home?" she asked anxiously.

He smiled suddenly, a brief, hard smile that caught her under the ribs. "I'll get you home."

She didn't want him thinking she was nagging for herself. "It's just that Mitchell worries if I'm late."

"Watching out for mom?"

She smiled, grateful for his easy acceptance. "Yes."

Mitchell *was* protective. More than that, he needed the routines they'd developed to pretend that everything was under control, that everything was all right. Rob used to mock Ann's almost superstitious adherence to their son's bedtime ritual. Her smile twisted. Though if she deviated from Rob's schedule, Rob's agenda, all hell broke loose.

Maddox lifted an eyebrow. "We'd better get you on your way, then."

She was embarrassed at being caught out dreaming like the goony girl he'd known in high school. "I...yes. Thank you."

He strolled back to his car, masculine power compacted into a pair of worn jeans. She looked away. Her face felt warm.

The sun, she thought. It struck through her thin blouse, rose up from the road in waves. A truck rumbled by on the other side of the road, dragging dust and exhaust in its wake.

"Here we go."

Maddox was back, exuding heat and competence. In one hand, he carried a gallon jug of water, and in the other...

"Duct tape?" she asked. "You carry it with you?"

"In my trunk, yeah." Straight-faced, he added, "Doesn't everybody?"

She almost laughed. Didn't, because she was afraid he would take offense. What if he hadn't meant it as a joke? Rob didn't like it when she found him funny. Though she hadn't found much to laugh about in her marriage for a long time.

"I will from now on," she said instead.

"Now, there's a picture." But Maddox didn't say it meanly. His voice was warm and amused.

She watched as he dried the hose with his handkerchief and bound it with the tape.

"That should hold you for a while," he said, setting down the jug of water. "Ten minutes or so. Don't sit in the carpool line too long."

"I won't," she promised.

He wiped his hands on the handkerchief he'd used for the hose. He had big, square hands and thick wrists. His fingernails were short and clean. Not buffed, like Rob's.

She looked up from his hands to find his hooded gaze on her face. Her blood drummed in her ears.

"Well." She floundered. She wanted to thank him. She wanted to apologize for throwing him out of her house last night. But her feelings were all mixed up with her therapist's caution not to take responsibility for things that weren't her fault.

She mustered her courage. "I'm sorry if I was rude last night."

He rolled his shoulders, shrugging off her apology. "Guess we ticked you off."

We. Maddox and Rob.

Rob had said—Rob made it appear—as if Maddox had sought her out to get her to change her story. And that she would not do. Her husband had tried to kill her best friend. She was sickeningly sure of that.

She was much less certain what Maddox was guilty of.

He unhooked the thin metal support and slammed the hood. He'd fixed her car. She would only be a little late picking up Mitchell because Maddox had stopped to help.

She cleared her throat. "I don't blame you for listening to Rob."

That earned her a dark, hot look. "No?"

She felt lapped by fire, but she did not drop her gaze.

"No. How could I?" She smiled crookedly. "I listened to him myself for years."

He didn't laugh, didn't answer right away. Slow, his teachers said all those years ago, but Ann knew better. Maddox was deliberate. She'd only seen him lose control once, and the memory still had the power to make her shiver. Now he reached forward, slowly, and deliberately tucked a strand of her hair behind her ear. His eyes never left hers. His hand was warm. His callused fingertips trailed up her cheek and along the curve of her ear.

Her nerve broke.

"I have to go," she babbled without looking at her watch.

"Annie—"

She shook her head. His fingers brushed her neck and fell away. "I can't be late. The camp charges ten dollars for every fifteen minutes past four-thirty. I have to go."

She sidled around the hood of her car, her heart beating, beating high in her throat like a lark rising in the morning. She fumbled with the door. Her hands were shaking so bad she could barely insert her keys in the ignition.

Maddox stepped back from the car. She fixed her attention on the temperature gauge, but she could feel him watching her, his gaze heavy and golden as the sun pressing through the windshield.

She was stupid. So stupid. Hadn't she learned by now that she was only attracted to men who were bad for her?

Yes, he'd stopped to help her. Yes, he'd fixed her car, his hands knowing on the engine and gentle on her cheek. But by the time she negotiated the end of the car-pool line and found a space to park and ran into the day camp office, the big round clock above the filing cabinet read four-forty-two.

So she was late after all.

The blond, ponytailed counselor smiled up from her desk. "Mrs. Cross! I was just about to call your husband."

Ann's heart squeezed. "Why? Mitchell…?"

"Is fine," the counselor assured her.

"Then…I don't understand. Did you expect him to pick Mitchell up?"

"Oh, no. He explained the first time that he couldn't do that. But he asked us to let him know any time you were late so he could pay the late charges."

Something was wrong. Rob had flatly refused to pay any part of Mitchell's camp fees. The boy belonged at home, he insisted. Ann belonged at home, taking care of their son. He'd never pay late charges for day care so that Ann could work.

Unless he had no intention of paying.

Unless he simply wanted to keep track of the days she was late, so he had evidence of her general unfitness as Mitchell's mother.

Panic ballooned inside her. She swallowed it.

"I don't want you to call him," she said as calmly as she could.

"Well, gee, Mrs. Cross—"

"I'm responsible for Mitchell's camp bill. I'm responsible for picking him up. And I'll take care of the charges if I'm late. Is that clear?"

The pretty counselor looked wounded. "Well, sure, Mrs. Cross. I just thought I was doing you, like, a favor."

Ann fought the urge to apologize. Rob had obviously already charmed this college girl—she couldn't be more than twenty—to his side. Rob got everybody on his side. Ann couldn't afford to forget that.

"Thank you," she said. "But I don't need any favors."

She wrote a check for ten dollars, which she also couldn't afford, to cover the late fee. And then she loaded her hot son into her broken car and nursed both through the drive home.

Ann tucked the phone beneath her ear and reached for a pencil. "How much?" she asked.

The mechanic told her. Her stomach rolled in dismay. "For both hoses? What if you only replace one?"

While the mechanic explained all the reasons why that wouldn't be a good idea, Ann scribbled and nodded and tried to figure what she could do without so that she could afford the repairs to her car. Mitchell drifted into the kitchen, wan with heat.

"All right," Ann said. "Is that the total? Could you possibly do it tonight?"

"What's for dinner?" Mitchell asked.

She held up one finger to hush him. "What about tomorrow? I see. No. No, I'll have to call you back."

"I'm hungry. What's for dinner?"

He looked hot. She felt limp. After being at the restaurant all day, she didn't even want to think about cooking. "How about a salad?" she suggested.

Mitchell pulled a face.

"Well, let me think about it." She scanned the short listing in the yellow pages, wondering who to call next. Rob had always taken care of the car. Both cars. He couldn't fix them, but he knew people who could.

Mitchell leaned against the window. "There's a man in our driveway."

"What?" she asked, distracted.

"That guy who was here the other night? When dad picked me up? He's in our driveway."

Ann stomped to the window and, sure enough, there was Maddox Palmer with his head under the hood of her car and a streak of oil on the butt of his jeans.

Her heart tripped, like she was fifteen again and he'd come cruising by her parents' farm. Only she wasn't fifteen. When she got her heart back under control, she was surprised to discover she wasn't flattered or anxious or grateful that Maddox was in her driveway making free with her car.

She was... Ann frowned. Well, really, she was pretty darn sure she was angry.

She cherished it, that lovely little lump of anger, as she marched out her kitchen door and parked herself right by the hood of her car, where he couldn't ignore her.

"What do you think you're doing?" she demanded.

She could see what he was doing, but it made her feel good to ask.

Maddox lifted his head, not smiling, but with a glow at the back of his eyes that could have been appreciation. Or maybe he was laughing at her. "Fixing your car."

"Why?"

"Because you're having trouble with it." A corner of his mouth quirked. "Didn't you ever hear you should call a policeman when you're in trouble?"

She crossed her arms against the temptation of that curving lip. "I called a repairman. My experience is that the police are not all that helpful."

He narrowed his eyes. "When you were arrested, you mean."

She meant when Rob hit her, but she chickened out of saying so. "I don't think your father likes me very much," she said instead.

"Darlin', the chief doesn't like anybody much. Including me. Though I guess you agreeing to testify against Robbo doesn't help."

His wry tone confused her. "Whose side are you on?"

He bent over the engine, presenting her with the long line of his back and that inviting smudge on his hip pocket. "I'm not on anybody's side."

"But you're here."

"I'm just doing you a favor."

I don't need any favors, she'd told Mitchell's camp counselor. But she did. She needed her car repaired.

"I don't want to owe you."

"So…" He looked over his shoulder, a gleam in his heavy-lidded eyes that about stopped her breath. "Make me an offer."

Oh, heavens. She twisted her hands together. "Jimmy's charges fifty dollars for two hoses and a half hour labor."

He shook his head. "I don't want your money."

"Dinner," she said suddenly. "You can stay for dinner."

"Tonight?"

"Yes."

"What are you having?" He sounded amused again.

"Does it matter? Not peanut butter."

He laughed. "Right. Okay, dinner. That'll be nice."

"Don't say that."

"Say what?"

"Nice. I am the poster child of nice," Ann said flatly. "I am inoffensive to the point of being a doormat."

He turned and regarded her thoughtfully. "Oh, I don't know," he drawled. "You've been pretty tough on me since I got back."

She was struck. Cheered. "I have, haven't I?"

Maddox almost grinned. Damned if he'd known another woman so tickled at the possibility that she might be a bitch. Which she wasn't really, not Annie, with her quick, shy smile and her low, warm voice and her remembering how he was getting tired of peanut butter.

No, Annie was nice, all right. It was good that she was growing a little backbone. When they were kids, she was too tenderhearted, too afraid of giving offense. Maybe now she'd put up some resistance when some low-life punk high on beer and hormones got her out in his car along the river road and went a little crazy on her, smooth and soft and willing in the darkness...

Don't go there, boy.

He cleared his throat. "So, who's been wiping his feet on your back?"

"Mmm?" she said. Her eyes were wide and unfocused, and for a second he wondered if she was thinking what he was, if she remembered.

"The doormat thing?" he prompted.

Her gaze cleared. She looked so appalled he figured he remembered, sure enough, and it wasn't good.

"I didn't mean... Nobody," she said hastily.

"My father?"

"He's just doing his job," Ann said, which was what the chief claimed, but Maddox thought it was generous of her to say under the circumstances.

He drummed his fingers against the fender of her car. "Rob?"

She turned white. "I need to start dinner. Thirty minutes?"

"Running away?"

She put up her sharp little chin. "Changing the subject. I don't discuss my marriage."

"Fine. It's not up to me to judge."

"Since you can't possibly know anything about it, I think that's fair. You haven't exactly kept in touch."

"Did I have a reason to? As I remember it, you got married pretty damn quick after I left town."

"Two years," she said quietly.

"You were eighteen!"

"Are you telling me now you were waiting for me to grow up? Because I don't believe it. You never wrote. You never even called."

"You were still in high school."

"Oh, please. Like that made a difference. You didn't have time for me when we were in high school, either."

Because he wanted her too much. Because she was fifteen to his eighteen, and it was up to him to keep his head, to protect her. And since he couldn't think straight when she was around, the best he could do was stay away from her, like a recovering drunk avoiding bars.

"I didn't want to hurt you."

She gave him a straight look. "I got over it," she said.

The screen door squealed, and then it was too late to explain he'd meant something different. Ann's son slipped out of the house, shoulders tight and eyes watchful.

Maddox frowned. He'd seen street kids stand like that waiting for something bad to go down.

"When's dinner?" the boy asked.

Ann turned to her son, her eyes crinkling as she smiled. The change made Maddox dizzy, made the blood rush from his head to places it didn't belong.

"Is that rude or just wanting to know?" she asked.

The kid's sullen expression melted. "Can it be hungry?"

"Hungry is acceptable," Ann allowed. "Forty minutes? Mr. Palmer is staying."

His gaze flicked to Maddox. Maddox didn't blame the kid for feeling doubtful. He was having second thoughts himself. The last thing he needed was to get involved with a witness. The last thing he wanted was to fall for his former teammate's wife.

But as Ann returned to the house, his eyes tracked her straight, slim back, the shining curve of her hair.

The kid stayed behind. "Did you hurt her?"

Maddox narrowed his eyes. "What?"

Mitchell's face was red, but his eyes were hard and adult. His thin hands closed into fists. "I heard you talking. Before. Did you hurt her?"

Maddox remembered. *I didn't want to hurt you.*

I got over it.

And the boy had heard. Hell.

Trying to buy time, Maddox took a step away from the car and shook out a cigarette. He put it in his mouth. Took it out and looked at it. He wasn't supposed to smoke around the kid.

Damn, damn, damn.

"I hurt your mother's feelings," he said. "A long time ago now. Did she tell you we knew each other a long time ago?"

"She said you rode the same bus."

"Yeah, we did. We were friends, kind of, even if she was younger than me. And a girl, at that," he drawled, hoping to coax the kid's humor.

But the boy didn't smile. "Did you hit her?"

"Hell, no," Maddox snapped, startled.

He saw the way the kid braced himself, and something inside him went "uh-oh." He didn't want to hear it. He didn't want to know. But a cop who didn't learn to pay attention to that small warning voice was just plain stupid. Or dead.

He tapped the cigarette against the box. "Is that what you thought?" he asked quietly. "That I hit your mom?"

The kid nodded jerkily, still stiff for a blow.

The back of Maddox's neck crawled. He heard Rob's rueful, easy confession the day they'd walked the links together: *You know I've always had a temper.*

Aw, man. Aw, hell. The carton crumpled in his hand as the reason for Ann's jumpiness clicked. Maddox choked down his anger, forcing words through his suddenly constricted throat.

"Well, I didn't. I never would. I never will. Okay?"

The boy met his eyes blankly. Not accepting what he said, Maddox thought, but considering it. It was a start.

"You figure you were looking out for her, asking me about it." He made it a statement, not a question.

The kid's head jerked again. *Yes.* He was obviously terrified. Compassion moved in Maddox, and then respect. Terrified, but determined.

"Good for you," he said.

Confusion widened those green eyes. Ann's eyes, in the boy's red face. "Sir?"

"That was the right thing to do," Maddox said, speaking man to man. "Your mother should be proud of you. You should be proud of yourself."

"It—I—" the boy stammered.

"Real proud. You're doing a good job taking care of

her.'' At least the nine-year-old was trying, which was more than Maddox could say for anybody else around Ann. Including, he thought with a spurt of disgust, himself. ''You want to give me a hand getting these hoses in?''

''I...'' The boy took a cautious step forward. ''I guess. Yes, sir.''

Maddox felt something loosen in his chest. ''Okay. Tell you what we're going to do. I'm going to put this new hose on here, see, and then you can screw the clamp in place. Got that?''

The boy squeezed in beside him, his small hands eager and unskilled. Maddox was grateful for the task that needed his hands, the boy who needed his help. Because the cop in him, the part that sought answers and solutions, wanted to storm the kitchen for a quick-and-dirty interview. He wanted to back Annie against the sink, into a corner, and interrogate her.

Why did you marry him?

Why did you stay?

What made you leave?

And the rest of him, remembering Rob smiling on the sunlit golf course, didn't give a damn about answers. The rest of him just wanted to find the son of a bitch and tear him in two.

Chapter 5

Ann frowned at the lump of meat defrosting on her kitchen counter. Half a pound of ground beef was dinner for her and Mitchell, but it wouldn't make a decent sandwich for mountain-sized Maddox. There was no way it could feed all three of them.

Well, she would deal with it. She was learning to deal with a lot of things: arrest, probation, separation, single parenthood... Dinner was nothing. She reached for a can of tomatoes and grabbed an onion from under the sink.

And the way that her heart fluttered and her palms got sweaty every time Maddox Palmer gave her one of those intense, hooded looks of his, well, that had to be nothing, too. Twelve years ago, he'd been out of her league. Now he was out of her orbit.

She chopped the onion into small, neat pieces. She was no good with men, anyway. She was terrible at sex. Nothing in her experience was worth risking her peace of mind and her son with some big, bad, violent cop who suspected her of framing her husband.

She scraped meat and onions into a pan and adjusted the heat under them. So why was she making him dinner?

Her cheeks flushed as she lifted the lid on a pot of boiling water. It was only payback, she told herself. She owed him for fixing her car. She couldn't afford to be in debt to Maddox any more than she could afford to be attracted to him.

At seventeen she'd been young enough and dumb enough to be dazzled by Rob Cross, duped by his perfect clothes and his perfect car and his perfect teeth into believing she'd found something special. For ten years, she had accepted Rob's judgment that he was the best she could do, the most she deserved. Her marriage was the price she paid for Mitchell.

She buttered sandwich rolls, sprinkling them with garlic powder and cheese before setting them under the broiler. Well, she wasn't that stupid anymore. She was learning to set her own terms. She wasn't offering any man her trust, her heart, or her loyalty again.

All Maddox Palmer was getting from her was spaghetti.

She went to the door to call him in to dinner and saw him head to head with her son under the hood of her car.

Misgiving shook her. Mitchell looked so small, all angles and bones beside Maddox's powerful, adult body. And he was teetering against the grill, poised to splash a blue gallon jug of—something—over her engine.

Maddox supported the wavering jug with one hand, her son with the other. "Right in there," he said, his voice calm, uninflected. "Easy, now. That's it. Good."

Ann released her breath. Nothing was wrong. Everything was…well, really, it was just fine. Unexpectedly light-hearted, she called, "Supper's ready."

They turned to her, two identical faces of masculine absorption.

And then Mitchell's grin split his face. "Mom!" He bounded toward her, flushed with accomplishment. "We did it. We fixed your radiator."

She beamed her approval. "That's wonderful. Thank you." Over his head, her gaze sought out Maddox. "Thank you both very much."

He followed Mitchell slowly, wiping his hands on a handkerchief. He looked big and male and competent.

"No problem," he said. He wasn't smiling.

Her own smile faded. Obviously his offer to fix her car hadn't included baby-sitting her son. "Yes, it was. I should... You need to let me repay you for the hoses."

He raised his eyebrows. "You're already making me dinner."

"Just salad and spaghetti." Cafeteria food, Rob called it. "Pretty basic stuff."

He gave her one of those dark, unreadable looks that made her stomach thump. "I have pretty basic appetites."

Oh, my. He couldn't mean... She'd never been good at... Ann caught a glimmer in his eye and stopped herself.

"I can *cook,*" she said. "So I guess you'll like it."

Maddox nodded acknowledgment. "Guess I'd better."

It was not, to Ann's mind, a promising start to their meal.

Dinner should have been a disaster. Maddox wasn't extroverted like Rob. He didn't try to be funny or charming. He didn't ask a lot of questions about who Ann had seen at the restaurant or what Mitchell had done at camp. But he ate the food she had cooked, and he listened. He didn't compete for the spotlight, or make it clear that how he spent his day was more important than how they spent theirs.

Gradually, Ann felt the tight knot in her chest ease. And Mitchell, who clammed up around his father, actually volunteered some story about somebody at the day camp named Sam.

"Is Sam your friend?" Ann asked, genuinely pleased he'd found something to like about the camp.

Mitchell ducked his head. "No."

She was confused. "But—"

Mitchell squirmed in an agony of embarrassment. "She's a *girl,* Mom."

Oh. Ann understood. Her nine-year-old couldn't be friends with a girl. It would make him a sissy, or worse.

"Sounds like she can shoot hoops," Maddox said casually, wiping the last of the sauce from his plate with a crust.

Mitchell looked up cautiously. "She stuffed Big Brian today when we played another camp."

"Good for her," Maddox said.

Mitchell relaxed. "We almost won."

"And good for you."

The boy turned red with pleasure.

"Thank you," Ann said later to Maddox, as they cleared the table.

He shrugged, making her conscious of his broad chest, his wide shoulders. Her acute awareness was embarrassing. She told herself it was because she wasn't used to having such a big man moving around her kitchen. "I didn't do anything," he said.

"You listened. You're a good listener."

"Goes with the job."

She sucked in her breath, reminded of who he was and why he'd come to see her last night. She turned on the hot water. "I guess getting people to talk to you would make you a good cop."

He leaned his hips against the counter by the sink, angling so he could watch her face. "Or a good date."

"Really," she said dryly.

"Oh, yeah. You wouldn't believe how many women want to talk about themselves."

"And that's your big attraction?"

He raised his shoulders again. He didn't have to explain his attractiveness to women, and they both knew it. "So, how about it? You want to talk to me, Annie?"

Her heart beat faster. "About what?"

"What's on your mind?"

"You're answering a question with a question again," she said crossly.

This time he didn't smile. He didn't move, either. He just stuck there at her elbow, big and silent and solid and somehow reassuring. No wonder Mitchell confided in him. She was tempted to confide in him herself.

Stupid idea.

She plunged her hands in the dishwater. "I don't want to talk about it."

"About Rob? About the case?"

"Both. Either. I'm trying to put all that behind us."

Maddox crossed his arms over his chest. "Difficult to do when you're a witness for the prosecution."

She closed her eyes briefly. "Yes."

"You know, you can't be forced to testify against him. You're still married."

"We're separated. And it's not that. He's Mitchell's *father*. I hate getting up in front of everybody and saying bad things about him."

"You don't have to," Maddox said in a flat, tight voice. "Confidential communications between spouses are exempt from—"

She jerked her head. *No.* "I have the right to testify to what he did. I have the responsibility."

"Why?" He hadn't raised his voice to her. Hadn't raised his hand. And yet his quiet, hard questions battered at her defenses. "Something else you 'owe,' Annie? You don't strike me as a vindictive woman."

"No. Maybe." She clenched her hands under the surface of the soapy water. "I can't forgive him."

The low voice was relentless. "You can't forgive Rob for what he did to Val?"

"No," she whispered. "I can't forgive him for what *I* did to Val."

"Stole from her."

Shame washed over her. "Yes. I hated what I was becoming. I hated what Mitchell could become."

"Which was...?"

"Somebody who used other people. Somebody who could hit other people."

The big, still body next to her grew, if possible, even more still. "Val?" he asked quietly.

"Val," she admitted, beaten down by his persistent questioning. "And—and me."

"Rob hit you," Maddox repeated without inflection.

Hit her, punched her, kicked her... She cringed from the judgment that must hide beneath his flat, expressionless voice.

She knew what he was thinking. What kind of woman put up with that abuse? What kind of mother let her child grow up at risk from her husband's temper, her husband's example?

"Yes," she said.

Maddox reached for her. She flinched as his hands closed on her shoulders, but his touch was light. His hands were warm. He turned her, so that her wet arms were between them, and studied her face in the light that fell from over the sink. His eyes were dark. His mouth was hard.

He drew his blunt finger along the line of her nose, over the tiny bump. "This?"

Her gaze fell to the center of his broad, solid chest. "He broke my nose. The day we left."

"Son of a bitch," he swore.

She was embarrassed. "He didn't usually touch my face," she felt compelled to add.

"No," Maddox said with instant understanding. A cop's understanding. "They don't. They don't hit where it shows, unless they're really far gone." His voice roughened. He tilted her chin to the light. "The kid?"

"Rob never hit Mitchell." She was sure of it. She would have left immediately if he had. "But..."

"But?" He returned his hands to her shoulders to encourage and support her with his touch.

"Children who live with violence are at greater risk of—"

"Becoming violent themselves," he finished for her. "They teach us that in the academy."

What they didn't teach, Maddox thought, was what made a fourteen-year-old boy from a supposedly stable home grab his daddy's hunting rifle and go gunning for his classmates. But that wasn't the issue here.

The issue was Annie, with her tender mouth and her guarded eyes and her brave determination to do right by her son.

She was either a very brave woman or a very good liar. And after his bright-lights-and-rubber-hoses interrogation, he was ninety-eight percent sure she wasn't lying. Not about Rob hitting her, at least. His hands tightened protectively on her shoulders.

But the cynical cop part of his brain recognized that the abuse she'd endured that engaged his heart and sympathies gave her one hell of a motive. Better for her if Rob rotted in jail.

Disgust with himself—with his doubts, with his methods—roiled his stomach. Rage—at Rob, at his father—pumped through his veins.

"I didn't want Mitchell to think the way we lived was normal," she continued painfully. "I didn't want him growing up to think it was all right."

"Not right," he agreed harshly. "Jeez, Annie…"

She was straight and stiff and fragile in his arms. He slid his hands from her shoulders to her neck, feeling the tension in her, feeling her pulse career in her throat. Excitement? Or fear? His breath came faster. He was some kind of creep if the thought of making her nervous turned him on.

He pushed his fingers into her hair, holding her still for his inspection. Her hair was silky fine, soft and slippery. She smelled like baby shampoo. Desire welled dangerously, adding to the explosive mix inside him. Cradling her head, he searched her face for the girl he'd known, the girl who had looked at him with adoration.

The green eyes meeting his were cool and blank. Her hands came up to curl around his wrists, to hold him away. Frustration shook him. He couldn't find her, couldn't get to her, couldn't protect her.

"I think you should go now," she said.

"Yeah," he said hoarsely. She was right. He ought to get out of here before he did something really dumb, something they would both regret.

He didn't move. Neither did she. Only that heartbeat in her throat, quick as a bird's. Her lips were pale and dry. She licked the lower one, and lust clawed his gut.

The need to touch her, to reach her, to make her respond, raked him. He kissed the bump on the bridge of her nose and felt her tremble. Hell, he was shaking, too. He kissed the corner of her wide, unsmiling mouth and felt the sharp intake of her breath.

Holding her still, he turned his head, just a fraction, and laid his mouth on hers. His heart jackhammered in his chest. Her hands tightened on his wrists, but she didn't pull away. He kissed her lips, long and softly, insistently, and felt them warm and cling in reply. But she was still holding back, holding out on him.

Heat exploded in his brain. He deepened the kiss, diving past her soft lips and her smooth teeth, driving for the heat and the heart and the depths of her mouth. She tasted like the sweet tea she'd served with dinner, and her lips were warm, and her tongue was velvet. He was kissing her. Kissing Annie. It blew his mind. He didn't even register if she kissed him back, he was a teenager again, hot and hungry, pushing into her mouth, desperate to possess, to plunder.

Her fingernails curled into his wrists. The tiny pain pricked through the overload of sensation, sliced through the haze in his head.

She was *not* kissing him back. Damn.

He dragged his mouth from hers. Her lips were red. Her face was pale. Her eyes were blank and wide.

Shock, he figured. He'd badgered her into revealing the worst secrets of her marriage, and then jumped her. He'd shocked her, disgusted her. Hell, he disgusted himself.

"Want to slap my face?"

Her eyes flickered. "Would it make me feel better?"

"I don't know," he said honestly. "It might make me feel better, though."

She angled her chin. Even with his body rioting and his emotions out of control, he admired her attempt at composure.

"I'm not particularly interested in making you feel better right now," she said.

He released her. "Yeah, I can see that."

Her hands twisted together at her waist. "What did you come for?" she whispered. "Answers?"

Her quiet question pierced his chest. That's what he'd told himself. Gather the evidence, get the facts, see if he could shake her story. That's the way he operated. Well, he had her story now, and all the evidence pointed to him being a jerk.

"That was part of it," he admitted.

She nodded. "Well, then, you can leave now. You got what you wanted."

Anger at her acceptance burned him. He would have preferred the slap.

"Not even close," he said harshly. "But I will."

He waited for that to register; watched her green eyes widen. And then he left.

The tables in the dining room needed fresh flowers. Ann collected a tray full of vases and eased through the swinging door to the kitchen, letting herself be distracted by the restaurant's prelunch buzz, the smells of baking bread and grilling vegetables.

She was *not* going to think about Maddox Palmer anymore. Her heart gave this funny little bump, and she scowled. She was not going to waste another second reliving and reexamining his surprising, hot, sweet kiss.

She entered the kitchen's work aisle in time to see Val MacNeill lay down her big chopping knife and put both hands on her back.

Thoughts of Maddox fled. Ann set down her tray in concern. "Honey, are you all right?"

Val turned her flushed face toward Ann and smiled. "Never better."

"You're not still…" Ann paused delicately.

"Throwing up?" Val asked cheerfully. She shook her head. "No, we're out of that stage. Now we're in the I-have-amazing-energy-and-a-fabulous-sex-drive-but-my-back-hurts stage."

Ann blinked. "Well, that's—that's good."

"Oh, yes. Con is much better at helping with the sex drive thing than with the nausea."

Ann laughed and began unloading her tray.

"What about you?" Val asked, reaching for her knife. "Any problems picking up Mitchell yesterday?"

"It was fine. I was a few minutes late, that's all."

"I'm sorry. I didn't mean to keep you, the time just—"

Dear Val, always taking responsibility. But Ann was responsible for herself now, or trying to be. "It wasn't your fault. I had a problem with my car."

Val pulled a sympathetic face. "Oh, too bad. Do you need time off to take care of it?"

"No, I—" Ann emptied the blue glass bottles into the sink, feeling her face begin to heat. "Actually, Maddox Palmer stopped to give me a hand."

"Mad Dog?" Val sounded more intrigued than appalled. "Well, well."

"It was just the radiator hose," Ann muttered.

"Do tell."

"There isn't anything to tell. I got a leak in the hose, and he stopped and fixed it with duct tape."

"That won't hold. You'll have to take the car to a garage."

"Yes. Well, no." She fumbled, rinsing bottles. "He came by last night and replaced the hoses."

Val stopped chopping peppers. She turned. "He did what?"

Ann cleared her throat. "He was only doing me a favor."

"Sweetie, you don't accept favors. Not from me, and certainly not from the chief of police's son."

"I didn't. I mean, he fixed the car, but I made him dinner to pay him back."

"This is getting more interesting by the minute. You cooked dinner for Mad Dog? Ate with him last night? How was it?"

"It was…fine. He was good with Mitchell."

"I adore my godson, but right now I'd rather know how the man was with you. Did he behave himself? Make a pass?"

So much for not thinking about him. About *it*. Ann began to refill the bottles one by one, concentrating fiercely on the water levels as if her life depended on getting them equal.

"He kissed me, if that's what you mean," she blurted, both embarrassed and relieved to get it out.

"Oh, boy. That is definitely what I mean. Did you like it?"

Ann remembered Maddox's hands in her hair, warm and coaxing, and his mouth on her mouth, hot and hungry. The stubble on his upper lip. The smooth thrust of his tongue. His strong pulse pounding against her grip on his wrists, his solid body—not pressing, not overpowering—but close and urgent. Maddox kissed like he meant it. Like he wanted her.

Her insides squeezed together. It was a novel and disturbing feeling, being wanted.

"He surprised me. I don't know. I think so." She winced from the uncertainty in her own voice. She sounded like such a loser.

Val's eyes sparkled. "Well, tell him to kiss you again so you can find out."

"I couldn't do that."

"Sweetie, it's been a year since you left Rob. Maybe it's time to live a little."

"Not quite a year. The divorce isn't final for two more weeks. Technically, I'm a married woman."

"And Rob is a creep. You deserve the chance to find out that not all men are like him."

Ann grabbed a bunch of daisies from the refrigerator and began stripping leaves from the lower stems. "I can't take chances. I have to think about Mitchell."

"I thought you said Mad Dog was good with Mitchell."

"Val, listen to yourself. 'Mad Dog.' What kind of mother dates a man with a nickname like that? I might as well go out with somebody named Viper or Spike."

"You know that name's left over from his football days. It doesn't mean anything."

"Really?" Ann tossed the leaves into the garbage. "Then why have you been using it ever since he came back to town?"

They exchanged looks.

"He can be a little…intense," Val admitted.

Ann shivered with the remembered heat of Maddox's kiss. "Yes."

"But that doesn't mean he's dangerous."

"Obviously, you haven't been listening to the gossip at lunch."

"So, is it Mad Dog you're worried about?" Val asked shrewdly. "Or what people will say about you dating him?"

"Both, I guess." Ann stared at the pretty, bright flowers

in the sink with their innocent and optimistic faces. She was a long way from innocent and years past optimistic. "I can't afford to ignore what people say. Not with the trial coming up. Rob still has lots of friends in this town, and I still have to live here."

Val sighed. "You're right. Of course, you're right. But I guess I'm so happy with Con, I want to see you happy, too."

Affection misted Ann's eyes. She wiped her hands on her apron and turned to hug her best friend since second grade. "I don't need 'happy,' honey. 'Safe' is good enough for me."

And Maddox Palmer definitely was not safe.

Chapter 6

"**Y**ou want to play policeman in this town, you have to put on the uniform." The chief drew himself up behind his desk, every starched thread in place, every button gleaming.

Maddox, sprawled in one of the brown vinyl chairs, felt like he'd been called down to the principal's office. "I thought you wanted me on this case."

"I wanted you to look into facts that could exonerate Rob. Not swallow that woman's stories."

That woman. Annie. A vision of her cool green eyes, her pale face framed by baby fine hair, rose up to accuse him.

"And if the facts support her stories?" Maddox growled.

"Then we'll bring them to the D.A.'s attention. God knows they're eager enough to use the rest of her testimony."

"Which is?"

"Anything going to motive. That Rob and Val had a history. That he was upset with her for offering his wife a job. And that while he was working at the bank, he encouraged

Ann to bring him the daily deposit bags from the restaurant.''

"She mention anywhere along the line that Rob also beat the crap out of her?"

The chief stiffened. "Where did you hear that?"

"From Annie."

The chief looked uncomfortable. "She never came to me."

Maddox shook out a cigarette and lit up. He'd never been able to do *that* in the principal's office. But he was a long way now from the nineteen-year-old truant who'd left town. "And you never encouraged her to. Is that why you want to believe she's lying now? So you can live with yourself for standing by while Rob took his fists to her?"

"I'm not defending myself or my actions to you."

"Some things can't be defended."

The chief's face flushed as red as the bricks on the county courthouse. "You know how tricky domestic situations are. If the woman involved won't file a complaint…but I run a clean department."

"Yeah? Then why are you so eager to get my investigation under your control?"

"For your sake, idiot. I want you to put a badge on again before you lose your head completely over that woman and do something we'll both regret."

"Like punch out Rob."

"Like get yourself fired for assaulting a civilian when you're already on suspension."

Well. The chief might actually give a rat's ass about him. Or about his career, at least.

"Thanks, Dad. I appreciate your concern."

"I'm concerned about upholding the law. I don't want to have to arrest my son in my town."

"So you're going to put me in uniform and let me make the arrests instead?" Maddox asked dryly.

The chief harrumphed.

It was a judgment call, and Maddox's faith in his own judgment had been badly shaken. He wanted action, damn it. He itched for the chance to wipe the blank look from Annie's eyes, to scrub away his self-disgust. But he was afraid of making another mistake.

He blew out a stream of smoke. "Let's say I do go to work for you. It beats moonlighting as a security guard. But what then?"

"Then I'll put you on the case. Officially, this time."

"What else?"

"Well, we're a small department. I can't spare any of my officers full-time on any one investigation."

"Which means what? You going to put me on rookie patrol?"

"I need somebody to start on swing patrol—three to midnight. But the schedule rotates. You'd do five-nines, just like everybody else."

Five days of nine-hour shifts and three days off duty. It was fair. Better than he'd expected. With the day-off rotation, he might even see a weekend.

Hell. He was thinking like this was a real job. Like he could ever work in Cutler, where everyone remembered every stupid thing he'd done in high school. Like he could work under the chief, who'd always figured him for a screw-up.

Like he had a choice.

Annie's flat acceptance still vibrated in his brain. *Well, then, you can leave now. You got what you wanted.*

He wasn't sure what he wanted. He only knew he couldn't leave Annie to face her detractors alone anymore now than he could when they were kids.

Anyway, it was only for a month.

He stabbed out his cigarette. "Where do I sign?"

The gym was hot and echoed with the slap of basketballs and the shouts of children. Ann stopped just inside the scarred double doors, hit by the smell of healthy young bodies and hot old ones, floor wax and sneakers and sweat.

She searched the knots of sliding, jumping children until she identified Mitchell's fair head and purple Spartans jersey. And then, with an old, reflexive fear, she looked for Rob.

He sat with the rest of the parents opposite the team's bench, his eyes narrowed on his son's play. His blond sideburns were dark with sweat. His mouth was compressed with annoyance. He looked like what he was, a former star athlete who played golf. She knew how hard he'd fought the deterioration of his physique, the collapse of his career. He still battled the loss of his standing in the community.

He did not see her.

Her shoulders sagged with relief. She'd come from weeding her garden, anxious not to miss Mitchell's first game. Her hair was stuck up with a plastic clip. Red clay shadowed her knees beneath the hem of her sensible shorts.

Rob hated her in shorts. Mrs. Robert Cross never wore them. She had never worn anything that could trigger her husband's uncertain temper. But Annie liked them. She liked the freedom and the coolness and the connection with the earth. She hadn't changed for Mitchell's game tonight. She was in too much of a hurry. And maybe she was too proud. But she was glad Rob didn't see her, all the same.

She slipped into the bleachers and sat down by the door.

The referee's whistle blew. Ann didn't know much about basketball, but as the quarter wore on even she could see that Mitchell played poorly. He ran aimlessly, seeming almost relieved when his teammates neglected to pass him the ball.

"Go on, grab it! Get it! Get in there!" Rob shouted from the sidelines.

Another player dribbled down the court. Mitchell slapped at the ball, earning a whistle from the ref and a reprimand from his coach.

''Reaching,'' the referee announced, his shaved head gleaming under the fluorescent lights. ''Red ball, on the side.''

Mitchell's face tightened. Ann's chest tightened, too, but her sympathy would only embarrass him. She looked away, toward the doors.

A police officer entered from the recreation center lobby, his shoulders wide, his body broadened by whatever it was policemen wore beneath their shirts. His hat brim shadowed his face, but Ann recognized the set of his head and the slant of his shoulders as he sauntered through the doors.

It was Maddox, his lawless energy contained in a blue police uniform wilting with heat. Her heart two-stepped in her chest. She pressed her hands together in her lap.

He took one step toward the corner, so that the door was no longer at his back. His hooded gaze panned the room: the running teams, the yelling parents, the teens' pickup game—shirts and skins—on the other court. He saw Mitchell and smiled.

And then he turned his head and stared directly at Ann.

Something fluttered low in her stomach. Like fear, but she wasn't afraid, though her mouth was dry and her blood drummed in her ears.

She waited for him to come to her. He would come. The certainty was both thrilling and distressing. And he did walk over to the bleachers, with the same casual prowl that caught her eye and broke her heart in high school.

He nodded. ''Annie.''

She said the first words to come into her head. ''You're in uniform.''

His mouth relaxed. ''I'm on duty.''

''But I thought—you said you were on leave.''

''From the Atlanta department, yeah.'' He angled his big body so he still had a view of the gym.

Ann blinked. On his dark sleeve, right above the stylized

star on his shoulder, were the words Cutler Police Department. "You're working here?"

"For the next month."

Through the start of Rob's trial. Something shriveled inside her. "Well, that should make our next interrogation easier." She was proud that her voice did not shake.

Maddox kept his head turned toward the teens' game across the court, where play and tempers were heating up over a foul call. "I've read your statement. I don't need to interview you."

"I thought you already had."

"Not in an official capacity."

"And unofficially?"

He shrugged. "I wanted to know what's going on with you, Annie. Is that so bad?"

She wasn't sure. "It depends on your reasons, I guess."

She couldn't believe she was talking to him this way, challenging him, and the high metal ceiling hadn't fallen on her head and the aluminum bleachers hadn't opened and swallowed her up.

You want reasons? Rob had sneered, his handsome face swollen with bourbon and frustration. *I'll give you reasons.* Reasons not to question. Reasons to be afraid.

Maddox rubbed his jaw with the back of his hand, recalling her to the present. He had big hands, square and clean. "Maybe I'm just taking a friendly interest."

"Is that what we are?" she asked dryly. "Friends?"

He looked at her sideways, and his mouth curled in that slow, knowing grin that did funny things to her breathing. "We used to be friends, remember? When we were kids."

"You beat up Billy Ward for calling me 'Chicken Legs.'"

"And you used to save half your dessert to give me on the bus. Chocolate chip cookies."

Because his mother had died, and he didn't have cookies

from home. She remembered. ''It was a long time ago,'' she said.

''You're still feeding me.''

''Once. I owed you for my car.''

''So.'' He crossed his arms casually on his broad chest, watching the action in the gym. Mitchell was sitting out, head bent, skinny elbows on bony knees. On the other court, the backboard rattled, and a shirt shoved a skin. ''What do I have to do to earn another invitation?'' Maddox asked.

''Why would you want one?''

''Maybe I'm still hungry.''

In her mind, on her mouth, she replayed his kiss, possessive, seeking, hot. *I have pretty basic appetites.* Her fingers curled in her lap.

''I'm sorry. I can't give you what you want. I can't be what you want.''

''You are what I want, Annie,'' he said in a low, rough voice. ''You've always been what I want.''

''Not always,'' she whispered, looking down at her hands. Remembering the river road.

''Even then,'' he said, instantly understanding her. ''But you were fifteen years old. Too damn young for what I had in mind.''

She wanted to believe him. It soothed an old hurt to believe he'd rejected her from kindness and not because he'd found her flat-chested, embarrassingly eager and dumb. She smiled sadly. ''And now I'm too old.''

''Twenty-eight. Three years younger than me.''

''Too married, then.''

Too damaged, she meant. Too much Rob's accomplice in the destruction of her own soul.

''Separated, you said. Almost divorced.''

The marriage is over. She'd told him that.

She sighed. ''It's not that simple. There's my record. The trial. Mitchell. You can't afford to be involved with me.''

''Why don't you let me be the judge of that?''

"Because," she said painfully, "I can't afford to be involved with you."

He drew breath to answer. And then the pickup game on the far court exploded. Half-naked bodies tangled under the hoop. Shouted curse words shook the gym. A ten-year-old Spartans player froze with the ball in his hands, and the ref blew his whistle.

Before Ann could blink, Maddox was gone, his hard shoes clacking on the wooden floor.

"Break it up. Break it up. Knock it off!" The last was an authoritative roar.

He stood aside a second while the sweaty players sorted themselves out, encouraged one with a heavy hand on his shoulder and plucked another from the floor. A father on the bleachers stood. The woman beside him stopped him with a hand on his arm.

Mitchell huddled with his teammates on the bench, chin down and eyes watchful. His trained response to violence, Ann thought, with a catch at her heart.

She looked anxiously back at Maddox, dark and solid in the center of a pack of teens.

I heard he shot that boy, and the department fired him.

He could handle it. Of course he could handle it.

"Tell me what's going on," he said.

The teens, black and white, shirts and skins, all of them sweaty and angry, crowded around. Words flew, punctuated with curses and gestures.

"Stuffed you, man."

"Knocked me down."

"Street rules. Show me blood."

Maddox listened, never reaching for his notebook or his radio, his face impassive. "This isn't the street," he interrupted. "You've got kids playing here, parents. I'm calling a technical foul."

"All right!"

"But I never touched him!" a tall black youth protested.

Maddox squinted. "Your name Burrell?"

The kid thrust his jaw forward. "So?"

"I used to play with a Jimmy Burrell. Know him?"

The kid's attitude leaked out like air from a ball. "My uncle."

Maddox nodded. "Good player. One shot," he said to the boy he'd pulled off the floor.

"But—"

"Take it," Maddox advised in a hard voice. "And get back to your game before I call the center off limits for the next thirty days. You want to get stupid, go someplace else."

Ann held her breath. Grumbling, the teen took the ball from one of his friends and stood at the free-throw line. The others jostled into position along the lane. Set. Shoot. Swish. Maddox caught the ball one-handed and bounced it to the other team.

And that was it. It was over. The teens slid and thumped down court, Maddox nodded to the referee, and the boys' teams resumed play.

Ann sat frozen on her hard aluminum bench, caught between relief and a sense of anticlimax. She watched Maddox stroll back along the far side of the court, nod to a parent, exchange a word with Rob. Uneasiness lurched in her stomach, but neither man glanced her way.

As Maddox passed the Spartans bench, he said something to Mitchell that earned him a quick, grateful look from the boy. *Thank you,* Ann thought. Without fuss, without thought, he'd done the right thing, defused a tricky situation and offered comfort to her son. She sighed. She would never in a million years have that kind of competent assurance.

And then, as Maddox paced the painted line toward her, she saw that beneath his black-brimmed hat his face was nearly gray.

He met her eyes and smiled crookedly. "Punks."

"You handled them very well."

He shrugged, dismissing her compliment. "So, I don't shoot every kid who pushes the line."

There it was, she realized. There was a reason for that gray look around his mouth, the lines of strain around his eyes. That boy he killed was only fourteen. Did he think about that every time he answered a call or went out on patrol?

"I'm sorry," she said. "It must be hard for you."

He shook his head. "Part of the job."

"A difficult one."

"I'm fine."

"Meaning, you don't want to talk about it," she guessed. "Or at least, not with me."

He raised sandy eyebrows. "There's nothing to talk about. I'm fine."

She hesitated. He wasn't angry with her, not yet. She didn't want to make him angry. But a friend wouldn't think like that. A friend wouldn't let her fear stand in the way of offering her help.

"I used to say that a lot," she said, looking down at her hands.

"What?"

"'I'm fine.'" She forced a smile. "It ranked right up there with 'I walked into a door.'"

"Jeez, Annie…" He sounded shaken.

"It's all right," she said quickly. "You don't have to talk to me. But you don't need to lie to me, either. I've heard enough lies—told them to myself, mostly."

"I am not lying to you."

Now he was mad, she thought with regret. And she hadn't helped him at all. She twisted her hands together. "I'm sorry. It's not any of my business. I'm not qualified, anyway."

"Qualified for what?" Irritation edged his tone.

"To help you with what's bothering you. For heaven's sake, look at me. I can't even deal with my own problems."

Maddox looked, and longing leapt up and grabbed his throat like a hungry dog. She was so damn pretty, pink-cheeked and earnest, her soft hair clipped back like a little girl's. But there was a bump in her nose and a ruler in her spine that reminded him she was all grown up, that made him think of her in purely adult kinds of ways. Inappropriate ways. Ways that involved white sheets and a dark room and long, uninterrupted hours to surround himself with her softness, to plunge himself in her peace...

He jerked himself back from that little fantasy. Like coming down from a bad marriage to an abusive jerk made her ripe for hard sex with a broken cop on temporary assignment.

She wasn't ready for him.

He wasn't right for her.

But she was braver and stronger than she gave herself credit for.

"You deal with your problems just fine," he told her roughly.

She slid him a disbelieving look.

"Seriously," he insisted. "It took guts to leave Rob. To get a new job. To start a new life. To make a home for your kid."

"Maddox, I work in a restaurant. My son has to go to day camp because I stole twenty thousand dollars from my best friend and I don't have any other way to pay it back."

He shrugged. "So, you found a way to meet your responsibilities."

She shook her head. A strand of fine hair slipped from her barrette and fell forward on her cheek. He wanted to touch it, just to tuck it back behind her ear. He wanted to do a lot of things to her, with her, most of them impossible. "You're making me sound too—"

"—straight? Brave? You are. You can handle a lot."

"But not you, apparently."

Was she reading his mind? He sucked in a hard breath.

He'd give everything he owned to have her handling him, her hands on him. Sweat collected at the base of his spine at the images conjured by her words. He was half aroused and way out of line.

He had to get a grip. He couldn't believe they were having this discussion in a hot gym full of people, with him in uniform and her husband glaring at them from across the court.

"I don't think we should talk about this now," he said tightly.

"Yes, you've made that very clear. And I'm working on accepting that it's somehow okay for you to have access to my house and my son and the inside of my car—and my police file—but I can't be trusted to know anything about you." Her voice was stiff with hurt.

Maddox swore silently. He felt like a heel. Served him right, too, for having his brain stuck below his belt buckle.

"It's not like that. I trust you."

Annie gave him one of those "oh, right" looks women were good at. "I'm trying to be understanding about this. Polite. But if you're going to hand me some line about trust, I—"

He couldn't help it. He chuckled.

"What?" she demanded.

"Some doormat you turned out to be," he said.

She turned as red as the referee's shirt. And then her eyes sparkled. "Don't change the subject."

"Darlin', I don't even know what the subject is. Except you wanting me to talk to you, and I don't have anything to say."

She collected herself, back straight, hands together in her lap like one of his grandmother's china dolls. "I want you to know that I admire the way you handled those boys back there. Even if it was hard for you, you did a real good job. And—and if you want to talk to me about it, you can."

She had guts, Annie Barclay. Her stubborn kindness prodded him on a level he'd kept carefully shielded since the shooting. He didn't let anyone get too close to the black gulf inside him: not the press, not his colleagues, not his girlfriend or his lieutenant. Even for Annie, Maddox wasn't peering over that edge.

"Thanks for the offer. But I don't go on about what happened. To anybody. Ever. I'm—"

Her eyebrows went up. "—fine?"

"Working," he finished grimly.

His radio squawked, and that was good, that made him a competent cop responding to a call and not a loser running from the concern in her voice.

He answered. "Go ahead."

"Assistance requested on a ten-fifty-four on Old Graham a mile past Spring Forest."

His city-trained brain grappled with the unfamiliar code. "Ten-fifty-four?"

The night dispatcher, Crystal, sniffed. "Do you copy?"

What the… He grinned suddenly. "Copy. En route."

Ann watched him, her green eyes big and anxious. "Is everything all right?"

"There's a cow in the road. Guess I'll go offer it a lift in the squad car."

She smiled. "Before it hitches a ride from a passing motorist?"

"Exactly." He panned the gym once—the pickup game, the running kids, the parents on the bleachers—before his gaze returned to her face. "You okay here?"

She nodded. "Take care."

Damn. Rob was watching them. But a patrol officer always responded to a call. And a cow in the road was a traffic accident waiting to happen. "You, too."

He left, regret dogging his steps like a rookie partner.

The Spartans lost to the Comets, twenty-six to fourteen. Ann bit her lip as the young players filed past one another, slapping hands and muttering over and over, "Good game, good game."

It hadn't been a good game for Mitchell.

Her son spent most of it on the bench. His coach put him in in the final minutes, when the game was irredeemably lost, but Mitchell still had time to fumble a pass and miss a rebound. Shoulders hunched and eyes lowered, he walked the gauntlet of the opposing team.

Good game, good game.

"He played a lousy four minutes."

Ann jerked at the sound of Rob's voice.

He stood beside her, hands in his pockets, scowling as the boys straggled by. "Did you see him waving his arms around out there?"

She drew a careful breath. *As long as your husband has visitation rights,* the therapist had cautioned, *Mitchell must forge his own relationship with his father.*

She'd witnessed Rob's disappointment when Mitchell showed no sign of developing into Golden Boy Junior. But she couldn't stand by while he picked on their son. "Coach told him to keep his hands up."

Rob snorted. "Well, he looked like a damn windmill. And you... What are people going to think of my wife coming out in public dressed like that?"

She'd forgotten she was still in her gardening shorts. "I was weeding. Before the game."

"It doesn't look right."

She caught her hands creeping to her hair and forced them to her sides. "You don't need to worry, Rob. We're almost divorced. You don't have to be embarrassed by how I dress anymore."

He eyed her critically. "At least you've got nice legs."

She was relieved by his mild tone; surprised by his compliment. "Thank you."

"You're an attractive woman, Annie," he said, moving closer. "I didn't tell you that often enough."

The hair on the back of her neck rose in warning. "Thank you," she said again. "Well… Shall I take Mitchell home? Since I'm here, I mean?"

"No. I'll take him out for some ice cream." Rob slanted her his All-American smile. "Cheer him up."

Just for a moment, he resembled the golden college boy who put on a sleek black tux to take her to her high school prom. Who put on a morning-gray one to do the right thing in front of God, her mother and the town as she walked down the aisle, wearing white and four months pregnant. Who held her hand in the hospital and cried after he knocked her down the stairs and she lost their second baby. Regret made a lump in her throat.

"Join us?" Rob invited, watching her carefully.

She could. It would be so easy. Mitchell would like it, the ice cream and her protection. For half an hour, she could pretend they were the family she'd once dreamed of.

She swallowed. "I have to get back to my garden."

It was getting too dark to work outside, and they both knew it.

Rob's eyes hardened, but his smile never faded. "Another time, then."

She'd made so many mistakes. The least she could do was learn from them.

"I don't think so," she said quietly. "Have a good time. I'll expect Mitchell around nine."

Back straight and knees shaking, she walked out to her car, leaving her old dreams behind.

Chapter 7

Rob used to tell her he would kill her if she left him.

He hadn't yet, but Ann had suffered a sort of social death when she moved out of the big house on Stonewall Drive. She quit more than her marriage. She left the flower committee and the garden club, the clique of wives who reapplied lipstick while their husbands clinched deals over golf, the circle of moms who gossiped and tanned while their children splashed in the clean blue water of the club pool.

She didn't miss it. She tried not to mind that women whose baby showers she'd attended avoided her eyes when she brought them menus at Wild Thymes.

"Stupid cows," Val fumed. "What do they think, that a felony conviction is something you can catch over lunch?"

Ann smiled, touched by her friend's loyalty. "I think they're more worried the divorce will rub off."

"They're jealous because you're free," newlywed Val said firmly. "They'd rather be you."

Ann rolled her eyes. "Honey, they don't want to be me. They don't even want to know me."

But something changed in the week after Rob brought Mitchell home from ice cream. Barbara Sue Evans called to invite Ann to a Pampered Chef party. Gladys Baggett stopped her in front of Silver & Lace Bridals and asked if she'd like to do the church flowers in August. Ann said "no" to the first request. She couldn't afford upscale kitchen gadgets even if she'd liked Barbara Sue. She said "yes" to the second. Everybody was on vacation in August, so her decorating the front of the church could hardly cause a schism in the congregation.

And then she telephoned Val to find out what the heck was going on.

"You tell me," Val said. "Mackenzie Ward told Mother you'd be at the club dance next Saturday."

Ann blinked, shifting the phone to her other ear as she unpacked Mitchell's lunch cooler. "Are you going?"

"I don't think so. Con's in Boston on business, and I'm not really up to an evening of committee discussions with Mother. But what about you?"

"No. Of course not. I'm not a member."

"Rob is."

"Rob is barely forking over child support. He's not paying for me to attend dances at the club."

"I suppose," Val said. "Although I can't see him taking Luella Hodges, either."

"Luella?"

"Hodges. Mother says he started seeing her—"

"You mean, sleeping with her?"

"Now you know Mother would never come right out and say that. Anyway, he took up with her after Donna from the bank left town. Didn't you hear?"

Ann threw out the foil wrappings and squishy apple from the bottom of Mitchell's cooler. She worried he wasn't eating enough fruit. "No. People don't talk to me about my husband's dates."

Val snorted. "I would have thought that was the first thing they talked to you about."

"I don't listen," Ann explained apologetically.

"Oh, Annie. You're too nice, did you know that?"

"Yes, but I'm working on it."

Maddox's rough voice stroked her memory: *Some doormat you turned out to be.* Sloshing a sponge around the bottom of the cooler, Ann smiled.

"Anyway, just be careful. I'm worried about what he could do," Val said.

He. Rob.

Ann collected her thoughts. "I already gave my statement to the prosecutor. I don't think there's anything he can do."

"I'm not worried about your testimony," Val said rather sharply. "I'm worried about you."

"Oh." Ann felt humbled and disconcerted as always by the proof of her friend's concern. "Well, he can't do anything about me, either. He's divorcing me. The court date's next Friday."

"Are you…okay with that?" Val asked delicately.

She had to be. She understood the blow her guilty plea had delivered to Rob's pride and reputation. After what she'd said about him, how could he not divorce her? "You know what Wednesday is, don't you?" she asked.

"Wednesday? We're closed. Fourth of July."

"Independence Day," Ann deadpanned.

After a heartbeat pause, Val laughed. "I guess you'll be fine."

"You bet," Ann said.

Sometimes, she even let herself believe it was true.

It took the state investigator listed in Rob's file four days to return Maddox's calls. Son of a bitch. Maddox hunched over the phone. This case was messy enough without some overworked State Bureau of Investigations desk jockey busting his chops.

''I've got the file in front of me,'' Maddox said, pushing the pages around on his desk. ''I wanted an update on the physical evidence taken from the fire scene.''

Detective Tyler Greene did not fall over himself answering his request. ''Is this the part where you tell me this is your investigation and you know how to run it?''

Maddox leaned back in his chair. ''No. This is the part where I tell you that up till now this has been somebody else's investigation and unless you help me out I'm totally screwed.''

There was a short pause on the other end of the phone. A brief laugh. ''I thought you said your name was Palmer.''

''Maddox Palmer. The chief's my old man.''

''My condolences,'' Greene said.

''Is this sympathy going to get me somewhere, or do I have to tell you sad stories about my childhood?''

''Spare me.'' But the detective's voice had warmed about twenty degrees. ''What do you need, Palmer?''

''I need to know if you have any indicators linking our suspect with the arson.''

''You having trouble with your case? Or does the chief still think your suspect is just misunderstood?''

Resentment still tinged the detective's tone. His father must have really yanked his chain.

''Hey, we're like the guys on Dragnet,'' Maddox said easily. ''We just want the facts.''

''So, what have you got?''

Maddox pulled out one of the three cigarettes he'd put in his breast uniform pocket that morning and looked at it. He'd picked a hell of a time to cut down. ''So far, all we can prove is aggravated assault. Both the victim and the ex-wife are willing to testify.''

''What, he beat the wife, too?'' Greene joked.

''As a matter of fact, he did,'' Maddox said flatly. ''But the defense will try to throw her story out on the grounds of relevancy. We've got motive and opportunity, but the victim was unconscious when Cross set the fire. So unless your lab can turn up evidence, we may not be able to make our case for attempted murder.''

''What do you want? An engraved lighter?'' the detective asked with heavy irony.

Maddox paused in the act of lighting his cigarette. ''How about a matchbook?''

''Look, we've got several hundred pieces of evidence from that fire, and they're all being identified and tested. Maybe there was a matchbook. Maybe there wasn't. When we have something for you, I'll let you know.''

''When?''

''Whenever the lab gets to it.''

''It's been a year,'' Maddox said.

''Victimless arson. It doesn't have priority. You know that.''

''A woman could have died in that fire.''

''But she didn't.''

''But the guy who set it is going up to trial in four weeks.''

Greene sighed. ''All right. I'll see what I can do. Holiday might slow things down, though. Lab's closed.''

''That's okay. I've got a big day Wednesday myself.''

''Writing traffic tickets?'' the state agent ribbed.

''Worse than that,'' Maddox said gloomily. ''I've got parade detail.''

Greene laughed.

The parade was over.

The floats—4-H and Channel Five and Little Dancers Studio—were coming down in the courthouse parking lot. A couple dozen kids carrying band instruments walked back to their parents and their cars. Men with lawn chairs and women with covered dishes drifted across the street to the park where the Rotary Club was firing the grills.

For the past three hours, Maddox had dealt with lost children, lost purses, lost tempers. He had ice cream on his uniform pants and sweat in his hat band.

And he was having, he realized with a sense of shock, the best time he'd had on the job in years.

He slowed a kid on a speeding bicycle shedding red, white and blue crepe paper. The ground was already littered with crumpled cups and busted balloons. Some poor public servant had a hell of a mess to clean up tomorrow. But it wasn't his mess. Maddox felt good.

He ambled toward the dunking booth, watching girls with braided hair and boys with balloons race across the wilted grass.

And then he heard the pops, coming from the line of trees on his right, and the whole scene cracked and twirled like a broken kaleidoscope.

Running children and screams. Falling children and blood. A woman teacher on the ground, covering an eleven-year-old girl with her body, while a skinny kid too young to drive sighted down his rifle...

Pop. Pop. Pop.

Fireworks.

Maddox shuddered. He wasn't there, in that Atlanta schoolyard. He was in Cutler. It was the Fourth of July. And there were some stupid kids with fireworks behind the cover of the trees who were due to get the lesson of their lives.

He strode over the littered ground, armpits drenched in sweat, relief burning like rage in his belly.

There were eight of them, a dozen if he counted the hangers-on: boys, ranging from almost ten to pushing fifteen, laughing and squatting by the stream that bounded the park.

Maybe he'd get lucky. Maybe they were launching their rockets over the water, and he wouldn't have to spend the rest of the afternoon tramping through the pines and poison ivy to search for smoldering fires.

The gurgling water and the boys' own noise covered the sound of his approach.

"My turn."

"I got it."

A tall kid in a baseball cap pushed away the boy at his elbow. "Watch out. I'm gonna light it."

"Don't," Maddox ordered from the top of the bank.

The older boy swore, and the circle rippled like water. The underbrush crackled as somebody bolted, and another child, all legs and a flash of white T-shirt, jumped for the opposite side of the stream.

"Stay there," Maddox warned. "Police."

The jumper froze and then turned, white-faced and defiant. Terrified. Nine-year-old Mitchell Cross.

Aw, hell. That made everything just perfect.

Maddox glared at the sullen circle from under his hat brim. "You boys know you're breaking the law?"

The tall kid balancing in the stream straightened slowly, not sure what to do with his height or his eyes or the rocket in his hands.

"My dad says fireworks are legal now," he said, trying for cool.

"Not these. Not in North Carolina. Not on public property, and never unsupervised. Hand 'em over."

"But my dad said—"

Maddox raised his eyebrows. "You want to involve him in this discussion? Maybe make an announcement over the PA?"

The kid fidgeted. Folded. "No," he muttered.

"Right. Turn out your pockets, I'll take what you've got. Now," he barked, and flushed the stiff and stalling boys into action.

He watched stuff bounce on the rocks and get lost in the weeds: rockets and cherry bombs, mortar tubes and strips of firecrackers... It would take forever to collect.

"Fine. Now get out of here. Not you," he added as Mitchell prepared to slink off with the rest. "You can help me pick up."

The boy said something to his shoes.

"What was that?"

Mitchell's chin jerked up. "I said, you can't tell me what to do."

Maddox sighed. "I can, you know. I'm bigger than you. I'm older than you. And I'm a police officer." He started down the bank, feeling his way along the rocks and ferns, and pulled a sample bag from his belt. "Here."

Grudgingly, the boy took the bag and reached for one of the yellow tubes lying on the ground. "That doesn't make it right," he whispered.

There was a kicker. This kid had a lifetime of somebody bigger and older and in authority throwing his weight around.

Maddox pushed back his hat with one hand. "So, you figure this shouldn't be my call?"

Mitchell stooped for another firecracker. "I wasn't doing anything wrong."

"You weren't doing anything smart, either." He regarded the boy's bent back for a minute. "Let's say I didn't come along. Let's say you got to choose. Don't you figure your mother's got enough to deal with right now without worrying about taking you to the emergency room?"

Mitchell's small hands clenched the evidence bag. Satisfied he'd made his point, Maddox turned his attention to the cleanup. They worked in silence and in the heat until the last bright yellow wrapper was retrieved from the rocks. Maddox took back the bag.

"Thanks." When the kid made no move to run, Maddox lifted an eyebrow. "What?"

Mitchell swallowed. "Are you going to tell her?"

"Hey, I'm a cop, not a snitch." But the boy didn't smile, just stood there, shifting from foot to foot, a desperate earnestness in his eyes. Maddox thought back to age nine, when everything he did was a disappointment to the grown-ups in his life.

"No," he said gently. "We don't want to worry your mom, remember? Just don't set off any more rockets, okay?"

The boy's head nodded jerkily. "We were supposed to go," he said.

"Go where?"

"To see the fireworks. At the fairgrounds in Raleigh? Dad said we'd go."

"So, are you?" Maddox asked, already feeling the answer in his gut.

"No. I told Mom I didn't want to. We wouldn't get back till late, and she has to be at work in the morning."

"That was real considerate of you."

Mitchell looked at his shoes.

Maddox tried again. "You're taking good care of your mother."

It was a damn shame there was no one around to take care of the pair of them.

Ann sat in her backyard, watching the stars and the flames of the citronella candles she'd set around the porch, wishing she could coax Mitchell from his room. He was reading *Droid Zone 12: The Undefended*. It was a lousy end to a disappointing day, but her son insisted he was fine.

Fine. She sighed. She wanted better than "fine" for Mitchell. She wanted better for herself. She felt itchy and restless in her own skin tonight, and it was more than the humidity or the mosquitoes.

She raised her wet glass of tea to the broken moon. "Happy Independence Day," she whispered.

The doorbell clunked from the front of the house, and her hand jerked and the tea jumped in the glass. Maybe Rob had changed his mind? But it was late, too late for the promised trip to Raleigh.

She hurried through the back door and down the hall before Mitchell could come down from his room. She flipped on the porch light, glanced through the peephole, and felt her heart slam into her ribs.

Maddox.

She had watched him that afternoon at the park, looking hot and dark and competent in his uniform. He was showered now, and wearing a plain-necked T-shirt and shorts. His calves were thicker and hairier than they had been in high school. No socks. She felt a little prick inside her and looked away.

Unhooking the chain, she opened the door. ''What are you doing here?''

His half smile faded at her abrupt tone. He held up a paper sack. ''I brought something for Mitchell. Can I see him?''

''He's upstairs. Reading.''

''Can you call him?''

Ann frowned. It was late. She felt vulnerable in her quiet house, in her restless skin. But maybe a distraction was just what Mitchell needed.

''All right.'' She moved to the bottom of the stairs. ''Mitchell! You have a visitor.''

She stepped back awkwardly to admit him, feeling the narrow hall close around them. She was very conscious of his size and his legs and his eyes on her face until Mitchell thumped down the stairs.

Her son stopped on the landing like a squirrel that had been marked by a hound. Ann bristled in defense.

And then Maddox looked up, and some unspoken reassurance flowed between them, and Mitchell's shoulders relaxed. Ann relaxed, too.

''You still up for fireworks?'' Maddox said, speaking directly to the boy.

Longing lit the nine-year-old's face, but he shook his head. ''I can't go. It's too late.''

''Yeah. I just got off duty myself. But it's the Fourth. Got to have fireworks.'' Maddox dangled the bag.

Ann felt a qualm. ''Oh, I don't think—''

"You said they were illegal," Mitchell interrupted.

"When did you say that?" Ann asked.

"Some kids got a little too patriotic at the park this afternoon," Maddox said easily. His look warned her to drop it there. "And it's true, they shouldn't have been shooting off rockets. Or mortars or firecrackers or anything that flies through the air and goes boom. But what we've got here are handheld and ground-based sparkling devices of no more than seventy-five grams of chemical compound. Perfectly legal."

"But aren't they still dangerous?" Ann protested.

"Sometimes dangerous is fun," Maddox said deliberately. "You just need to take precautions."

He held her gaze with his hooded eyes until her breath rushed out. She was pretty sure he wasn't talking about fireworks anymore.

But he did take precautions.

He wet a patch of grass with the hose and put out a bucket of water. He told Ann where to sit, and Mitchell where to stand. And then he set off whistling, crackling explosions of color, shimmering fountains of light. Mitchell whooped with excitement as sparks flew up and rained down, dazzling, twinkling. Magic.

Maddox lit wire sparklers, blue and green and gold, for them to hold, and the soft showers flowed over Ann's hand and never burned her at all. She leaned back on her elbows, watching her son dance and Maddox move, a black shadow against the glare. He set off showers and smoke snakes until the backyard was a blur of light and fog and Mitchell glowed.

When, half an hour later, Ann came down from tucking her son into bed, she was glowing, too.

"Thank you," she said sincerely. "He was really looking forward to— He really enjoyed the fireworks."

"Why the hell didn't his father take him?" Maddox

asked, and a little of her pleasure went out, like the sparks on the damp grass.

"Rob was annoyed with me," she confessed. "This morning he offered to give me a lift to some dance at the club, and when I said no, he—"

"Took it out on the kid," Maddox finished grimly.

She shrugged. It was true. "Anyway, it was nice of you to make it up to him."

He sat on her porch steps, solid and warm, like a rock breathing absorbed heat into the night. His legs took up a lot of room. "It wasn't much."

She skirted his knees to sit down gingerly beside him. "It was wonderful. And thoughtful."

He made a disgusted sound. "Jeez, you're easy."

She stiffened with offense. "Excuse me?"

"You're too trusting. You ever think maybe I didn't stop by just to light sparklers for the kid?"

"Then why did you come?"

His deep voice reverberated, making her shiver. "Maybe I want to see if I can light you up, too."

Her heart thumped. She twisted her hands together in her lap. "Are you talking about...?"

"Sex. Yeah."

She wrenched her head to glance at the upstairs windows, as if their words could somehow penetrate her son's curtained, closed and darkened bedroom.

"Well, I'm not," she said crossly. "I don't talk about sex."

"Okay. Why don't we do it instead?"

She snickered before she could feel shocked, and then she felt guilty. "No."

He didn't say anything, didn't pressure her. It was almost disappointing.

"I'm no good at it," she explained desperately to the dark.

And the dark answered back, "Maybe you are. Maybe old Robbo wasn't any good."

The possibility was too frightening to think about. She didn't want sex. She couldn't. "You sound like my therapist," she muttered.

"My mistake."

"Anyway, I never was any good at it. Remember?"

"I remember I was terrible." He turned his head, and his dark, hooded gaze trapped hers. "I've improved some."

All the air left her lungs. "I'm sure," she said dryly, when she could breathe again.

"You don't believe me."

"I don't believe we're having this discussion."

"I think," Maddox said deliberately, "you should give me a chance to prove it."

The heat must have gotten into her blood. Or the fireworks. Or the moon. She was sitting on her back porch talking about having sex with Maddox Palmer as if she were a fifteen-year-old virgin arguing with her boyfriend about getting to second base. It was ridiculous. It was appealing.

She blushed in the darkness. "What kind of chance?"

Maddox went, if possible, even more still. "You could let me kiss you."

Oh, yes, her blood demanded.

Oh, no. "I told you, I can't afford to get involved."

"This isn't involvement. This is sex."

It sounded wicked. It sounded...fun.

"Just a kiss?" she asked uncertainly.

His smile gleamed like the crooked moon. "Of course. What kind of a man do you think I am?"

"I don't know."

"Why don't you come over here and find out?" he invited.

Her head spun. She couldn't possibly...could she?

Balancing herself with one hand on his chest, she leaned over. Cautiously, with her eyes open to see what he would do, she pressed her lips to his. His lips were warm. His eyelashes were thick and short. He didn't *do* anything.

She drew back.

"Well?" he asked hoarsely. His heart pounded under her hand.

"I think you're very nice," she said solemnly.

"I think I'm out of my mind."

She almost giggled. "Can I do it again?"

He leaned back on his elbows, so that she tipped into him a little. His legs stretched over the steps. He had very long thighs, she noticed. "Be my guest."

She drew a deep breath and leaned forward.

"Maybe you should try it with your eyes closed this time," he suggested.

Her pulse thrummed. "All right."

She tucked her hair behind her ear, angled her head, and closed her eyes. The night breathed around them.

"You okay?" Maddox asked finally.

"I'm sort of afraid to do this," she confessed, opening her eyes again.

"Then don't."

"I'm more afraid I'll miss my chance."

His chest expanded as he inhaled, a sharp, quick breath. And then he let it out slowly. "Take your time." He lay back on the hard planks of the porch, crossing his arms beneath his head. "I'm not going anywhere."

Well.

Impelled by curiosity and yearning, she flattened her palm on his chest. The knit shirt was soft, the body beneath it warm and hard. She flexed her fingers and felt his muscles tighten, but he didn't grab at her. He didn't even move.

Encouraged, she dipped her head and kissed his wide, firm mouth. It was nice. It was very nice. He must have shaved before he came over, because his jaw was smooth and he smelled all clean. She parted her lips a little, tasting him, and he opened his mouth, but he didn't stab at her with his tongue. He didn't hold her down with hard, cold hands and open her up with unforgiving fingers....

She pushed the thought away, kissing him, kissing Maddox, concentrating on the textures and the warmth of his mouth, the slick inside of his lip, his strong, smooth teeth. She kissed the dent in his chin, like the careless imprint of a sculptor's thumb, and eased closer, enjoying the solid support of his chest and the way her breasts felt flattened against him.

She wanted...something. She kept kissing him, because that was almost it, that was almost enough, and it just got better and better and warmer and moister, and she didn't have to worry at all because he kept his strong arms anchored behind his head on the porch. She let herself fall into him, fall into his mouth and his kiss and his hot, broad body.

She wriggled against him, trying to get closer, and then cried out in pleasure, in protest, as his hands swept lower and clamped on her hips and dragged her over him. He was burning up. He was completely aroused. And she was straddling him, her knees on either side of his hard thighs and her fanny sticking up in the air.

Ann moaned and pulled back.

The hand on her butt tightened and then slowly relaxed. The hard arms fell away. Maddox dropped his head. She winced at the sound of his skull hitting the porch.

"I'm sorry," she blurted. "I can't do this."

His face gleamed with sweat. His eyes were nearly black. "Okay," he said through his teeth.

She struggled to sit up. "I'm sorry."

"I said it's okay." He gulped in air. "I was too rough."

"No."

"Yeah, I was. I scared you."

"No." She twisted her hands together. *I am responsible for my own life,* she recited silently. *I can decide for myself what is best for me.* "*I* scared me."

He rubbed his face with his hand. "Look, it's all right. You didn't want to."

"I did," she practically shouted at him, frustrated by his patience and his total lack of understanding. "That's what scares me. I can't make that kind of mistake again."

He shook his head, curling up effortlessly from the floor. "You lost me."

"I'm just getting out of one bad marriage. I can't afford to get carried away."

He gave her his hooded look. "Darlin', I'm not saying something didn't come up between us, but I don't remember marriage being raised."

Her cheeks burned. Something had "come up," all right. "I'm just saying the two aren't necessarily separate issues."

"They are for me."

"Well, not for me," Ann snapped. "I got married once because I got pregnant, and I'm not going to risk it again!"

Chapter 8

Dear Lord. She'd told him. Of course, most of the town knew or guessed. What else could you expect from a Barclay? She covered her mouth with her hands.

"Pregnant," Maddox repeated. He sounded poleaxed.

Ann nodded. She couldn't even look at him.

"Mitchell?"

She nodded again.

His breath whistled out. "That explains a lot."

She put her chin up against the familiar accusation. "Why Rob would marry me, you mean."

"No. Why you would marry him."

Without anger to brace them, her shoulders slumped. "Oh."

He rubbed his jaw with the back of his hand. "And why you're not big on unprotected sex with me."

Really, he was being nice about this. The thought only depressed her further. Even with a nice man, she didn't have any luck.

She sighed. "So, here we are, back where we were thirteen years ago."

"Not quite," Maddox drawled. "You're not a fifteen-year-old virgin anymore."

Not *that* nice, she thought, startled. "Is that supposed to make me feel better?"

"Well, it makes *me* feel better," he said frankly. "I won't have to run myself in for statutory rape."

She bit her lip to keep from smiling.

He reached out his big hand. She sat very still as he smoothed a strand of hair behind her ear. His touch was light, but it reached down deep inside her.

"If it's protection you need," he said, "I'll bring some next time. Just in case you decide to live dangerously."

She felt the draw of him all the way down in her belly and did her darnedest to ignore it. "I don't think I'm ready for dangerous."

His smile was an invitation to trouble. "It's like messing around with fireworks. Nothing wrong with it, as long as we take the proper precautions."

She crossed her arms against temptation. "Uh-huh. I bet that's what you told Tom Creech in eighth grade right before you two blew up the chem lab."

Maddox laughed.

The judge peered over her reading glasses at the elderly shoplifter before the bench.

"How many years would you say we've been going steady now, Mr. Nash?"

"Your Honor—" the defense attorney protested.

Maddox smothered a grin and edged toward the courtroom door. This was going to take a while. For his first day in court, he had half a dozen cases on the calendar—a DWI, a Peeping Tom, a couple of speeding tickets—but he wouldn't be called until the judge got through with the lawyers. Plenty of time for a smoke.

He slipped out past a couple of cops from nearby Benson and a highway patrolman built like a mountain. He was used to waiting to testify. That didn't mean he couldn't think of things he'd rather be doing. He could follow up on last night's B and E. Return Detective Greene's call. Drive Annie Barclay out on the river road and show her everything he'd learned in the past twelve years...

Yeah, right. Like *that* would impress her.

He prowled the long passage to the building's only smoking area, the lobby connecting the civil, criminal and superior courts.

Ann was struggling free of a lousy marriage to an abusive jerk. She wanted safe. She needed gentle. She deserved somebody with money and class. Somebody like Rob.

Maddox's jaw set. Not Rob. Marriage to the Golden Boy had cost her.

He found a spot against the wall with a view of all the doors and took out his first cigarette of the day. Ann didn't want a man who smoked. Hell, she didn't want a man, period. But he thought, or at least he hoped, he had a shot at changing her mind. Maybe he wasn't rich or smooth or subtle, but he'd take a bullet in the head before he'd touch her.

No, that wasn't true. Maddox dragged on his cigarette. He'd like to touch her. A lot. It remained to be seen if she'd give him the chance.

He blew smoke. Two nights ago on her porch he'd established Ann could still respond to him. His blood ran hot at the memory of her sweet little body pressed against his, her soft hair brushing his chin as she bent to take what she wanted.

As she hadn't wanted Rob, all those years ago. The knowledge stirred Maddox at a gut-deep level, surprising and gratifying. She hadn't married the one-time quarterback for his money or his blond good looks. She hadn't fallen for his perfect hair, house, manners, teeth, clothes. She hadn't preferred Rob, the way everyone had always preferred Rob.

Although she must have wanted him once upon a time. Or she wouldn't have let him knock her up.

Son of a bitch.

Maddox stabbed out his cigarette in the dirty sand by the door. He looked up to see Rob Cross promenading across the lobby.

For a second Maddox thought he was imagining things. But it was Rob, all right, gliding across the fake marble floors, his steps only a little quicker than they were on the golf course. He had a laugh for his lawyer and a smile for the lady, yellow and brittle as cured tobacco, who guarded the information desk. It was a good act, and it played well to a receptive crowd.

It pulled Maddox like a drug deal going down.

Rob's blond hair and heavy shoulders disappeared through the paneled doors of civil court. So he wasn't here in connection with his felony trial. Both the room and the timing were wrong. Frowning, Maddox tailed him into the high, crowded chamber.

It only took a minute at the back of the room to figure out that the court was running divorces like train cars through a tunnel. Rob was getting a divorce. From Ann. Today.

Satisfaction almost robbed Maddox of breath. No way did he want to interfere in that.

He eased back toward the door. And then he saw her, Annie, sitting straight and quiet and alone, near the front of the room.

Her thin, squared shoulders snagged his heart. What the hell was she doing here? Only one party needed to show in an uncontested divorce. Rob's lawyer had already handed the decree to the judge. Rob himself stepped forward to testify, suited, serious and handsome. He answered the judge's questions in a low, sincere voice, the perfect picture of a responsible husband sorrowed by his wife's disloyalty.

Yeah, a good act. And even though it would leave Ann

free, Maddox found himself resenting it. He leaned against the doorway, crossing his arms against his chest. Maybe he'd stick around. Not that his undisclosed presence was likely to do Annie any good. But he found he couldn't leave her sitting there all alone.

The judge, gray-haired, black-robed and closely shaven, looked up from the judgment in his hand. "Mrs. Cross?"

She stood, dwarfed by the courtroom and her husband's splendid appearance. Maddox felt his jaw tighten.

"Yes, sir?" she asked in a faint, clear voice.

"The court is not used to seeing both spouses appear in cases of this kind. Did you have anything you wanted to say?"

She shook her head, making her smooth hair swing. "No, sir."

"Nothing to add? No objections? All issues of custody and support resolved?"

"I guess. I mean, yes, sir." Her hands fluttered at his evident displeasure. The room was very quiet, the judge waiting, the lawyers waiting, the other plaintiffs waiting for her to finish so they could get on with their scheduled divorces and their lives.

She put up her chin, saying softly, "It's just…I was there at the beginning, and I thought I should be here at the end."

Her words, plain and brave and decent, restored dignity to the train-station rush of the court. Maddox could have saluted. In the no-fault atmosphere, her quiet acknowledgement of past misjudgments and mistakes, her simple assumption of responsibility, stood square and true. Her sincerity trembled in the high-ceilinged room like the echo of a bell.

Rob's face flushed. His lawyer looked down.

The judge cleared his throat. "Very good, Mrs. Cross. Divorce granted."

Ann blinked. She felt a little stunned. She'd come for

closure. And now she had…what? Freedom? Could she really be free?

Rob's lawyer approached the bench to collect the papers from the judge. Ann gathered her thoughts and her purse and turned to go. She did not look at Rob. She did not want to check her reactions in the mirror of his mood, to let his response define hers. It was over.

Her shoes made too much noise as she walked between the rows of chairs, awkward as a mourner at a funeral. She was here to bury her beaten-down hopes, to mark the death of her naiveté. She didn't feel free. Her bones felt heavy. Her head felt light. She almost stumbled into someone on her way out of the courtroom.

Someone broad and solid in a dark blue uniform.

"You should have been the one to divorce him," Maddox growled over her head.

She raised her gaze from the center of his chest—he blocked her way like a building—and stammered, "Wh-what are you doing here?"

"It's my court date." She must have looked confused, because he explained. "I get assigned once a month to come in and testify on all my collars." He stooped to examine her face with his cop's eyes that saw too much. "Are you all right?"

"I'm fine."

He raised one of those sandy eyebrows at her, and she flushed, the memory of her own words rising between them. *I've heard enough lies—told them to myself mostly.*

"Really," she insisted. "It's just a little hard to take in that it's over."

"It's not right." Maddox's mouth was grim. "He was the one at fault. You should have been the one filing for divorce."

She smiled, touched that his sense of justice was offended on her behalf. "It would never work that way. Rob controlled the marriage. There was no way he would give me power over the divorce. And after all the things I said about him… I may have left him, but *he* had to divorce *me*.''

Maddox scowled. ''That's bull.''

His anger didn't frighten her. Later, she would think about that, and wonder. But right now, his wrath warmed her.

''That's the way it had to be. It's all right,'' she reassured him gently. ''I got what I wanted. What I needed.''

''Ann!''

She flinched at the sound of her husband's voice. Ex-husband's voice, she reminded herself firmly, but his change in status didn't seem to have any effect on her nerves.

Rob sauntered toward them flashing his ''trust me'' smile. She tightened her hold on her purse.

''You sure got out of there in a hurry. You didn't give Henry a chance to hand you your papers,'' he reproached her.

She fought the urge to apologize. ''He can mail them.''

''Oh, I wouldn't let him do that. You can't leave without your papers.''

She felt the slow crawl of blood in her face. He made her sound like a dog. As if all she needed to go out in public now was a collar and a new keeper. Without her willing it, her gaze flickered to Maddox.

''Hey, MD.'' Rob's genial tone never faltered, but his eyes were cold and hard. ''I didn't expect to see you here.''

Maddox lifted his brows slightly. ''Yeah, a cop in a court-house is a real unusual sight.''

''Ha, ha. So, what are you doing here?''

Ann held her breath. Rob might not want her, but he could get ugly if he thought someone else did.

''I've got a case over in criminal court,'' Maddox said finally. ''I saw Annie and thought I'd come over and say hello.''

''Well, wasn't that friendly,'' Rob said. He turned back to Ann. ''No hard feelings, I hope?''

She exhaled. ''No. No hard feelings.''

"Good. You know my offer's still open for Saturday night. Just to prove to everyone we can be civilized about all this."

She didn't feel very civil. And she had nothing to prove to anyone at the club. "Thank you, but no."

"I wish you'd reconsider." Rob stepped closer, dropping his voice confidingly. "We wouldn't want Mitchell to think his parents can't get along like reasonable human beings, now, would we?"

It was a threat, made in the same rich, persuasive voice that talked her out of her panties and virginity at eighteen and into marriage four months later. The same voice that kept her captive for ten years, that made her doubt the screaming wrongness of her life and the bloody evidence in her mirror.

Stop making a fuss.
You're overreacting.
If you were any kind of wife to me…
If you just wouldn't make me so angry…

If she made him angry, he would take it out on Mitchell. She moistened her lips. "I don't want to be any trouble."

"Then say yes." Rob smiled charmingly. "I'll pick you up around seven."

Maddox stiffened. It's over, she'd told him, but she was wrong. As long as Rob had power over their son, it would never be over.

Her stomach churned. She didn't want to go with him. But she didn't want to antagonize him, either. For Mitchell's sake. Maybe if she gave him one more night to play the wronged but generous husband he would leave them alone?

She swallowed. "Actually," she said, "I already told Val I'd go with her. Con's on a consulting trip, and she wanted company. Maybe we'll see you there."

It was a partial capitulation, a promise of public support. But was it enough to appease him?

Apparently so, because he nodded. "That might do. And

for God's sake, wear something nice. I don't want people thinking I'm not giving you money.''

He wasn't, except for minimal child support. But she wasn't eager to go there. Not with Maddox bridling at each new proof of Rob's continued hold on her. She just wanted to get away.

''I'm sure I have something.''

''The blue thing's not bad. At least it covers you decently.''

That had always been important to Rob, that she cover the parts of herself he wasn't interested in any longer. *Just because you acted like a slut in high school doesn't mean you have to dress like one now.*

She bit her lip. She wasn't sure what she said in reply. She was too conscious of Maddox, seething and dangerous beside her.

And Val. Oh, dear. Val wasn't going to be happy with her, either. She'd just committed her best friend to an evening of committee talk *and* Rob. Rob, who had tried to kill her. And now Val would have to acknowledge him at the club.

No wonder Rob oozed satisfaction as he left.

Ann closed her eyes, trying to shut out the crowded lobby and the knowledge of what she'd done.

''What the hell was that about?'' Maddox asked.

His tone should have upset her. But at least Maddox was direct in his anger. She knew where she was with Maddox.

She opened her eyes. ''There's a dance at the club tomorrow night. Remember? Rob offered to give me a ride.''

''And you turned him down.''

''And he backed out of taking Mitchell to the fireworks.''

''So now you're going to do what he wants?''

Her hands were shaking. She folded them together. ''No. Not exactly.''

''No? What—*exactly*—do you think he's after?''

His voice was rough. He was big and intimidating and

scornful, and she still wanted to crawl into his pocket. Boy, did she have lousy instincts.

"I don't know," she said wearily. "Maybe it's just what he says. Maybe he wants people to see him as the wronged, understanding husband for one night."

"Or maybe he can't let you go."

She blinked. "He just divorced me."

"In my line of work, that's usually the most dangerous time. You're leaving his control."

A memory swamped her of the emergency room the night Rob broke her nose. Bright lights and efficient hands, white linen, red blood and pain. The nurse had given Ann the phone number of the women's shelter, printed on an anonymous slip of paper to hide in her shoe. *You don't want him to know you're leaving, honey,* the tired nurse explained. *There's no telling what he'll do.*

She knew. He'd told her. *I'll kill you.*

She felt his past threats in her flesh, like deep, enduring bruises, and along her bones, like old fractures.

She folded her arms at her waist. "He's been better this week. Friendlier."

Maddox looked down at her with his cop look, strong and skeptical and in charge, and she had to fight a burst of resentment.

"You ever ask yourself why?" he asked.

"I'm not stupid. Of course I wondered."

"He saw us together Monday night at your son's ball game. Could be he's worried."

"That I'm involved with you," she said flatly.

"Or that I'm involved with you. Maybe his lawyer warned him about letting a key witness for the prosecution play footsie with the cops."

"What difference would that make? I thought the investigation was over."

"Not until trial."

"Have you…" Her mind grappled with the possibilities.

Rob guilty. Rob vengeful. Rob locked up. Her head pounded. She *so* did not want to deal with this. She had enough to deal with. But this entire mess was her fault, because she hadn't had the guts to stand up to Rob in the first place. She owed it to Val to see it through to the end. She owed it to herself.

She took a deep breath. "Have you found out anything new?"

Maddox hesitated, as if debating what to tell her. So he didn't trust her. She wasn't surprised.

"Not yet," he said. "But if I do, you can bet old Robbo is going to want to find some way to undercut your testimony."

"He can't do that. The police have my statement."

"Sure we do. But if he can produce forty witnesses to swear you let him twirl you around the dance floor the day after your divorce, he can poke holes in your story about what an abusive jerk he is."

She winced. Everything he said was true. But it shamed her that he saw it so clearly.

"Well, that explains his interest in me very nicely."

Maddox frowned. "I think you should be aware of his motives, is all."

"Yes. Thank you. Obviously, a man would need an ulterior motive to come after me."

"I'm saying Rob would," he said carefully.

Above her raging headache, her thoughts darted quick as swallows. "You're thinking anyone would. You did yourself."

Maddox stiffened. "What the hell are you talking about?"

"You came to see me because Rob asked you to straighten me out."

His expression wiped clean. "Well, I guess you've got me figured. Me and old Rob, we're one and the same."

She should have known he wouldn't deny it. But even

through her distress, she recognized she was being unjust. Guilt pinched her.

"I didn't mean it like that."

"Sure." His tone was dismissive. Flat. Accepting of judgment.

She'd hurt him, Ann realized. It simmered in his eyes. It radiated from his stiff, unyielding posture.

The knowledge shook her. She was almost more afraid of his pain than his anger. She hadn't known she had that kind of power over him. She was pretty sure she didn't want that responsibility. Her life was complicated enough without her taking on a big, tough cop with his own emotional baggage.

Chicken. Bad enough that she didn't defend herself. Was she really such a coward that she would strike out at the one person who might be trying to help her?

She sighed. "I'm sorry."

His face was still carefully blank. "I don't want your apologies."

If they weren't in public, she would have risked touching him. She would have liked to touch him, the angles of his face, the hard curve of his biceps beneath his uniform sleeve.

"Why not?"

He shot her an annoyed look. She wasn't sure if that was an improvement over the granite cop face or not. "I don't want your pity."

"Well, good, because I don't feel sorry for you. But I do appreciate that you're trying to help."

"I don't want your damn gratitude, either."

She put up her chin. "Maddox...I'm a convicted felon on probation. A witness in an attempted murder case. Before you get mixed up with me, maybe you should think about what you *do* want."

The memory of his words whispered between them, roughening her nerve endings. *You are what I want, Annie. You've always been what I want.*

"Is that an offer?" he asked quietly.

Her heart skipped. What would he do if she said yes? She flushed. "No."

The corners of his eyes crinkled suddenly. "Not used to turning down sex?"

There was so much tender amusement in the question that she smiled cautiously back. "I'm not used to having the choice," she said without thinking.

His grin disappeared as if it had never been. Tension coiled his muscles. He was angry. And even though his fury wasn't directed at her, Ann's heart stumbled.

She hurried into speech. "I didn't mean—I'm not used to a lot of things. That's all I meant. I need to have control."

"Control of what?" he asked through his teeth.

"Things." Her hands fluttered. "My life."

"And you think I'd threaten that?"

"Without meaning to, maybe. I just can't afford to let myself get involved with anyone right now."

"What the hell am I supposed to say to that?" he asked bleakly. "If I try to change your mind, I'm doing exactly what you're afraid of."

She winced at the bitterness in his voice. "I know," she said. "I'm sorry."

"Don't apologize," he snapped.

"I'm—" She stopped, twisting her hands on her purse.

"Hell, I'm sorry, too." He blew out a short, explosive breath and then rubbed his jaw with the back of his hand. "Okay," he said, visibly clamping down his temper. "Fine. You're in control. Now figure out what you want." His hooded gaze stabbed her, hot and compelling. "Because from where I'm sitting, as long as you're alone and miserable, Rob is still calling the shots."

Chapter 9

Ann balked on the clubhouse steps smack between two marble planters as big as bathtubs.

"I still think this was a mistake," she said.

Val, glowing in a green-patterned gown that pulled slightly across her stomach, patted her arm. "It'll be fine. We'll sit with my parents—"

"Who are friends with all Rob's friends."

"—and we'll leave right after Rob notices you're here."

Ann fussed with the catch on her black evening bag. "I don't want you to have to talk to him."

"I won't."

"You may not be able to avoid it. If he comes over—"

"He won't. He's too afraid of my husband."

"Your husband isn't here."

Val looked at her sharply. "You're whining."

"I know," Ann said humbly. "I'm sorry. I'm terrible company. Let's go."

Val laughed. "Nice try. No." Her expression gentled. "Sweetie, we'll be fine. Come on."

"I don't feel good about this," Ann muttered.

"Well, you look good," Val said, tugging her up the terraced steps. The trees outside the tall windows were twined with fairy lights. Piano music filtered through the glass. "I'm glad you borrowed the dress."

The dress. Another lurch of misgiving fixed Ann on the spot. Black and fitted, it flared at her hips and floated around her calves. She'd borrowed Val's dress as a flag of defiance, hoping some of her confidence would shake out of the folds. Only now, facing the arena of her last defeat, Ann wondered if the dress had been another mistake.

Her hand crept to finger one of the spaghetti straps that threatened to slide off her narrow shoulders. "Are you sure it's not too much? I feel naked."

"It looks great," Val said firmly. "And you look wonderful. What I'd give to have your bones."

Ann smiled. "Bones are all I have. No cleavage."

"You don't need cleavage in that dress. No one's going to be able to take their eyes off you."

"Dear Lord." She felt light-headed. "I can't breathe."

"You'll be fine. We'll be fine. You'll see."

Ann had never been comfortable at the club. Even after she learned how to transfer her olive pit to her plate and not to call the towel attendant by name, there were a thousand subtleties of conversation that marked her an outsider: fashionable resorts she hadn't seen, sorority sisters she hadn't met, clothing designers she'd never heard of.

She never broke the plane that separated her from the club wives, never found the topic that made her one of them. Oh, she pretended. Maybe they pretended, too. Maybe behind their double-foiled hair and manicured hands they kept their own secrets: a child's failure, a malign growth in the breast, a morning cocktail, a husband who extracted payment for the SUV and new living room drapes in pain and fear and blood. But they didn't talk about these things over tennis lunches or drinks poolside. They never confessed the flaws that might have made them kin.

It was better coming as a guest, Ann decided as she trailed Val through the gleaming lobby. Entering the chilled and scented dining room, she could almost pretend she was in some upscale department store at Christmas, admiring the larger-than-life displays and perfectly dressed and posed mannequins.

Val's parents, Edward and Sylvia Cutler, were propped at their table like a pair of dummies. He could have modeled Better Clothing for Men. She was a breathing display of Ladies' Jewelry. Tanned and toned and cool and polite, they managed to greet Ann without making one reference to the fact that she and her ex-husband had robbed their daughter and their bank of twenty thousand dollars. It didn't matter. Ann still felt as if the word Thief was tattooed on her forehead.

"Smile," Val hissed at her as they made their way to the bar for a drink.

"Everybody's staring." Ann excused herself softly.

"It's the dress. Oh, shoot, there's Mackenzie."

"Val, darling!" Mackenzie Ward, her Outer Banks tan set off by her white silk pantsuit, bore down on them like a yacht in full sail. Her bright eyes flicked over Ann's bare shoulders. She did not say hello. "I wonder if you would mind coming over to our table? Charlene Wilks is throwing her niece's bridal shower, and I told her all about your darling little restaurant, and she's just dying to talk menus with you."

"Maybe another time? I—"

Ann was not going to cost Val another penny—or a lucrative catering contract. "You go ahead," she said. "I'll be fine."

"No," Val said.

Mackenzie tucked her hand in Val's arm. "Charlene is just going out of her mind planning this thing. The niece doesn't eat meat, and her sister breaks out in spots if she so much as looks at fish, so you're their only hope.''

Val tossed her head, making her earrings dance. ''Really, Mackenzie—''

Ann fought the flutter of panic in her stomach. ''It's all right. I want you to go.''

She needed her to go.

If she could find Rob while Val was discussing tapenade and strawberry tarts with the bride-to-be, she might be able to keep the two of them apart.

''Well… If you're sure…'' Val said doubtfully.

''Positive,'' Ann lied.

''We'll only be a minute.'' Mackenzie Ward flashed her teeth at Ann, reward for her cooperation. ''I'll bring her right back.''

Ann nodded. Val was dragged away, throwing worried looks over her shoulder. Just for a second, Ann warmed herself with her friend's obvious loyalty and concern. And then she drew a deep breath and went in search of Rob.

She bumped around the edges of the room, trying to scan the chardonnay crowd without snagging anyone's attention. Most of her old social circle seemed as eager to avoid her eyes as she was to miss theirs. Occasionally someone would stare back and then deliberately look away. Ann felt the heat crawl into her face. She might be tolerated in town, but she wasn't welcome here. She accepted that. This was Rob's turf.

But where was Rob?

She braved the bar again, but she couldn't get past the anteroom where men were lined six and eight deep to bring their spouses drinks.

''…doing here?''

''…on the fourteenth hole.''

''…see what she was wearing?''

She did her best to shut out the voices, to ignore the pit-deep conviction they were all discussing her. Craning her neck, she searched for her ex-husband's blond head and heavy shoulders in the crush. Someone stepped on her shoes. An Armani-wearing golfer rushed the bar, forcing her back into a potted palm.

She wanted to go home, back to her son and her garden.

The memory of Maddox's deep voice taunted her. *As long as you're alone and miserable, Rob is still calling the shots.*

She ignored him, too. What did he know?

"Are you all right?" a man asked gruffly behind her.

Maddox?

Her heart leapt. She turned, battling resentment and gladness.

And found herself looking up at the red-faced, gray-haired, hard-jawed chief of police. Wallace Palmer. Maddox's father.

Her heart plummeted from her throat to the tips of her black silk shoes. Would he ask her to leave?

But what he actually said was, "Can I get you a drink?"

"N-no," Ann stammered. "Thank you."

The chief looked almost as uncomfortable as she felt. Maybe it was being out of uniform? His summer jacket and starched white shirt sat oddly on his squared shoulders.

"Looking for someone?"

Ann blinked. She didn't know what to tell him. He'd been Rob's fan and then Rob's champion. As far as she knew, the chief hadn't been in on the deal that traded her guilty plea in return for her testimony in Rob's embezzlement trial.

"I'm here with Val MacNeill," she said. The victim. The woman her ex-husband stood accused of trying to murder.

Wallace Palmer nodded. "I saw her parents. Sylvia looks well."

"Um…yes." Ann twisted her hands together, practically backing into the palm tree. Fronds tickled her shoulder blades. This was awful. Awkward. Why didn't he go away? The police chief always struck her as more a public servant than a social leader. For the first time, she wondered if that made him an outsider here, too.

The thought gave her courage to ask, "Are you—that is, you're not working tonight?"

"No." He unbent enough to give her a small smile. "Though maybe I should be. In case the bar runs out of ice and this crowd, you know, gets out of control."

He'd actually made a joke. To her.

Cautiously, Ann smiled back. "That could get ugly."

Chief Palmer cleared his throat. "It looked like it was getting pretty ugly already. Let me get you that drink."

She was touched by his stiff gallantry. "Oh, you don't have to do that."

"Humph. According to my son, I haven't done enough for you in the past. The least I can do now is fetch you something."

Unexpected tears stung her eyes. Oh, dear. She was not—she absolutely was *not*—going to lose it because Maddox's father was being kind. She bowed her head, grateful for the screening palm. "Thank you," she whispered. "That would be…very nice."

He hesitated. "White wine?"

She nodded. His shiny brown loafers squeaked away.

"Whew." Val's cheerful voice forced Ann's head up. "If Charlene Wilks had been in charge of my bridal shower, I would have eloped."

Ann struggled to answer in kind. "Be nice. For all you know, your mother's recruited her to host your baby shower."

Val laughed. "Bite your tongue. Why are you hiding out in the decorations? Did you see Rob?"

Ann bit her lip. "Not yet."

And now she didn't want to. Not with Val standing beside her. But before Ann could ferry her friend back to the safety of the Cutlers' table, Rob entered the bar, big and blond, affable and assured. Ann shrank back into the palm tree.

But of course he saw her anyway. Or maybe he smelled her fear, like a predator scenting prey. Under the sleek black dress, Ann felt a thin trickle of sweat crawl down her spine. Rob used to tell her she would never get away from him. They were bound together in pain and shame and blood. Maybe he just *knew* she was here.

Ann grabbed Val's arm. "Should we go sit down?"

Val lifted her perfectly arched brows. "Are we in a hurry?"

"Yes," Ann said baldly.

But it was already too late.

Rob negotiated the crowd around the bar as easily as Moses parting the Red Sea. He waited until she met his eyes before he smiled, cool and knowing. A chill chased up the back of her arms.

Once she would have screamed when he looked at her like that, as if he had an enjoyable secret only she could share. Once she would have run. But screaming never brought help. And running only brought him after her.

She stayed where she was, sick and dumb, trapped between her friend and a stupid plant and sapped by a familiar paralysis.

She still heard, dimly, polite laughter from the dining room, the persistent flourish of the piano, the clink of glasses and bottles. At the edge of her vision, she saw the sudden consternation on Val's face and movement in the lobby. But all of that was wavy and distorted. None of it penetrated the fishbowl world she shared with Rob.

He stopped in front of them. "Isn't this nice," he said.

The movement at the corner of her eye stabilized into a large, dark mass on her right, solid and close enough to distract her.

Maddox—it was Maddox's voice, now that she heard the real thing she wondered that she'd ever confused it with his father's—said, "Turn around."

A different kind of tension gripped Ann. Even out of uniform, he looked dangerous. It was more than his ill-fitting jacket or unruly hair and slouching posture. He broadcast menace.

But for Ann, Maddox carried with him the promise of rescue, the possibility of comfort, as much a part of him as his badge or his gun. And that promise was the most dangerous thing of all. She couldn't trust anybody else to solve her problems ever again.

Rob stiffened in offense. "Excuse me?"

Maddox gave him a hard look from under hooded lids. "Turn around and walk away."

He didn't raise his voice, but Rob heard him. The man next to them, waiting to give his order to the bartender, heard him, too. They were attracting attention. Maddox gave no sign that he observed the sidelong looks, the suspended conversations in the bar. But Rob would notice. Rob would care.

Ann shivered.

"You can't talk to me like that," Rob said, low and cold. "You don't belong here."

Maddox shrugged. "I'm here now. And you're leaving."

"You're not even a member."

"I'm a member of the Cutler Police Department. And I'm telling you if you don't turn around and walk away, I'm going into the dining room to find Judge Brailsford and get a restraining order that will keep you away."

Rob sneered. "You can't. He won't. I haven't threatened her."

"Threatened who?" Maddox asked, real quiet.

But Ann could still hear him. Everybody standing around could hear him. Beside her, Val watched the two men with fascinated interest.

Rob made an abrupt gesture. Ann flinched. "Her. My wife."

"Ex-wife," Maddox growled. "And the restraining order

NO COST! NO OBLIGATION TO BUY!
NO PURCHASE NECESSARY!

PLAY THE

7 LUCKY SLOT MACHINE GAME!

Just scratch off the silver box with a coin. Then check below to see the gifts you get!

YES!

I have scratched off the silver box. Please send me the 2 FREE books and gift for which I qualify. I understand I am under no obligation to purchase any books, as explained on the back and opposite page.

345 SDL C6ND

245 SDL C6M7
(S-IM-0S-12/00)

7	**7**	**7**	WORTH TWO FREE BOOKS PLUS A BONUS MYSTERY GIFT!
🍒	🍒	🍒	WORTH TWO FREE BOOKS!
♣	♣	♣	WORTH ONE FREE BOOK!
🔔	🔔	🍒	TRY AGAIN!

Offer limited to one per household and not valid to current Silhouette Intimate Moments® subscribers. All orders subject to approval.

The Silhouette Reader Service™ — Here's how it works:

Accepting your 2 free books and gift places you under no obligation to buy anything. You may keep the books and gift and return the shipping statement marked "cancel." If you do not cancel, about a month later we'll send you 6 additional novels and bill you just $3.80 each in the U.S., or $4.21 each in Canada, plus 25¢ shipping & handling per book and applicable taxes if any.* That's the complete price and — compared to cover prices of $4.50 each in the U.S. and $5.25 each in Canada — it's quite a bargain! You may cancel at any time, but if you choose to continue, every month we'll send you 6 more books, which you may either purchase at the discount price or return to us and cancel your subscription.

*Terms and prices subject to change without notice. Sales tax applicable in N.Y. Canadian residents will be charged applicable provincial taxes and GST.

If offer card is missing write to: Silhouette Reader Service, 3010 Walden Ave., P.O. Box 1867, Buffalo, NY 14240-1867

BUSINESS REPLY MAIL
FIRST-CLASS MAIL   PERMIT NO. 717   BUFFALO, NY

POSTAGE WILL BE PAID BY ADDRESSEE

SILHOUETTE READER SERVICE
3010 WALDEN AVE
PO BOX 1867
BUFFALO NY 14240-9952

NO POSTAGE
NECESSARY
IF MAILED
IN THE
UNITED STATES

is for Mrs. MacNeill. I figure a murder attempt is threat enough to have you thrown out.''

The charge rippled through the room like a rock tossed in a pond. No one was comfortable with the reminder that one of their own was accused of the attempted murder of the banker's daughter.

Rob turned an ugly red. ''You're making a mistake, MD. The police haven't proved anything.''

''It's three weeks to trial. What do you want to bet I can turn something up?''

Rob's anger was a palpable thing. It pulsed against his collar and escaped like sweat into the air. Ann shrank inside her skin. Did anyone else smell it? Did anyone else feel it?

Because Rob smiled his I'm-the-good-guy smile and shook his head in bemused acceptance. ''I'd try to tell you how wrong you are, MD, but unlike some people, I don't relish making a scene.'' He nodded to the lineup at the bar. ''I'll leave the nice folks here to enjoy their evening.''

It was retreat with dignity. But it was a retreat. Ann could calculate the cost in the set of Rob's shoulders and the tiny tic in his right cheek. And she wondered as he stalked away: now that she wasn't there to take the force of his anger, who else would pay for the damage to Rob's pride?

Val blew out an exaggerated breath. ''Mad Dog Palmer. This is quite a reunion.''

Maddox turned his attention from Rob's back. ''Now you know why I never made it for homecoming.''

She grinned appreciatively. ''We missed you.''

''Did you?'' he asked, but his eyes were on Ann, demanding a response she wasn't sure she knew how to give.

Her body didn't know that. Her stupid body was ready to give him anything he asked for. She blushed.

A handsome giant in a wilted suit entered through the tall glass doors that led to the lobby. He paused, surveying the room, and then strode purposefully toward them.

"Am I late?" Con MacNeill asked.

Val's whole face lit up. "I thought you were spending tonight in Boston. What are you doing here?"

He kissed her, a brief, hard kiss. "Annie's cop called me. I caught an earlier flight in." His astute blue gaze took in Maddox, big as a house and much more hostile. "You Sergeant Palmer?"

Maddox nodded. "Maddox Palmer."

"Con MacNeill." He offered his hand. They shook, testing grips.

Val hugged her husband's arm to her breast. "What is this, a wrestling match? You already missed the countdown, MacNeill."

"What happened?"

"That's what I'd like to know." Chief Palmer appeared from the direction of the bar, bringing Ann's drink and a cloud of displeasure with him. "You overstep your authority, MD?"

Ann sucked in her breath. There was enough testosterone swirling around to qualify the club bar for Danny's Roadhouse on a Saturday night. So, she felt a little shaky surrounded by oversize, overbearing males. So, she had reasons of her own to doubt Maddox's stepping in. That didn't mean she wasn't grateful to him for rescuing her friend from an uncomfortable confrontation that was largely Ann's fault.

"Val and I were just thanking your son for his preventive police work," she said softly.

The chief snorted. "Is that what it was?" But his eyes, as he handed over her wine, were surprisingly approving. "I guess you think you're entitled to some police protection."

"Overdue," Con MacNeill said in his brief, cool way.

Val squeezed his arm.

"Maybe," the chief said.

Ann went still. He believed her?

Rob had said the police would never believe her. He explained it to her, over and over, punctuating his words with his fists until she finally accepted it as true. The chief would think—because Rob would tell him—that Ann was only bored. Or jealous. Or insecure. Or vindictive. He would never believe that Rob could simply beat her up. Or maybe he'd wonder just enough to drop a warning word to Rob, and she and Mitchell would be worse off than before.

Wallace Palmer's grudging admission now was validation on a level Ann had not sought or expected. *According to my son, I haven't done enough for you in the past.* It made her want to cry.

"You apologizing to her?" Maddox asked.

"It's none of your business what I'm doing," his father snapped. "You just think twice before you go committing the resources of my department again."

"I got a call from Tyler Greene," Maddox said. "SBI. The lab results are in."

Ann's hands tightened on her wineglass.

The chief stiffened like an old dog that's spotted a squirrel. "And?"

"And they've got something on a matchbook. I told him to run it for ink residue, see what they could identify."

"So?"

Maddox shrugged. "Holiday weekend. He'll get back to me."

The chief looked sour. "Your timing stinks."

"Yeah." He looked at Ann. "But eventually I get it right."

Ann's pulse sprinted at the heat in his eyes. She took a hasty sip of wine.

Con lifted his eyebrows.

"Well," Val said brightly. "This is too much excitement for me for one night." She smiled at her husband. "Want to take me home, MacNeill?"

"You'll have to drive, Dixie. I caught a cab from the airport."

"Oh, but—" Ann stopped. She was not imposing on Val any further.

"I've got my car," Maddox said. "You can ride with me."

His car smelled like him, leather and tobacco and man. It had deep, flat seats, to accommodate his legs, and a complicated-looking radio. Maddox didn't turn it on. They drove with the air conditioner on and the night closed out, and the silence pulsed around them.

Ann cleared her throat. "The last time you drove me home, we ended up out on the river road."

His hands flexed on the steering wheel, but his voice was neutral. "Don't worry. I won't drag you into the back seat tonight."

"You wouldn't need to," she said without thinking. "You've got bench seats now."

She felt his tiny jolt of surprise, instantly controlled, and bit her tongue. "I shouldn't have said that. It must be the wine talking."

He gave her a quick, assessing glance. "You drunk?"

"One glass of Chablis. But I didn't eat much," she offered in excuse.

"It's okay. I wasn't planning on getting lucky, anyway."

His bluntness brought her chin up. "I don't get lucky in the back seats of cars. I get pregnant."

"That was how…?"

She twisted her hands together. "Prom night."

"Well, there's a real mood breaker," Maddox said savagely. Reaching into his breast pocket, he pulled out a crumpled cigarette and held it up. "Third one today. If you're counting."

This was awful. They were practically snarling at each

other. What was she doing, rehashing old, bad sex with the man who'd rejected her in high school?

"I don't want to do this," Ann said shakily.

"Yeah, you already made that clear."

"No, I mean, fight with you." She closed her eyes. "I don't want to fight with you."

There was a charged silence in the car.

"Fighting's not so bad," Maddox said slowly. "If you do it right."

"I'm terrible at it. I have trouble expressing anger."

"Is that so?"

Ann nodded earnestly. "I saw a counselor over in Chapel Hill for a while. She said I need to work on the discrepancy between my feelings and my body language."

"Yeah? So I should take the fact that you're pressed up against the door over there as a sign that you're really ready to have screaming sex with me?"

She snickered and then clapped her hand over her mouth.

He raised his sandy eyebrows. "Maybe not." The glow from the dashboard edged his smile with green light. "Though if you change your mind, I've got condoms."

Arrogant man. But she was smiling, too. "Am I supposed to find that reassuring?"

"Sorry." He didn't sound sorry. He sounded distracted. "So, I'm not smooth."

"I don't want smooth," she said, deciding it was true. Rob had been smooth. "Honest is better. And it was—" How did you thank a man for buying birth control? Especially when he set off a hum in your blood that made you feel like you might actually one day be tempted to use it. "—considerate."

"Yeah, I'm a prince." He said it absently, like his mind was somewhere else.

She was disappointed. After the condom remark, she didn't think she would have to work for his attention. To get it back, she said, "Of course, you making the purchase ahead of time does create a certain level of expectation."

"No expectations. No pressure. I told you, the next move is up to you." He shot her a sideways look. "Though it would help if you weren't wearing that dress."

She straightened defensively. "What's wrong with my dress?"

"Nothing's wrong with it."

Rob had always criticized her clothes. Ann forgot about not wanting to fight. "Val loaned me this dress. I think it's pretty, and it's cool."

"It looks great. It makes me hot, that's all."

"Oh."

"Yeah. Oh," he repeated grimly.

Ann stared out the windshield at the white road markers flickering past. He wasn't distracted at all, she thought dazedly. He was thinking about her dress. He was thinking about her. She made him *hot.*

The possibilities made her dizzy.

She knew better than to live her life at the mercy of her hormones. She really did. She had firsthand experience of the consequences of one unplanned, uncomfortable act.

But Maddox bought birth control.

She twisted her hands together in her lap. So, then, if pregnancy wasn't the issue, what was?

Could she make love with him? Could she give herself up to him? Could she risk letting another man invade her body and control her responses?

Unbidden, Maddox's words came back to her. *From where I sit, as long as you're alone and miserable, Rob is still calling the shots.*

She was still afraid. But she was more afraid of letting Rob control her life than she was of sex with Maddox. She had something to prove now, to him and to herself.

Ann snuck a glance at him, hard and silent on the other

side of the car. It wouldn't be awful, she reassured herself. She moistened her lips. She had liked kissing him. She liked the feel of his warm, firm lips, his broad, solid body. She liked the way he made her feel.

She wanted to feel that way again.

If she didn't look at him, she could probably say it.

"If the dress bothers you, I could take it off."

Chapter 10

A tree jumped into the headlights and away as the car lurched toward the curb and then straightened.

Maddox gripped the wheel. "Jeez, Annie." It wasn't only the car that was out of control. His pulse was racing. His body surged. "Where the hell did that come from?"

From the corner of his eye, he saw her wince. "I'm sorry," she said stiffly. "I thought I was responding to your comment."

Damn. She was apologizing again. He might know squat about women, but he knew Annie well enough to realize that was bad.

"No, no. That's great. Take off anything you want. Just—" He was sweating. His hands were clammy on the wheel. "Look, would you mind if we stopped somewhere first? Before I run us both off the road?"

"Stopped somewhere? You mean, like for coffee?"

"No. Someplace private."

In the dim glow of the dashboard, her knuckles were white. "Not a motel."

"No." Something inside him twisted at her obvious distress. Besides, he wouldn't last five minutes with her in a motel. "Somewhere we can talk."

"You want to talk." Her voice was expressionless.

"First. Yeah." This was not going well, he acknowledged. Maybe on her turf, she'd be more comfortable? "How about your place?"

"No. My baby-sitter…and then Mitchell will still be up."

His fingers drummed the steering wheel. "We're grown-ups, for crying out loud. It shouldn't be this hard to find a place to be alone."

Ann's faint smile filtered through the dark like starlight. "It's because we're grown-ups that it's so difficult."

"So, what did we do when we were kids?"

But the answer already throbbed in the air between them, as impossible to ignore as another couple on a double date. Teenagers in Cutler parked on the river road.

I don't get lucky in the back seats of cars, she'd told him. *I get pregnant.*

Maddox cracked the window and flicked out his unlit cigarette. Birth control or no birth control, he wasn't going to be another bum who hurt her. "Never mind," he said. "Bad idea."

To his surprise, she didn't immediately agree with him. "You said we needed privacy."

"To talk, I said."

"We can talk. I need to thank you, anyway. What you did, keeping Rob away from Val…I'm very grateful."

Her soft, precise voice cut under his skin. Her shoulders gleamed in the dim interior of the car. She was killing him. "How grateful?" he asked grimly.

"What do you mean?"

Trees arched over the road screening the sky. The moon played prisoner behind their branches. Without him ever making a conscious choice, he'd already taken the turnoff for the river. But the cop in him persisted in questioning her.

If Ann was offering herself to him out of some misplaced sense of obligation, she deserved better. And he deserved to know.

"This little road trip down memory lane... Is this how you say thank you? Because I don't want some sacrificial virgin."

She came back at him with the fragile humor that was part of her new toughness and part of her old appeal. "You said it yourself. I'm not a virgin anymore."

Near enough to make him sweat, he thought. "How about a sacrifice?"

He felt her straighten up beside him. "You were right. This was a bad idea. Take me home now, please."

"Annie—"

"You don't have to drive all the way to the river to tell me you don't want me. Again. Spare us both that."

Maddox swore silently. Rob had broken more than her nose. He'd battered her self-esteem. What Maddox saw as respect for her, she would take as rejection. He still wasn't sure she was ready for this. For him. But telling her so wasn't getting either of them anywhere.

"The only thing I'm trying to spare you is another lousy car-sex memory. I want you so bad I can't see straight, all right?"

No answer. The tires rumbled on the road. Maddox glanced over. Her profile was turned away from him. She clenched and unclenched her hands in her lap.

"If you can't see, it can't be safe for you to drive," she said reasonably, a little quiver in her voice that just about did him in. "You should pull over. There!" She leaned forward suddenly, her shoulders pale and slender in the dark. Her finger stabbed at the windshield. "There's a place to stop."

Maddox stared in disbelief. It was no more than a widening of the road, a gravel strip where fishermen could leave their cars and tromp down the soft bank. Shrubs half screened it from the road. High trees separated it from the water. As make-out spots went, this one wasn't scenic. It was barely even private.

She had to be pretty damn desperate to suggest stopping here.

He'd have to be horny or crazy—or both—to listen to her.

He pulled over.

The car bumped off the road and jolted down the slight incline. He took it as deep into the bushes as he dared, cringing as the branches shrieked across the paint, and cut the engine and the lights. His pulse thudded in his ears. He wondered if she could hear it in the silence.

He unrolled his window and angled against the driver's side door, facing her. "Now what?"

She dipped her head. Her hair slid forward, a whisper in the darkness. "I was hoping you had some ideas."

Too many. The images exploded in his brain: Annie under him, open to him, astride him, her tender mouth, her slender thighs parting to take him. Blood rushed from his head. His groin was heavy. His tongue felt thick.

I need to be in control, she'd said. And he was dangerously close to losing his.

Oh, damn. He wrapped his hands around the steering wheel again to keep from grabbing for her. He should never have thrown away that cigarette.

"Tell me what you want, Annie," he said hoarsely. "I'll do it. Whatever you want, however you want it. You tell me."

"I don't know." The words burst out of her. "How can I tell you? I don't know."

He was too old for this. Too big and too clumsy to be fumbling around in a car. Particularly with Annie, who deserved gentleness and respect. And a bed.

But there was no way he was going to crush her courage by denying her now.

Maybe this was his chance to prove to both of them that he could get it right.

"Okay," he said. "Then we'll have to make it up as we go along."

He could kiss her, he decided. She had liked his kisses. He eyed the yard of cushioned vinyl that stretched between them. The outline of her head was a deeper shadow against the darkness outside. She was still pressed tight against the door.

She was scared. And he was terrified of screwing this up.

"Of course, it would help if you'd come over here," he said, as gently as he could.

The outline moved as she nodded. The vinyl squeaked as she scooted toward him. Her scent—anxiety and shampoo and something sweet that was hers alone—tickled his nostrils. Her knee pressed his thigh.

Maddox was sweating. He started to shrug off his jacket, and she jerked and froze.

"Relax," he murmured. "I'm just getting rid of the old country club uniform, okay?"

"Yes. Sorry."

He decided to let this apology pass. He struggled out of his jacket. She helped him when his elbows stuck in the sleeves. Taking the jacket from her, he folded it over the back of the seat between them, feeling awkward as a bridegroom.

"Should I—should I take off my dress now?"

Oh, yeah, his body clamored.

"No rush," he said. "How about I put my arm around you instead?"

She laughed, a quicksilver fall of amusement that surprised them both. "You wouldn't have said *that* when we were teenagers."

"Probably not," he admitted wryly. "My body had two gears in those days, Full Stop and Full Speed Ahead. Guess you remember."

"I remember 'Stop.'" The humor in her voice didn't hide the hurt.

Hell. It wasn't only Rob who had shredded her confidence as a woman.

"That's okay. That's a good word for a woman to know. You say it, and I'll listen to it. I promise. But, Annie—" He risked a touch, cupping her delicate chin in his clumsy hand to turn her face to his in the dark. "I'm not saying it tonight. You want me to stop, you're going to have to say so."

He felt her nod. He felt her throat move as she swallowed. He found her lips and kissed her, keeping it light, keeping his hands to himself and his tongue in his mouth. His pulse roared in his ears.

He raised his head. "All right?"

She nodded again, her smooth hair brushing his jaw.

"Your turn," he suggested.

Her lips were warm and closed. Her breathing was erratic. She leaned into him, her small, sweet breasts flattening against his rib cage, and it became really evident she wasn't wearing a bra under that pretty nothing of a dress. His sex leaped in celebration.

Whoa, boy.

He itched, he burned for her like he hadn't burned for a woman in years. But this wasn't any woman. This was Annie. Deer-shy, man-wary Annie. With ruthless control, he throttled his eager body, forcing himself to give her time, to let her explore, while everything inside him churned and steamed. Gradually, she increased pressure, experimenting with slant and fit, and finally, shyly daring, testing him with her tongue. He nearly bucked off the seat.

She lifted her head. "Your turn," she said, her voice breathless and warm with satisfaction, giving his words back to him.

He wanted to strip off her dress and drape her over his lap and go crazy. His hands were shaking. Hell, he was shaking. He buried one hand in her hair, massaging her scalp, letting the fine strands slip through his fingers. Her neck was very close to his mouth. He kissed the column of her throat and felt her shiver. He almost growled. He kissed her again, indulging in the feel and the smell and the taste of her, the softness of her skin, the catch of her breath. Her pulse beat under his lips. Her skin was smooth and warm.

When he got to her bodice he stopped. He didn't trust himself that far. He kissed the velvet curve of her breast, rising gently above the square neckline of her dress, and then undid his shirt buttons, silently offering himself to her. *Your turn.*

Shyly, she kissed his neck. Her hand parted his shirt, flattened on his chest.

"You're hairy," she said on a note of discovery.

He had to clear his throat before he could speak. "Yeah. Me and King Kong."

"I like it."

Her neck bent and she kissed him again. Her legs curled up on the seat as she angled against him. Her lashes tickled his throat. She tasted him as he'd tasted her, her lips parted and moist. He groaned.

She jolted, her head almost clipping his jaw. "Should I stop?"

"No," he croaked. "No, this is—you're doing great."

"Really?" With the windshield behind her, he could not see her face, but her voice was pleased and excited.

"I swear. Don't stop now."

She kissed his mouth, softly, as if in gratitude, and then his throat some more. She wriggled around on the seat beside him as if she were trying to climb into his lap. His lap wanted desperately to cooperate, but the steering wheel got in the way. He slid along the seat. She made a low, assenting noise and arched against him.

He nuzzled her cheek, finding her mouth with his in the dark. They kissed, warm and slow, and his blood rose, fast and hot. She burrowed closer, her hands sliding into his open shirtfront.

Her soft hands petting him almost wrecked his control. He reached for her breast; stopped. Slow, he ordered himself. Easy. And he kept his movements gentle and unhurried until she twisted against him, until he could feel her breath quick on the side of his face and the riot of her heart close to his palm. Only then did he glide his hand over the silk of her dress and close it smoothly over her breast. Her nipple pushed into his palm. He hissed in satisfaction and lightly scraped it with his thumbnail.

Ann gasped. Her head was a swarm of bees, a buzz of sensations. Honey flowed in all her veins. She couldn't think. She could barely breathe, and it was—well, really, it was wonderful. Her breasts tightened at Maddox's touch. Her whole body tightened. She wanted him to touch her just like that everywhere. How shocking. How lovely.

And it was as if Maddox knew what was happening to her, because his hand slid from breast to thigh and from the outside of her hip to the gathered fold of her skirt, right there, right between her legs. She was glad it was dark. Her face burned, but she did not move away. He touched her there, brushing her lightly, stroking her softly, until she just had to open for him so that he could go on touching and touching her.

"That's it," he whispered. "A little more. Yeah, that's it. You are so pretty, darlin'. You are so hot."

She *was* hot. She squirmed and opened her legs some more. She was practically riding his hand, and he went on touching her through her panties, firm and knowledgeable. Tears sprang to her eyes. She thought she would die from the pleasure of it, from the pleasure of his caring touch and fierce concentration.

"You could take off something now," he suggested huskily in her ear. "If you wanted."

That sounded like a good idea. She scrambled on the

broad, flat seat, struggling to rid herself of her clinging underwear. One of her high heels fell into the passenger well. Her hip bumped the steering wheel.

His big hands spanned her hips, steadying her. "Easy, Annie."

She was embarrassed. But then his hand smoothed down her skirt to her knee and glided back up along her bare thigh to the place that waited and wept for him.

He sucked in his breath. "Oh, darlin'."

The awe in his voice, the movement of his fingers, made her forget her awkwardness. They caressed her and she danced.

He drew them away slowly, slowly, and she moaned at the loss. He kissed her, his tongue warm and urgent, and then brought his hand to his mouth. She watched, her heart jerking in her chest, as he tasted her on his fingers. Even in the dark, she could see his eyes glitter.

"Your turn," he rumbled.

All her insecurities crashed in on her. She drew back shakily. "I don't think—I've sort of reached my limit here."

Under her hands, his muscles coiled, but he did not move. Only his broad chest rose and fell with his breath.

"Is this 'stop'?" he asked quietly.

"No," she said. She felt like such an idiot. "I just—I don't know what to do."

His hand reached up. She willed herself not to flinch. Tenderly, he tucked a strand of hair behind her ear and then cupped her cheek.

"You want me to take over for a while?"

She closed her eyes in gratitude, nestling her face against his warm, square palm. "Yes. Please."

Please. She winced. Such a Nice Girl thing to say, she thought.

But Maddox didn't mock her. He kissed the doubt from between her brows and the tears from the corners of her eyes. He reached up under her hair and urged her head down onto his shoulder. She could feel the pounding of his heart and the tension in his arms. His chest was sweaty. But he held her, simply held her, his hands undemanding on her back and hip. He was solid and warm and real, and her starved heart shuddered with wanting him. After a long time, she sighed.

"All right?" he asked again, low and deep.

She nodded against his shoulder. He kissed her cheek. Such a short distance from her mouth, she thought fuzzily. Such a little thing to turn her head. She turned to him.

Mouth to mouth, they kissed, long and sweet. And desire rose in her again, dark and dizzying deep inside, dancing on her skin. She trembled. He touched and coaxed and caressed her, and the heat rolled in through the open windows and built up between them.

She was close, Maddox thought, heat pouring through his veins in sheer male jubilation. He was holding on to the edge of oblivion by his fingernails, but she was close to going over. He wanted that. He wanted to push her, wanted to feel her fly.

He tried to keep her with him as he yanked at his belt buckle, as he fumbled with his zipper. Sex in a car. What a joke.

But it didn't feel like a joke, not with Annie warm and willing above him. It felt like heaven. It felt like everything he'd ever wanted, all wrapped up in a green-eyed girl who tasted like salt tears and wine and honey.

He dug in his back pocket for his wallet, lifting his hips. She made a choked sound in the back of her throat and wiggled closer. He dragged in air. He was going to lose it.

"Easy," he whispered. "Don't try so hard. I've got it. I've got you."

It would be simpler if he laid her along the seat, but he didn't want to come down on top of her, didn't want her to feel trapped or confined. He tried to deal with the condom one-handed. He couldn't see. And he was distracted with

Annie rubbing against him, all soft silk and smooth skin and slender curves, so it took a long time.

She kissed his jaw, missing his mouth in the dark. Her small, capable hands fluttered over his, making the ache worse. "Should I—" She touched him, and his body strained toward her. "Can I help?"

"Yeah. That would be good," he said through his teeth.

So she helped, and that took a long time, too, because she was shaking damn near as much as he was and probably had less idea what she was doing. It was torture, but it was the kind of torture a man got down on his knees and prayed for.

Eventually he was covered, and she pulled her dress out of the way, and he was there, almost inside her. Almost there. Almost home. Ann was breathing hard and trembling, but not with fear. It wasn't fear, was it, when she gripped his shoulders so tight? He couldn't stand for it to be fear. But he couldn't see her face, couldn't see if there was welcome in her eyes.

"Annie…"

She shuddered.

Oh, damn. His heart died within him. He was a dead man. "Annie, it's okay. We don't have to—"

"Now!" she cried sharply. "Maddox, please!"

She didn't have to tell him twice.

He thought, *She wants this.*

And he thought, *She wants me.*

And the knowledge and the relief together were too much for him, and he went into her, and she was hot and tight and wet and there. In his arms. *Annie.* He pushed into her, and she made a soft sound above him in the dark and kissed the side of his face and totally blew his control. He was just so damn glad to be with her, all the way with her, all the way inside her, at last. He started moving, rocking into her, and she tried to move with him, but he was too far gone. He was lost in her, so lost in the clasp of her body and the beat of his blood and the way her hands touched him that he couldn't stop, couldn't slow, couldn't breathe.

She tightened around him, and he emptied himself into her in hard, dark jets of abandon.

Ann wrapped her arms around Maddox, holding on for dear life. She absorbed the uncontrolled pounding of his heart, took in the force of his powerful body as he shook beneath her, and it made her glad that she was doing that to him, with him, that he felt this way because of her.

Everything inside her was warm and relaxed, and it hadn't hurt at all.

She smiled into the crease of his neck, not caring that her borrowed dress would have to go to the dry cleaners and she'd somehow lost a shoe. It didn't matter. She could do this, she thought, with relief and gratitude. She could please a man—this man—and enjoy it.

He exhaled into her hair. His hands relaxed their tight grip on her bottom. He stroked her there, and she sighed.

"Damn," Maddox said. "That didn't go the way I planned it at all."

She stiffened. A little of her pleasure leaked away. "Excuse me?"

"I was too quick." He raised his hand and tucked her hair behind her ear, his touch lingering on her neck and jaw. "I left you in the dust back there."

She was reassured. "Oh, that's all right. I had fun."

"I should have had more control."

She shook her head, forgetting he couldn't see her in the dark. "I liked it," she insisted shyly. "I liked knowing I could make you feel like that."

"But you didn't—"

"No," she said hastily. Embarrassed, now that she understood what he meant. What he wanted. "I don't. It's all right. It's not you. I just don't."

Seconds ticked by, measured in the beat of her pulse.

"Ever?" Maddox asked at last, his voice neutral in the dark.

Heat crawled in her face. She levered away from him, one hand on his naked chest, her legs awkwardly placed to either side of his hips. "I don't want to talk about it."

"Okay. Take it easy. Hey." He gentled her, tempted her back to him with soothing strokes and murmurs. "It's okay. Come here. Just put your head… There we go. We won't talk."

He settled her against him, her head on his shoulder. His arms sheltered her. His warmth cocooned her. His breath stirred her hair.

"We could try doing something about it instead," he rumbled.

Oh, dear. She should have known Maddox would take her failure as his challenge. Ann thought of the inevitable embarrassing fumbles, the growing sense of shame and defeat, the having-to-pretend, and her heart sank.

"It's too much work," she blurted.

"I think I'm up for it," he said, real dry.

"I didn't mean—"

"You won't have to do a thing," he promised.

He kissed the hollow of her neck, and she shivered with new desire.

"Well, you don't have to do anything, either," she said, a little pettishly, and he laughed.

"Yeah, I do. This time I'm carrying the ball all the way to the end zone."

"I am not—" she said, but he kissed her open mouth, stopping her words, stealing her breath.

"Yeah, you are," he said, his voice rough and confident.

Irritation licked along her nerves, a welcome heat that joined and danced with the warmth collecting lower down.

"You sound sure of yourself," she said.

She felt him smile against her cheek. His hands moved in

the dark, sneaky, irresistible. "Sure of you," he whispered. "You're such a soft touch, Annie."

"Such a doormat, you mean."

"Nope. Kind. You always were nice to me." His warm lips cruised from her jaw to the point of her chin. "Soft." He rubbed her mouth gently with his until she sighed and opened for him. "Sweet." He stroked inside, and everything inside her tightened and then softened until she was melting on his lap.

"Maddox?" Her voice shook.

"Shh. I had a thing for you back then, you know," he told her, while his large hands petted and soothed her. "Big-eyed Annie with the pretty hair. I used to watch you up on the bleachers watching me at practice, and I'd imagine touching you like this." He demonstrated, and she trembled, wanting him. "And this."

She was shocked. Pleased. "You did not."

"Did, too," he said solemnly, and she smiled.

He kissed her, long and sweet and slow, until her heart turned over in her chest.

"Of course, I didn't really know what I was missing," he whispered. His breath was warm against her lips. "But I had a great imagination. You want to know what else I thought about?"

Her face flamed. She was hot all over, dying with embarrassment and delight.

"I'm not sure you should tell me," she said, trying for humor, but his big, patient hands were making it hard to joke. Hard to think.

"How about I show you instead?" he suggested, and her blood flowed thick and hot.

He sounded so impossibly wicked. He felt so incredibly good, and, just as he'd promised, she didn't have to do a thing. He kept touching her, praising her, and everything in her strained toward him, toward…something.

"Maddox?" she said again, panicked as the tension inside her wound higher and tighter.

Control. She wanted—needed—control, and he was stealing it from her, taking charge of her body with his large, square hands. They slid around her, possessing all her curves, claiming all her secret places. He was hot, pressing inside her. She opened her mouth to breathe. And he kept on, kept at her, stroking, sliding, pressing, until the spiraling tension broke in a great gasping shock, and her mind let go, and her body pulsed with deep, drenching pleasure, coil after coil of it, and she cried out.

He held her, cradled her against his broad, damp chest, kissed her forehead and her eyelids as she shook and gulped against him.

"Now, that was worth waiting for," he drawled.

Chapter 11

Ann felt a chill in the pit of her stomach that a moment ago had been flooded with warmth. She tried for dignity and for distance, but both were beyond her while she sprawled on Maddox's chest with his hand still up her skirt.

"I'm sorry if I took too long. I haven't had a lot of practice."

"I wasn't complaining, darlin'. It's nice to know I can give you something Rob can't."

The chill spread. She struggled to sit up. "Is that what this is about? You proving you're better than Rob?"

His words came back to her with distressing clarity: *This time I'm carrying the ball all the way to the end zone.* She looked around for her underwear.

"What are you talking about?" Maddox asked, no longer sounding lazily amused.

She found her panties dangling from the radio knob and snatched them up. "I don't like being used."

"Neither do I," he said.

She stopped with one ankle through the leg hole in her underwear. "And what is that supposed to mean?"

He reached a long arm over her head to flick on the cabin light. "You weren't this fussy an hour ago when you were hell-bent on proving you were over your ex."

She flinched from his scrutiny. There was enough truth in his accusation to make her uncomfortable. "You think that I accepted a ride with you because I wanted sex?"

"I don't know what to think," he replied evenly. "You're the one who offered to take her clothes off."

Her hands were shaking. She abandoned her underwear at her knees to raise her head and glare at him. She wasn't any better at standing up for herself than she was at sex. She had no experience with either one. But even the horrible fear that she was making a big mistake didn't stop her from saying, "I didn't hear you object to parking with the quarterback's girlfriend."

"Because I wanted you."

"Because you wanted what Rob had."

"Back in high school. I for damn sure wanted what he had then. The respect. You. That doesn't reduce what happened between us tonight to some old locker-room rivalry."

She folded her hands and raised her eyebrows. "'Carrying the ball to the end zone'?"

"Well, I did, didn't I?"

"Yes." She bit her lip. "Thank you."

"Hell, Annie, I don't want you to thank me. I just want you to let me—"

He broke off. Possibilities trembled between them. Inside Ann, some soft and unprotected part of her she thought had died quivered to painful life. Her hungry heart quaked with frustration, with hope, with...

"Let you—what?" she whispered.

He shrugged. "Help you."

Disappointment tumbled her dreams before she'd even

started to build. "No. Thank you. I've had enough of being 'helped.'"

"Take care of you, then."

Worse and worse. "I don't need someone to take care of me. Rob did that, and I let him go on doing it, until I couldn't take care of anything. I need to handle things myself."

He narrowed his eyes. "I can't let you do that."

"That's your problem."

"No. It's my job."

Realization settled coldly in her chest. He was a police officer, trained and sworn to protect. Obviously, he'd decided she needed his protection. It was her own stupid fault if she longed to be something more than an obligation he met and left behind.

"For how long?" she asked steadily. "The next two weeks?"

"Two and a half."

She bent for her shoe, intent on hiding her red face, her trembling hands. "Well, thank you very much, but I'm not interested in being your pet police project this month."

"You know, in court you can't jump from collecting the evidence to sentencing the defendant without going through a trial. But I guess you decided to skip that part." His voice was rich with disgust. He patted his empty breast pocket for a cigarette and then swore.

"I'm s—"

"So help me God, Annie, if you apologize, I'll—" His jaw clamped shut.

She cringed, but not from fear. Under the anger, she could hear the hurt in his tone. She had hurt him, and he'd never intended anything but kindness toward her.

She swallowed regret, thick and hot as tears in her throat. She had to protect herself. Rob had broken her spirit. Maddox could break her heart.

"I think you should take me home now," she said.

He exhaled. "Fine. Whatever you want."

He started the car. She stared out the window. The ride home passed in silence, stony on his part, miserable on hers. Her skin was delicately abraded, her emotions raw.

He pulled up at her curb. The block was quiet. The outside security light shone. Through the living room window, she could see the glow of a lamp and the flicker of the TV.

Maddox turned to her, propping one arm on the steering wheel. "I already figured you're not inviting me in for coffee. Can I walk you to your door, or is that considered overprotective now?"

She didn't want him to come to her house. She would be too tempted to beg him to stay. She moistened her lips. "It's not necessary. Julie, my baby-sitter, is here, and I have my key."

His eyes were flat. "Right."

Obeying an impulse she refused to examine—risking his anger, risking rejection, risking her whole small store of courage—she leaned across the wide bench seat and pressed her lips to his cheek. His skin was rough. He jerked under her touch.

"Good-night kiss," she explained to his surprised face, and scrambled out of the car.

If he called her name, it was lost in the slamming of the car door. And maybe he thought better of it, because she didn't hear anything as she hurried up the walk.

She did not look back. She fumbled with the lock and the dead bolt and flicked the porch light once to let Maddox know she was safely inside. Locked away from temptation, in a prison of her own choosing. She felt the weariness of her self-imposed punishment in her shoulders. She felt its loneliness in her soul. She closed her eyes a moment, as if that would bring her rest or peace.

At least this time, she chose the bars that kept the world at bay.

With her palms pressed flat to the metal door, she listened to the sound of Maddox's car as he drove away.

Then, summoning a smile to greet her baby-sitter, she walked into the living room, dropping her little black bag on the back of the couch. "Hi, Julie, I'm home."

Rob looked up from the brown recliner, where he slumped watching TV. "It's about time," he said.

Driving down the darkened street, Maddox smacked the steering wheel with the heel of his palm. Damned if he knew what had happened.

He'd just fulfilled his high school fantasies with the girl of his dreams. Okay, so he'd rushed to the party, but she'd been satisfied. He ought to be on top of the world.

He felt lousy.

He felt... Never one for self-examination, he searched for the word. Frustrated.

Not sexually frustrated. His body still had the revved-up hum of a well-oiled engine allowed to race. He hadn't felt so relaxed since...before the shooting, in the early days of Sandra. A long time. But he was frustrated all the same. Something had been missing from their little car encounter, and it wasn't just that he hadn't had a chance to see Annie, really see her, without her clothes on.

Thank you very much, but I'm not interested in being your pet police project this month.

Hell.

He'd suspected things were moving too fast. He'd tried to talk her out of it, hadn't he? But when she offered to take off her dress... His body tightened in memory. Well, he'd seized the chance to replay their high school fiasco on the river road, to get it right this time for both of them.

It should have worked. He'd taken care to *make* it work, to give Annie the experience she deserved, even after he scored early in the game. He'd certainly been satisfied. Maddox frowned, driving on autopilot down streets he hadn't cruised in a dozen years. Maybe not quite satisfied. He wanted to do it all over again, slower, in a bed, in the light. But still, it was great car sex.

And Annie had been satisfied, too, damn it, sweet and soft, wet and eager. *His,* shuddering in *his* arms, moaning at *his* touch, crying out at the last. Desire pulsed through him, and he almost turned the car around.

Bad idea. She wouldn't want him with the baby-sitter there. She wouldn't want him with her son sleeping upstairs.

Hell, who was he kidding? She didn't want him anyway. She didn't want to be helped, didn't want anyone taking care of her.

And it was a good thing, too, he was glad about that— wasn't he?—because he was the last guy she needed taking care of her. He remembered enough of the academy course in domestic violence intervention to know that Ann needed to trust her own decisions. And he needed to get back to Atlanta. Back to the pimps, the pushers, the teenage shooters, the jokes and jargon and chaos of the squad room. Back where he belonged. He had what it took to make it there.

He pulled into his father's driveway—God, he felt like a teenager again—and sat for a minute with the engine running. Two and a half weeks. The sooner he left, the better. Because he'd never made it in Cutler. He didn't have what it took to make it for good with a woman like Annie.

But she'd kissed him good-night.

He shook his head. See, that was the kind of thinking that could get him into trouble. Annie was vulnerable. She might claim she wanted less from him, but he knew she dreamed of more. Only she deserved to find it with some nice guy with clean hands and a good heart. Somebody with a big, loving family and a low-risk, high-paying job. Somebody safe.

Deep down, Maddox figured she knew that.

He'd be a lot better off once he accepted it, too.

* * *

Everything inside Ann screamed. *Get out, get out, get out, get away.* She did her best to ignore the howling warnings, keeping her face a mask, her voice quiet.

"Where's Julie?"

"Afraid I murdered your baby-sitter?" Rob stood, enormous and out of place in her small, neat, shabby living room. She took one step backward and he looked at her in disgust. "Oh, what do you think, Ann? I paid her and sent her home. She thanked me for her tip."

"I'll pay you back."

He made an impatient gesture. "Don't be stupid."

She would send him a check, although he'd probably tear it up. But she would not fight with him. She would not give him the opportunity to fight with her. She had to protect Mitchell.

"And Mitchell?" she asked.

"In bed."

Safe, then. She drew a shallow breath of relief. Once in bed, their son knew not to come down. Because no nightmare could be as bad as what happened after bedtime in the house on Stonewall Drive.

"Is that where you've been? Bed?" Rob asked.

"No, I—" *Don't apologize, don't explain.* "No."

"I saw you get out of his car."

"I didn't see yours."

"That's because I'm smarter than you. I parked down the block. What were you doing with him, Ann?"

Ann swallowed. No point in pretending she didn't know who Rob was talking about. "He gave me a ride home from the club."

"Are you putting out for him? Is that why he's switched teams all of a sudden?"

"I think you should go now," she said.

Rob strolled forward, his hands in his pockets, his head thrust forward. Ann stood her ground, her heart hammering. How could she run, with her son hostage upstairs? She was guilty of so much. But she would never leave Mitchell to face Rob's wrath alone.

"You look like a whore," he said in a pleasant, conversational tone. "And you smell like sex. I wouldn't have thought you were enticement enough to make MD forget where his loyalties lie."

"Don't touch me," Ann said.

Rob lifted his brows. "Touch you? I could do a lot more than touch you, dear wife."

He was close enough for her to smell the remembered scent of his after-shave, the bourbon on his breath. Her skin crawled. She opened her mouth to breathe.

"Ex-wife," she said stiffly. "And I'll call the police if I have to, Rob."

"And tell them what? That I was here baby-sitting our son while you screwed Maddox Palmer out on the river road? That will impress his daddy."

"You followed us?" She shuddered. It was too creepy, the thought of Rob out there in the darkness while she and Maddox…

Rob shook his head. "I assumed you'd both run true to type. Sex in the back seat was all you were ever good for."

She forced herself not to recoil from his verbal slap. "Too bad you didn't figure that out before we got married," she said quietly.

"It was too late then," Rob said self-righteously. "You were already pregnant. I wasn't about to let you spread it all over town that I ignored my responsibilities."

"I wouldn't have done that."

"No? But you're doing it now. You're testifying against me." He leaned in even closer, his eyes feral. "It doesn't look good. I'm disappointed in you, Ann. I'm trying to be friends with you. I'm trying to show people there are no hard feelings. And you just aren't cooperating. Maybe MD isn't the one who needs to reexamine his loyalties."

She could feel the violence building in him. It reached out to her in waves. "What do you want?" she asked.

"Ann, Ann," he reproached her. "You don't want to make me tell you. A loving wife should know. You just think about it. You think about where your best interests lie. Not with the cop. Not with Val. With me."

Realization settled sickly in her stomach. Val. This was about Val. This was about betraying her friend—again—by recanting her testimony when Rob went to trial. "I can't do that," Ann protested. "I gave a statement."

"You better do it. Or I'll make you sorry, do you hear me?" He towered over her. He bent, so that his hot breath tickled her ear and sent cold chills down her spine. "I'll make you very, very sorry," he whispered.

Maddox was stepping out of the shower when his pager beeped from the back of the toilet. He frowned. He wasn't on duty tonight. Unless a traffic stop had gone bad, and the dispatcher was signaling for help…

Hitching a towel around his waist, he checked the number before dialing it in. It wasn't Crystal at the station. "Palmer."

"Hey, Mad Dog, it's Tom. Creech? Got a call to a possible ten-sixteen."

Domestic disturbance. Maddox frowned at the clouded mirror. "You need backup?"

"No, I'm okay. No drinking, no weapons, no assailant on scene. It's just the reporting party on this one is Ann Cross. You told me to let you know."

He was already in his room, yanking open bureau drawers. "Medical assistance?"

"She said no. I figured I'd assess, drive her to the ER myself if it looked bad."

"Copy." A hanger rattled to the floor as he grabbed his uniform pants. "Show me en route in five."

"You want to cover?" Tom sounded surprised. "I'm just going to take a report."

"That's affirm. Thanks for the heads up, Tom. Call Crystal for me?"

"Will do. I'll go run interference on a party in Grand Oaks. Noise complaint."

"Juveniles?" Maddox guessed, shoving his feet into his shoes, reaching for his holster.

"Twelve-year-old girl. Birthday party." Tom chuckled. "Guess the neighbors don't like boy bands."

Maddox grunted and signed off. Even as he pocketed his keys and methodically checked and strapped his equipment belt, his mind was leaping ahead to Annie, frightened, threatened, hurt.

Annie, telling him she didn't need or want his protection.

His gut burned. His jaw set. She was getting his protection now, whether she wanted it or not.

Crossing town, he put the blue light up and the gas pedal down. *No assailant on the scene,* Creepy had reported, but as Maddox stopped in front of Ann's house, he checked all the approaches, anyway. No Rob. No sign of Rob's car.

He pressed the bell and stepped back so she could get a good look at him through the peephole.

The door cracked open. Ann stood in the gap, her face in shadow, her arms folded protectively across her middle. She still had on the sexy black dress she'd worn to the club, but her hair was tumbled and one narrow strap had slipped off her shoulder. He wanted to reach through the opening and pull it up for her, to set it right.

"What are you doing here?" she asked.

"You called."

She didn't budge from the doorway. "I called 911. I didn't know you were on duty."

"I am now. Are you going to let me in?"

Her head tilted. "Did you bring your superhero cape with you?"

Her wry humor caught and cut him as easily as a knife. "No. But I've got my badge and notebook."

"And a note from your father?"

"I don't need one. This is an official call, Annie."

"I never called before," she whispered.

His heart wrenched. "I know. Let me in."

She shuffled back from the door. The light from the lamp slid across her face, and he let himself hope. Her eyes were sunken and her skin looked tight, but he didn't see any cuts. No swelling. None of the puffy redness that would bloom into bruises by morning.

And then he remembered what she'd told him. *He didn't usually touch my face.* And his own response: *They don't hit where it shows.*

"Are you all right?" he asked roughly. He would kill the son of a bitch, badge or no badge.

Her head wavered up and down. "Fine."

His blood pumped hot. He forced himself not to jump and roar, but enough of what he was feeling must have escaped into his face, because she looked at him with wide, dry eyes that had seen too much violence. Like the eyes of a survivor at an accident scene, or the flat gaze of the old-young children on the bad streets of Atlanta.

"No, really fine," she insisted. "He threatened me. He didn't hit me."

"Mitchell?"

"Was upstairs the whole time."

He would have to accept her assurance for now. Concentrate on the job, aid the victim, make his case. For now. He took out his notebook. "Okay. Why don't we sit down and you can tell me what happened. Starting with when you got home."

She perched on the edge of the couch. He sat in the brown recliner, the only chair in the room big enough for him, and wondered why she stiffened. He wanted to hold her, wanted to tell her that everything would be all right, that he would make it all right. But she didn't want him that close, and he didn't know if he could fix anything yet.

So he asked his questions and wrote down her replies. She was a good witness. She kept her times and events in order, clasping her hands in her lap like a polite child while she described how her home and her freedom and her safety had been violated. Her evidence was unemotional and clear.

Maddox was afraid it wouldn't be enough.

"...and then he left," Ann concluded.

"Is that when you called the police?" Why not me? he wanted to demand. Why the hell didn't you turn to me?

"I—" Her throat moved as she swallowed. "It may have been a couple of minutes after that."

Her words trembled between them. *I don't need someone to take care of me. I need to handle things myself.*

Ann was scared and cold and sick inside. She wanted Maddox to hold her, wanted to crawl onto his lap and beg for the strong comfort of his arms, the rough reassurance of his voice. She squeezed her hands together to keep from reaching for him.

A muscle bunched in his jaw.

She knew what her distance cost her. She was less sure how it affected Maddox. But that betraying muscle... He'd never let anyone bully her, not even Billy Ward back in middle school. Sudden gratitude made her offer,

"I never called before. But tonight your father—I thought it would be all right. Because you'd talked to him."

His hooded gaze met hers straight on, acknowledging her concession. "You did the right thing," he said. "Tomorrow we'll go see a magistrate, get a warrant."

It sounded so straightforward.

"But he didn't hit me."

"He threatened you. That might be enough, given your history of abuse and him being on probation."

She nodded. "All right."

"In the meantime, you should get somebody to stay with you. Val, maybe?"

"You figure I should ask my pregnant friend, the friend I stole from, to leave her husband and her bed and defend me with her frying pan from the man who tried to murder her? No."

He almost grinned. Scowled, instead. "What about your mother?"

Her brief enjoyment faded. "We don't—we're not close," she said with difficulty. "She could forgive me for getting pregnant and marrying Rob—how else could a girl like me catch a prize like him?—but she still can't find it in her heart to forgive me for divorcing him."

She'd shaken that granite police face. "Annie—"

"It's all right," she said quickly. "I don't need anybody. We'll be fine."

And he respected her boundaries. He didn't even suggest that he sleep on her couch.

Ann told herself she was glad. She would have said no, anyway. Instead, she said good night, and locked and dead-bolted her door, and went upstairs and cried herself to sleep.

But in the morning when she looked out her window, she saw Maddox's big blue sedan, as if he'd driven right out of her restless dreams to park in front of her house. Not in her driveway—the neighbors would talk—but across the street. Just for a moment, she had it back: the squeak of vinyl, the rush of heat, the scent of tobacco and sex and Maddox moving under her, thrusting inside her.

She blinked. The car stayed stubbornly at the curb. So she wasn't hallucinating. Maddox must have camped out in his car all night. She didn't know whether to be thrilled by his determination to protect her or mad that he'd do such a thing without once asking what she wanted.

She jerked a brush through her hair and reached for her shorts. When she sallied forth ten minutes later, she still wasn't sure if she were visiting the troops or going into battle.

His window was open. She stopped in the street, clutching a coffee mug, and demanded, "What are you doing out here?"

Maddox scrubbed his face with one large, square hand. The slanting light revealed the bags beneath his eyes and exaggerated the creases in his forehead. He needed to shave. "Good morning to you, too."

She fought the twist of concern. "That was a stupid thing to do, sitting up in your car all night."

He gave her one of those level, unreadable looks that made her stomach flutter. "I'm used to it."

She remembered their conversation from the gym. "Another part of the job?" she quoted dryly.

He must have remembered, too, because his eyes narrowed. "We weren't going to talk about it, you said."

It. The shooting. She held out the mug to him. "Maybe we should."

"Thanks." He sipped the hot coffee. "Why? You worried about me hanging around your kid?"

"Maybe I'm worried about you. Did you ever talk to anybody?"

"Darlin', they made me talk to everybody. The division commander, the investigating shoot team, the D.A.'s office, the P.I.O.—that's the Public Information Officer—and the shrink."

"And?" she prompted softly.

He shrugged. "And they all said the same. Clean shoot. Hell, I saved a teacher's life. I must be some kind of cop, huh?"

Her heart wrenched at the bleakness in his voice. "Is that how you felt?"

"No." He stared into the mug cradled in his large hand. "I kept wondering—I still wonder—if there was something else I could have done."

It was a bigger admission than she'd expected. More, perhaps, than she knew how to deal with. Ann studied him a moment. "Do you want to know what my therapist would say?"

He looked up at her. "Sure." His lashes were thick and short. Something warm and liquid and addictive as caffeine spread under her ribs.

"My therapist told me that no one is the cause for another person's violent behavior. So you can't take responsibility for that boy's decision to fire that gun any more than I should accept the blame for Rob beating me."

"Damn it, that's different."

"You're right. I chose to stay in my marriage. You didn't have any choice about being in that schoolyard. It seems to me that if I can forgive myself, then you certainly should be able to forgive yourself." She waited for him to absorb that one, watched his jaw tighten and his full lips compress. Had she said enough? Too much? What would this man accept from her, anyway?

"Do you want to come in for breakfast?" she asked.

"You don't have to feed me, Annie." A corner of his mouth quirked. "Though I wouldn't say no if you offered your bathroom."

She'd had sex with this man on the front seat of his car. It was stupid to blush because he asked for indoor plumbing.

"You can wash up while I'm cooking," she said briskly. "How do you like your eggs?"

He caught her eye. "I'm partial to over easy," he drawled. "But I'll take whatever you give me."

Her heart beat faster. "Breakfast in fifteen minutes."

He caught her hand through the open window as she turned away. His hand was warm and callused, his voice warm and earnest. "Annie. Thanks."

Her fingers tangled and tightened with his. She felt herself color. "Fifteen minutes," she repeated, and hurried back to the house.

She left the door unlocked behind her for the first time since she and Mitchell had moved in. She heard Maddox come in and go up the stairs, listened to the water gurgle through the pipes as she sliced a tube of Jimmy Dean sausage and counted bread for toast. As she pulled the egg carton from the refrigerator, she caught herself humming.

Oh, no, she thought, jolted back to reality. She was not playing house, no matter how seductive she found the combination of hot sex and intimate conversation. Wasn't her marriage to Rob painful, living proof that she didn't belong in the full-page fantasy of some glossy women's magazine? Once she'd carried those articles home like talismans, as if decorating with pillows or creating colorful meals using seasonal vegetables or knowing the seven secrets of happy marriages could magically transform her into the kind of woman whose husband kissed her when he came home.

She was smarter now. She knew what she was. She knew what she could have. And Maddox Palmer was not on the list.

But when he walked into her kitchen a few minutes later, his wet hair showing the tracks of her comb and his chin still rough with stubble, her heart lifted with happiness. Her mind blanked with lust.

"Smells good," he said with a smile.

The impact of his smile traveled all the way to her stomach. She was in very big trouble.

She adjusted the heat under the frying pan. Act casual, she ordered herself. "Find everything you need?"

"Yeah. Thanks. Though I don't know..." He rubbed at his jaw with his hand. "Think I should have used your little pink razor?"

She laughed. "The one I use for my legs? Not unless you want to visit the judge with blobs of tissue stuck all over your face."

And there it was, out between them, the reason he was standing in her kitchen on a sunny summer morning while she cooked his breakfast. Rob. The threats. The trial. Her smile faded.

After a moment, his did, too.

"Maybe not," he said, and took his place at the table. She noticed he sat in the same spot, facing the door.

"I'll get your eggs," Ann said.

She glanced over her shoulder as Mitchell shuffled in, his T-shirt hanging out and his hair sticking up where he'd mashed it against his pillow, and she had another reminder of where her priorities should lie.

"Hey, Mom. You cooking *sausage?*"

And then he saw Maddox. His eyes flickered. Ann watched helplessly as he assembled and reassembled the shards of evidence—his mother going out last night, the closed bathroom door this morning, and now the man sitting at the breakfast table—into a damning picture.

His bright, nine-year-old face closed into the watchful, old man's mask she hated.

"What's he doing here?"

Chapter 12

Ann dithered. What could she say? She didn't want to flounder through an explanation of her sex life to her nine-year-old son. But was the other half of the truth any more acceptable? Could she really tell Mitchell that she was trying to have his father—the father who still had custody on alternate weekends—arrested?

She tightened her grip on the spatula. "Mr. Palmer had to work last night. So I invited him for breakfast."

Mitchell's gaze slid sideways to Maddox, big and imposing in his uniform. "Why?"

Maddox spoke up. "Because I'm hungry, and your mom is nice. And because I'm driving her to the police station this morning."

The boy's face pinched. "Is she under arrest?"

"No," Ann said quickly. She rescued Maddox's eggs before the yolks turned completely hard, and slapped the plate in front of him. "In fact, we might not go at all."

"We're going," Maddox said.

"But…it's Sunday."

He stabbed his eggs with a fork. "I've already called the dispatcher. Magistrate will meet us there at nine-thirty."

"I can't. Mitchell—"

"Can wait in the hall. He'll be perfectly safe. It's a police station."

She felt control of the situation slipping away. "I need to make him breakfast."

Maddox swabbed his plate with a piece of toast. "I'll make him breakfast. You get ready."

"But—"

"I can handle eggs, Annie," he said gently. "We'll be okay."

Maddox watched her think that one through, and he thought, This is what her life is like, all the little decisions rushing in on her, one after another, like waves at the beach. Only nobody ever told her she could swim. And he felt bad for her, and admired her, too, that she waded in anyway, even when the footing was treacherous and the next big one could knock her down.

He knew from his time on the force that it took most abused women an average of seven support contacts with authorities—the cop on the scene or the nurse in ER or a social worker with a telephone number—to finally find the courage and resources to leave. Annie had done it cold. But the residue of doubt still clung to her like dirt on a window, clouding her decisions.

Could she leave him alone with her son?

Could she make the complaint against her husband?

She looked at the clock. Looked at her sullen kid. And then, finally, she nodded. "All right. Mitchell, put your dishes in the sink when you're done."

Maddox waited until her soft tread went up the stairs before he asked the kid, "*Are* we okay?"

Mitchell shrugged. "I guess."

"Why don't you tell me what you think is going on, and we'll see if we can figure it out."

The boy thrust out his chin, the gesture enough like Ann's to cause a pang. "I heard my mom crying last night."

Damn. But Maddox filed away his own reaction to Ann's distress. He'd deal with it and with her later. "And you're worried maybe I was responsible for that."

Another shrug.

"I told you I would never hurt your mother."

That earned him a quick, scornful look. "Sure."

Maddox didn't blame the kid for not believing him. He'd probably spent his entire life listening to grown-ups lie.

"Did you hear anything else last night?"

Mitchell turned red. "I didn't listen at the door, if that's what you mean."

Another problem to be dealt with at another time. "Downstairs. Did you hear anything downstairs after your mother came home?"

"Like what?"

"Did you hear anybody?"

From red, Mitchell's face turned to white. "Did he come here?"

"Your father? Yeah. He was here."

"Did he hit her?"

"No." For the first time in years, Maddox gave thanks for the stiff-necked martinet who'd raised him. He might have had issues with his old man, but at least he'd never had to worry about him beating up on his mom.

"Are you—" the kid's throat moved as he swallowed "—are you going to arrest him?"

Tricky question. What answer did Mitchell want to hear? Rob was still his father. But Maddox wouldn't lie to the kid.

"I don't know yet. That's why we're going to the police station to talk to the judge."

"Good," Mitchell said fiercely. "I want you to make him stay away from her. I wish he would stay away forever."

"Hey," Maddox said, startled.

"Mom won't say anything bad about him, because I still

have to see him. But I'm not stupid, whatever he thinks. I don't want him to hurt her anymore.''

Maddox cleared his throat. ''No,'' he said slowly. ''Not stupid at all.''

The words jerked out, propelled by guilt and fear and rage. ''I didn't do anything. Before. To stop it. I didn't do anything to stop him.''

Jeez, the kid was only nine years old. Only eight, when his mother packed their bags and left. What did he think he could have done against a grown man's fists?

But pointing that out wouldn't help Mitchell. It didn't respect the seriousness of his feelings or his boy's need to be a man.

''Sometimes it's hard to know what to do,'' Maddox said, as simply and honestly as he could. The kid's willingness to accept responsibility earned him that, at least. ''Sometimes you just do what you can at the time, and hope you don't screw up.''

The kid looked at him with his too-adult eyes. ''Did you ever screw up?''

The memory of the Atlanta schoolyard rose to haunt him. And the memory of Ann's soft voice raised in his defense. *It seems to me that if I can forgive myself, then you certainly should be able to forgive yourself.*

He shrugged. ''Like I said, sometimes you don't know. You do what you have to. Like today, going to see the magistrate.''

Mitchell gave a decisive nod. ''Okay. Let's go.''

Maddox regarded the boy with affection and an uncomfortable, astonishing pride. ''Glad to have you with me on this. But let's have breakfast first.''

''I'm sorry, Mrs. Cross,'' Judge Westcott said.

The magistrate, an imposing African-American woman in her forties, was dressed for church in black straw and peach linen. They must have caught her on her way to services,

Ann thought guiltily. But the judge didn't sound annoyed at this waste of her Sunday morning. She sounded almost sympathetic as she continued. "But without any chance of a successful prosecution, I can't issue a warrant. He didn't hit you, you said?"

Ann felt Maddox stir protectively beside her. "He doesn't have to hit her. Communicating a threat is still a crime."

"You don't need to tell me the law, Sergeant Palmer. Unfortunately, this threat is too vague to justify an arrest at this time."

"How about interfering with a trial witness?" Maddox asked, radiating frustration and heat.

But the judge stayed cool. "That is certainly a reasonable interpretation of what he said. But those were not, in fact, his words. Or did I miss something? Did your ex-husband instruct you not to testify?"

Ann shook her head, feeling more inadequate than ever. "No. He told me to reexamine my loyalties. That I should think about what was in my own best interests or he'd make me sorry." She swallowed. "'Very, very sorry,' he said."

Judge Westcott sighed. "Yes. Vague. Now, with your past history of abuse, if he actually threatens to beat you, I think we could establish probable cause. If he comes back—"

"If he comes back, he could put her in the hospital," Maddox interrupted savagely. "Or the morgue. Why don't we work to prevent that?"

Ann fought not to flinch from his graphic image, from his naked anger. Forget the odd, dark thrill she felt at Maddox losing it in her defense. She didn't appreciate his attitude.

Neither did the judge, apparently. She drew herself up. "I will excuse your tone, Sergeant, since you are here as a friend of the complainant. I certainly sympathize with your frustration. Now I will do my job, and I suggest that you do yours in protecting this young lady. Are we clear?"

"Yes, ma'am," he said woodenly.

"Good." She looked at them over the tops of her half glasses. "I believe that's all."

Ann was shaking. Rob was right. There wasn't anything she could do to stop him.

Maddox took her arm as they left the room. Automatically, she looked for Mitchell on the long benches that lined the hall. Her heart jumped into her throat. Two figures sat side by side on the bench where she'd left her son: Mitchell, in baggy shorts and big sneakers, and the red-faced, gray-haired chief of police.

Both stood as Ann and Maddox approached. Her son in the shadow of the big, stiff man reminded Ann irresistibly of a squirrel perched on the steps of the town's Confederate soldier. The image should have made her smile.

Ann had seldom felt less like laughing.

"Miz Cross. Ann," Wallace Palmer amended, almost shyly. "I met your boy. He tells me you're in to see Judge Westcott?" Over her head, his gaze sought Maddox. "How'd that go?"

Maddox's mouth tightened. "Not so good."

"Probation violation?" the chief inquired.

It took Ann a second to realize he was referring to Rob's probation and not hers.

"Communicating a threat," Maddox replied.

"Get your warrant?"

"The judge felt the threat was too vague to prosecute successfully," Ann said. She was proud of her steady voice.

Wallace Palmer's brows pulled together. "Want me to go talk with her?"

"No point," Maddox said. "She's right. We'll have to get him another way."

Ann didn't like the shuttered look on Mitchell's face. She didn't like the grim determination in Maddox's voice or his father's accusing frown. She was tired of dealing with all this swirling testosterone, fed up with male needs and agendas and demands. "I'm sure Chief Palmer has other things to do now. Perhaps we could discuss this another time?"

Like tonight. Next week. *Never.*

"Of course," Wallace Palmer said. "I was getting through some paperwork when I saw Mitchell here and thought I'd take a little break."

His wave encompassed the bench, and for the first time Ann noticed the discarded candy wrapper, the half-empty can of Dr. Pepper. Mitchell's favorite. He'd rot his teeth. She turned on the clueless police chief, prepared to give him a piece of her mind.

Wallace Palmer smiled tentatively. "When MD was that age, he could eat enough to fill a truck."

And she melted. "Well, it was very kind of you," she said sincerely.

The older man turned an even deeper shade of red. "It was nothing. Growing boys, and all that." He coughed. "Actually, I thought of inviting you all to join me for lunch over at Arlene's."

Ann's stomach lurched as if she'd hit a speed bump at fifty miles per hour. She'd never been the kind of girl who got invited to take meals with the family. And when the family was the chief of police—and the meal was at the most popular Sunday spot outside the First Baptist Church—well, the very idea made her shudder.

Sometime between can-I-get-you-some-coffee and would-you-like-to-take-that-home-in-a-box, word would be winging to Rob that his ex-wife was in a booth with the Palmers, father and son. Ann might as well take out an announcement in the paper. Or paint a bull's-eye on her face.

I'll make you very, very sorry...

"Oh, I couldn't possibly," she said politely. "You two go ahead."

Maddox frowned. "I'm not leaving you alone."

The chief of police nodded. "No. Well, then..."

An awkward silence fell as Wallace Palmer examined the

tips of his polished black shoes and Mitchell looked curiously from one grown-up to another.

And Ann thought, his son has been gone twelve years. He'll only be in town for two more weeks. How many special times together had they denied themselves, these two proud and stubborn men, how many Saturday games and Sunday dinners and Christmas mornings?

The invitation fell out of her mouth before she could stop it. "You're both welcome at my house. For dinner?"

Maddox shot her an are-you-nuts look. She ignored it. Maybe this was a big mistake. Probably this was a big mistake. But her heart didn't feel that way.

"I'm making fried chicken," she told Wallace Palmer, as if she had it all planned. "I'd love to have you."

"Well, that would be real nice. I'd enjoy that. Thank you," he added stiffly.

Maddox raised his eyebrows. "How much fried chicken?"

She flushed. Her freezer was empty, and she suspected he knew it. "Enough."

"Tell me what to bring," Wallace urged. "A man can't practically invite himself to dinner and then show up empty-handed."

Ann smiled at him, touched by his unexpected enthusiasm. "You just bring your appetite."

"We'll do the grocery shopping when I drive Annie home," Maddox said.

He was taking charge again. It was comforting. It was admirable. It was annoying.

Ann didn't want to object in front of his father, but when they stood in the checkout line half an hour later and Maddox pulled out his wallet, she asked, "What are you doing?"

He turned to her with unconscious male arrogance. "Buying dinner."

"You don't have to."

He set down his wallet and relieved the cashier of a five-pound sack of potatoes.

"Hey, thanks," the girl said, flipping her hair over her shoulder in a flirty gesture.

"No problem," Maddox said.

To which one of them, Ann wasn't sure. She took a deep breath, releasing it slowly. "I mean, I don't want you to. I can provide for myself and my child."

"Sure you can. But I eat more than you do."

"But I invited you to dinner."

"And my father."

She was confused. "What?"

He looked back at her, his dark eyes unreadable. "You invited my father, too."

"Well...yes." Oh, dear. Maybe Maddox wasn't the only one to overstep his bounds. She knew he didn't get along with his father. Had never gotten along, really.

Mitchell was standing motionless beside the cart, not looking at the gum and candy bars, alerted by the impatience in Maddox's voice, the tension in hers. She wanted to tell him it was all right, that everything was all right, but she wasn't sure herself.

"Mitchell, honey, why don't you go look for a *Droid Zone* book?"

He nodded, moving away, but she could still see him, stiff-shouldered and watchful in the magazine aisle.

"Why, Annie?" Maddox asked quietly.

"Why did I invite your father? Well, I— He seemed—" She would not be intimidated. She moistened her lips. "I just thought it was the nice thing to do."

"Uh-huh." He unloaded a foam tray of chicken parts onto the conveyor belt. "So, it's okay for you to be nice and invite my old man to dinner, but not okay for me to be nice and pay for it?"

Put that way, she sounded unreasonable. She tried to explain. "I don't want you to think... Just because we have a—a relationship doesn't oblige you to buy my groceries."

He pushed the cart out of the way so that he was standing right in front of her, close enough for her to see that his stubble was tipped with gold and his eyes were flecked with green. She could feel his heat. She could smell his skin, and her heart stumbled in her chest.

"This isn't payment for what happened in my car last night, Annie," he said, soft and close. "This is me, trying to be nice to you. I haven't had a lot of practice, so you'll have to tell me if I get it wrong."

Sorry if I took too long, she'd said in the car, after he made her...after. *I haven't had a lot of practice.* Did he remember?

She studied his face. His eyes were grave, but a smile lurked at the corners of his wide mouth. He remembered. Something inside her lightened.

She smiled back. "I guess you're getting it right. I guess we're getting a lot of things right."

His look was warm enough to toast bread. "Good" was all he said.

"And it's not payment?" she asked, needing to hear it again.

"No." He reached up to tuck her hair behind her ear. She felt his whisper warm against her lips. "If I were paying for last night, I'd have to do better than chicken and potatoes. I could give you the moon, maybe. Or the stars."

She blinked. Nobody had ever said such things to her. She'd certainly never expected lovely, extravagant words from Maddox Palmer. They shook her heart.

"Mom." Mitchell was beside them, his tone jealous, his eyes suspicious. "I'm ready to go."

She dragged her attention back to her son. "Did you get a book?"

"No. I read all those already."

"Okay." She was warm and flustered. She turned back

to the cart, making sure she had control of her breathing and a hold of her purse.

But she let Maddox pay for her groceries.

"That's one good cook," Wallace Palmer said as he stood with Maddox on Annie's back porch. They could see her through the screen, moving with quiet competence between the table and the sink.

Maddox grunted in agreement. Ann leaned forward to turn on the water, and the light over the sink illuminated her thin face. He got an ache in his chest and a hunger in his gut that all the looking in the world wouldn't ease.

"And a nice woman," his father observed.

Maddox reached for a cigarette and then reconsidered. Mitchell ran around the yard, chasing a balsa-wood glider the old man had brought. The gesture had surprised Maddox, but the kid was happy with it.

"She's too tenderhearted for her own good."

"I'm beginning to see that," Wallace said. "But a man could do worse."

Maddox shoved his hands into his pockets. "Don't go there, Dad."

"She's local, too."

"What difference does that make?"

"I'm just saying, is all. If you were to think of settling down, staying here—"

"Why the hell would I do that? I've put twelve years into building a career and making a life in Atlanta."

Some career, he thought bleakly, where he shot a child in a schoolyard to protect the lives of other children. Some life, where he drank too much with the other cops getting off shift to delay going home alone to an empty apartment.

"I can't come back," he said, more quietly.

"Seems to me you are back."

Maddox watched Mitchell crash the glider into a tree. "For two more weeks."

Wallace rubbed his nose, his gaze returning to the kitchen window. "Maybe you just need a good reason to stay."

Maddox ignored the jab of longing. "Uh-huh. Why do you think she asked us to get out of her kitchen?"

"She needed room. To put the leftovers away, she said."

"She needs space. And security."

"We can increase the number of drive-bys on our patrols."

Maddox appreciated that the chief was taking the threat to Ann seriously. But he still missed the point. "Thanks. That'll help."

"But…?" Wallace prodded.

Maddox shrugged, uncomfortable with such frank speaking. But if his father was harboring some crazy idea about him staying in Cutler, it was best to set him straight before somebody got hurt. Before Annie got hurt. "Rob did more to her than bust her face. She needs someone safe now. Someone reliable."

"So?"

Maddox took his hands back out of his pockets. "That's not me."

"It could be you."

"That's not what I remember you saying."

The chief reddened. "Hell, MD, that was in high school. You weren't a bad kid."

"Just a screw-up."

His father eyed him. "You're still a screw-up. But you've improved some."

Maddox laughed.

It felt all right, standing on a back porch with his father on a summer afternoon, with his belly full of fried chicken and Annie's boy running around on the grass. And when Annie came to the back door to call them in for dessert, it felt damn near perfect.

He wanted this, Maddox realized. He could spend every Sunday scooping ice cream for Annie while she smiled and blushed at his father's awkward compliments and Mitchell locked himself to the back of a chair with a pair of handcuffs.

He was still grimly aware that Rob was free. And until Maddox found a way to tie that son of a bitch to Val MacNeill's attempted murder, he might stay free.

But at least for now Maddox had a shot at protecting Ann. All he had to do was keep his head and remember that in the long run she was better off without him.

Ann glared at Maddox, trying not to be distracted by the sunburned hollow revealed by his open collar. In his wilted uniform, he looked tired and sexy and hot. "No. You are not spending another night in your car. We'll be fine."

"You need protection," he repeated stubbornly.

He was wearing his closed cop face again. Ann sighed. Despite her annoyance, his determined care of her shot straight to her defenseless heart. She needed protection, all right. But not at the cost of her independence. And not at the risk of his safety.

"Next you'll tell me to buy a gun," she grumbled.

"No, I won't. You can't," he explained when she blinked. "You're a convicted felon."

Ann crossed her arms. She didn't even know why she was arguing with him, except that what she really wanted was to join him in the front seat of his car and beg for a repeat of last night, and there was very little chance of that with her son upstairs brushing his teeth.

"Rob has a gun," she said. "Two guns, if you count the hunting rifle he bought for Mitchell."

Maddox's grim face got even grimmer. "You never told me he was armed."

"Because I never thought of it that way." It was true. Cutler was still country, where pickup trucks sported gun racks and every boy went deer hunting. She bit her lip.

"Can't you—I don't know—confiscate them or something?"

"Not in the state of North Carolina. A man has a right to his guns. As a felon, Rob can't buy them or transport them, but if he already owned a gun before his conviction, he has the legal right to keep it in his home. That's the law."

She thought of Rob leaning close, whispering, *I'll make you very, very sorry,* and shivered. "And you have to uphold the law."

Maddox's mouth set. "I won't let him near you."

"It's all right. It doesn't make any difference, really. Rob never threatened me with a gun."

"Not while he could get at you with his fists."

She dropped her chin.

"Annie," Maddox said gently. "You need to be protected."

"Not by you."

"You have other volunteers?"

His dry tone brought her head back up. "That's not what I meant. I don't want you fighting with Rob." Especially if her ex-husband was armed. She couldn't stand it if Maddox was at risk because of her. She had enough trouble living with what her cowardice had done to Val, what it might have done to Mitchell.

"What's the matter? You think I'll lose it and shoot somebody?"

She was surprised. He sounded almost…hurt. "Of course not. You're not that kind of cop."

"You don't have any idea what kind of cop I am," he said flatly.

Ann swallowed. She wasn't the only one living with ghosts and regrets. *I heard he shot that boy, and the department fired him.*

She laid her hand on his arm, feeling warm, hair-roughened skin and solid muscle. "I know what kind of man you are," she said as firmly as she knew how. "I am sure you would do the right thing."

"But you'd like me to do it someplace else."

His bleak assessment raked her heart. Sure she would. She'd be better off if Maddox Palmer were out of her sight, out of her reach, like liquor in a locked cabinet or candy in the freezer. He was bad for her.

But that was her fault, her lack, her problem. Not his. Somehow she had to convince him of that. For some reason he cared what she thought of him—her, Annie Barclay, whose opinion never mattered to anybody.

"I'd like you right here," she said. "I'd feel a lot safer. But I don't want you sleeping in your car."

His hooded gaze burned into hers. "What are my alternatives?"

Her heart beat hard and fast. "The couch?"

He nodded curtly. "You got yourself a deal."

As she went to get pillows and a blanket, Ann wondered if she'd wound up with more than she'd bargained for.

Chapter 13

"What's this I hear about Mad Dog's car spending the night in your driveway?" Val asked Ann as they closed the dining room the next day.

Ann's heart bumped. Her hand jerked so that she squirted Sta-Green Environmentally Friendly Cleaner from the painted tabletop to a chair. "It's all over town already?"

Val tossed her a towel. "Depends what you mean by 'all,'" she drawled. "I heard the two of you went shopping for groceries—"

"Mitchell was with us."

"And then his father came for dinner—"

"He lives alone. I was just being polite."

"And that Mad Dog's car was parked in front of your house all night."

"He slept on the couch."

"Oh." Val sounded disappointed. "So, there's nothing going on?"

Despite herself, her mouth curved in a smile. Biting her

bottom lip, she bent her head over the table. "I didn't say that."

"Oh-ho." Val plunked down in an abandoned chair. "When?"

"Saturday night. When he drove me home?"

Val nodded. "So...how was he?"

"He was—" Heat crept into Ann's cheeks at the memory of Maddox touching her in the dark. "Well, it was different."

"Different, good, or different, I-must-have-been-out-of-my-mind?"

"Both, I guess. Mostly good."

"Mmm." Val put her feet up on the chair opposite, her eyes amused and sympathetic. "Good enough that you think you'll do it again sometime?"

Ann's face was burning now. "I've thought about it," she confessed, and Val laughed. "But I've got other things to consider."

"Like what?"

"Mitchell."

"They don't get along?"

Ann attacked another table with her spray bottle and rag. "They get along fine. But I'm not going to invite the man to my bedroom with my son sleeping down the hall."

"Good point."

"And there's the fact that I just got divorced. My therapist warned me about becoming involved in another potentially abusive relationship."

Val dropped her feet to the floor. "You don't trust him?"

"I don't trust myself. I don't want to make the same mistakes."

"Oh, honey." Val stood and hugged her, trapping the spray bottle and wet towel at Ann's sides. "You won't. You're not the same woman. And Maddox is definitely not the same kind of man."

Ann let herself be comforted by the conviction in Val's voice. She sniffed. ''You think?'' she asked hopefully.

''What do *you* think?'' her friend replied.

Ann closed her eyes a moment, washed by the memory of Maddox's lovemaking and his warm, rough voice saying, *I'd give you the moon, maybe. Or the stars.*

''I think I'm confused.''

''Well, you'd better get unconfused quick,'' Val said. ''Because guess who just walked into the restaurant.''

Ann opened her eyes and saw Maddox, broad and solid with his thick, sandy hair that his short cut couldn't tame and that ''I'm dangerous'' slouch that his uniform couldn't disguise, and for an instant she wasn't confused at all. Her heart gave a great leap, and her body shouted ''yes,'' and she smiled, purely glad to see him.

He didn't smile back.

He had on his flat cop face, watchful, impersonal. He stood back politely while Val welcomed him, and the ''yes'' inside Ann changed to ''uh-oh.''

Maddox Palmer was trouble, her mother had warned her. It felt like her mother was right.

''Sorry to walk in like this when you're closed,'' he said civilly. ''Your door was open.''

Val pulled a face. ''I forgot to lock it. Bad habit. What can I do for you? Or could you be here to see someone else?''

''Yes, I am. Is Mr. MacNeill here?''

Val's twinkle faded. ''Con? He's in Raleigh today.''

''Why?'' Ann asked.

Maddox's hooded gaze turned to her. ''I'd like to talk with him,'' he said.

''He'll be back around five, five-thirty,'' Val said. ''I can tell him you want to see him.''

''Thank you. I understand you two have a house on Fargo Street?''

Val's brow creased. ''That's right.''

"And before that, before your marriage, you were living with your parents?"

"Well, I was. Con stayed in a motel."

"Which motel?"

"Beyer's. Out on I-40?"

"What difference does it make?" Ann asked.

Maddox only looked at her, his mouth grim, his shoulders tight.

"The lab tests," she breathed. "You said you'd have the lab results today. Something on a matchbook."

"So what?" Val asked.

"Where was the matchbook from?" Ann demanded.

Maddox paused before he replied. "Beyer's Motel."

Val flipped her braid over her shoulder. "Why does it matter?"

He answered slowly, apparently choosing his words with care. "The defense has argued that the fire was set as part of an insurance scam."

"That's ridiculous," Val snapped.

"Your restaurant wasn't insured?"

"Of course it was insured. And the insurance company paid up when Rob burned it down."

"But you were having financial difficulties before the fire."

Ann felt sick. In her worst nightmares, she'd never imagined that in trying to protect her from her husband, Maddox could end up targeting her best friends. "She was only having trouble because I was helping Rob embezzle money from her account at the bank."

Maddox acknowledged her with a nod. "Understood. But the defense will argue that the insurance money sure came in handy."

Val was starting to look mad. Ann was glad. Anger was preferable to the cold, sick feeling in the pit of her own stomach.

"Are you saying my husband set that fire? That he'd risk my life to collect on the lousy insurance?"

"I'm telling you what Rob's defense team will say," Maddox said. "They'll be looking to establish reasonable doubt."

"By throwing suspicion on Con? That's stupid. He was at the bank with my father when the fire started. Or are you going to argue that my father was in on this scheme, too?"

Maddox rubbed the back of his neck. Ann felt an instant's sympathy for him and squashed it. She was on Val's side in this. She would not betray her friend again, whatever it cost.

"I'm not arguing anything," he said evenly. "But unfortunately the lab just established a direct connection between the motel where your husband was staying and the fire scene."

Ann cringed. She could either stand by while Maddox built a case against Con MacNeill or she could open her mouth and humiliate herself.

It was some choice. It was no choice at all.

"What about Rob's connection with the motel?" she asked.

Maddox's brows drew together. "What connection? He never signed the guest book. I drove out this morning to check."

"But he stayed there," Ann said. "Not overnight, but—"

"When?" The question cracked like a gunshot.

"About the same time, I guess. A year ago? When he was—seeing—Donna Winston."

Shame pumped heat to her face. She could just imagine what Maddox was thinking.

She was not only spineless enough to let her former husband beat her up, she was gutless enough to put up with his cheating.

Maddox pulled out his notebook. "Well, that would explain why he didn't sign his name. Do you have any proof

that he took this woman to the motel? Credit card receipts
or—''

"My mother told her," Val said wryly.

Maddox raised his eyebrows.

"She was only trying to help," Ann said.

"I'll bet," he muttered. He turned to Val. "Did your
mother see them there? Rob and the other woman?"

Ann hugged her elbows. "I don't think so."

Val shook her head, making her earrings sway. "Somehow I don't see my mother dropping by Beyer's Motel for
a little afternoon delight."

"Good point." Maddox flipped the notebook closed. "I'll
go talk to this Donna, then."

"She left town," Ann said. "After the trial."

And, oh, how she'd envied her husband's girlfriend for
being able to leave it all behind: this town, the scandal, the
lowered voices in the post office, the sidelong glances in
church.

Ann firmed her mouth. The heck with it. Let everybody
talk about how she wasn't woman enough to hold on to her
husband. She could live with the whispers. But she couldn't
live with herself if Val and her husband were suspected of
arson.

"I can go to the house," she offered. "I know where Rob
kept the bills and things. Maybe there's a charge from the
motel."

"I don't want you anywhere near him," Maddox said.

Which sounded fine, but didn't get them anywhere. "I
could go when he's at work," she said tentatively.

"No. We'll subpoena the records if we have to. What I
would like is a recent photo. Do you have one? I want to
see if I can jog some memories at the front desk."

"And if you can't?" Val asked.

Maddox looked grim. "Then we'll track down this
Donna, get him some other way. What time do you get
home?" he asked Ann.

"I pick Mitchell up at four-thirty."

He frowned. "My shift isn't over till ten."

"That's all right. We'll be all right."

She hoped.

Tonight was Rob's night to take Mitchell to basketball, but she didn't tell him that. She couldn't live her life hostage to his schedule. She wouldn't make him responsible for her safety. She needed to be responsible for herself.

"Maybe I'll drive by," Maddox told her. "See how you're doing."

"Maybe you shouldn't. People will talk."

Val lifted her eyebrows. "Seems to me they're talking already."

Maddox stuck his thumbs through his beltloops. "Trouble?" he asked.

"No," Ann said firmly. "But if there is, I know what to do."

"Yeah? What?"

She smiled, hoping he could see the faith in her eyes, willing him to give her his trust in return. "Call a policeman."

He sent her a slow, appreciative grin that warmed her down to the soles of her shoes.

But trouble, when it came, wasn't anything a gun or statute book could protect her from.

Rob brought Mitchell home from basketball at eight-thirty.

On time, Ann thought, with a prick of relief. But when she opened the door, she knew right away that something was wrong. Mitchell brushed past her in the doorway with his shoulders hunched and all his features drawn together—lowered brow, pursed mouth, pinched chin—as if he could somehow disappear behind the blank, white mask of his face.

Ann's heart constricted. "How'd it go?" she asked, her voice as false and bright as a ring from a gum machine.

Mitchell shrugged.

"Tough practice?"

He shook his head.

Rob lounged in the edges of the porch light, hands in his pockets. "He did all right."

From Rob, this was praise. But Mitchell was still pulled in on himself.

"How about a snack?" Ann asked.

"Not hungry. I'm going upstairs," Mitchell said. And he ran to his room as if pursued by monsters.

Ann watched his thin legs disappear up the steps and then glared at Rob. "What did you say to him?"

"Aren't you going to invite me in?"

"No. What did you say?"

"You really don't want to have this discussion on the porch where everyone can hear us. Invite me in."

Bad idea, she thought. But this was her baby, running hurt and scared.

She jerked the door wider. "Fine. But if I need to, I'm calling the police."

Rob's brows flicked up. "Oh, please. Don't be so melodramatic."

She didn't answer him. He sauntered past her, and she smelled his cologne and the starch from his shirt. She wondered who did his ironing now, and if he ever hit them for creasing his collars.

Don't think about that. Think about Mitchell.

"What happened?" she demanded. "What did you say to him?"

He leaned one shoulder against the wall, watching her, his eyes bright with enjoyment. "I was just honest with him. I told him to expect things to change around here."

"What things? Nothing's changing."

He laughed bitterly. "Everything's changed. My life, my career, my reputation—and all because of you. Maybe it's time you knew what that felt like."

She recognized the danger. She just couldn't figure out what direction the attack would come from. "What are you talking about?"

Rob's face hardened at her sharp tone. He shifted closer along the wall. "I told Mitchell he might have to come live with me."

Her chest collapsed. He was toying with her, she told herself. She didn't have to play by his rules any longer. But it was hard to resist his bluff when he dragged her baby into the game. She sucked in her breath.

"That—you can't do that." She forced the words out.

"I can do anything I want."

"The consent order—"

"Can be challenged. I've talked with my lawyer."

"So have I." She struggled to repeat what the pleasant young woman provided by legal services had told her, as if the lawyer's assurances were a magic spell that could ward off evil. "Custody arrangements can't be challenged unless there's a change in circumstances material to the well-being of the child."

Rob nodded. "Precisely."

"But—"

"You're screwing a cop, Ann. Having sex in the presence of a minor child. You're unfit to have custody of our son."

"That's not true!"

"That's for a judge to decide, isn't it?"

"But I didn't—" She stopped. Maybe she hadn't made love with Maddox in her house. But she had taken him as her lover. Would the court look at that? Judge her for that? People in this town gossiped. Kids overheard things. What would Mitchell hear? And what would he think?

"His car was in front of your house all night," Rob continued inexorably. "Two nights. Wallace Palmer was here Sunday afternoon. Did you do them both, Ann? Did you do them with our son watching?"

"Why are you doing this?"

"You have to ask? I will not let you bring me down, do you hear me? I won't let you destroy what's left of my reputation in this town. My God, Ann, why are you doing this to *me?*" His voice broke with betrayal. "I married you!"

Guilt struck her heart. Guilt and regret for the misguided choices and the wasted years.

"Maybe it would have been better for both of us if you hadn't," she whispered.

His hand flew up. She shrank into the wall.

And then his fist opened and he patted her cheek in a parody of a caress.

"I'm not going to let you upset me," he said. "You're not running to your boyfriend with marks on your face so he can take you to the judge to tell another bunch of lies."

"I never lied, Rob."

"You lied your whole life, you mealymouthed little bitch. Carpooling around town in your khaki skirts, acting like the perfect wife and mother and all the time squeaking if I so much as looked at you sideways. You never helped me. You never fit in. You never were a wife to me."

She knew better than to defend herself. She really did. But...

"I tried," she said.

"Oh, tell me how you tried," he sneered. "By testifying against me? By divorcing me?"

She was momentarily surprised. "*You* divorced *me,* Rob."

"Of course I did. How would it have looked if we stayed married while you said all those awful things? At least this way, everyone has to wonder if you're just a lying, vindictive slut."

She'd thought—she'd hoped—his words had lost the power to hurt her. But she still flinched from this assault. His accusations hit too many old bruises.

I saw you leave the party with Mad Dog Palmer...

The Barclays are all white trash, anyway.
He had to marry her, you know.
Put on a slip, for God's sake, you look like a whore.
You're such a slut.

She shook her head to clear it of the voices. "Get out. I don't have to listen to this anymore."

"Maybe not. And maybe it doesn't bother you that Mitchell will hear it." Rob straightened away from the wall. "But it bothers me. I don't think you can provide a fit environment for our son."

"I won't let you have him," she said fiercely. "I will never let you have him, do you hear me?"

"It's in your hands."

"What do you mean?"

"We don't have to be enemies, Ann. I'm prepared to be reasonable. But you've got to understand that I can't ignore talk. It doesn't look right, you playing the bitch for Mad Dog Palmer. And I don't like it that he's poking into things, stirring folks up again."

"I can't help that."

"No, but you can hurt. It hurts me, Ann, that you have so little loyalty after so many years. It hurts me right here." He laid a hand on his starched white shirt front like a bad actor feigning heartbreak.

And as suddenly as that, he killed her sympathy. He didn't have a heart. At least, not one that Ann had ever been able to reach with her touch or her tears or her pleas. If he had a heart, he could not threaten to take her baby from her.

She lifted her chin. "Maddox must really have you worried if you're coming after me again," she said steadily.

Rob's face turned red and ugly. "He doesn't have anything. He's a stupid cop, and you're a stupid slut. But you better be smart now. You better listen, and understand good." He towered over her, big and intimidating, hissing the words into her face. "If you go to court, then so will I.

And you figure out who will pay once I get custody of Mitchell.''

"I will always want you to live with me," Ann told Mitchell solemnly as a vow. "I would never want you to live anywhere else."

They sat side by side on his bed, in their old read-me-a-story position, their backs to the wall, their legs stretched out across the mattress. Mitchell's legs were almost as long as hers now. His feet, in white basketball shoes, were bigger. But he was still hers. Her baby.

He stared at his knobby knees. There was a purple scar on the left one from when he was six and she'd taught him to ride a bike. "Dad said since you had, like, a boyfriend, you might not want me anymore."

Rage erupted in her chest. Her hands shook with it. She folded them in her lap, so Mitchell wouldn't see.

"No," she said, as quietly and firmly as she could. "Your father was—" Lying, she thought. "Mistaken," she said.

"I don't think he likes Mr. Palmer very much," Mitchell offered.

"No. I don't think he does."

He twisted his head, regarding her sideways. "Do you?"

She trembled on the brink of disclosure. Because she was trying so hard to be truthful now, and she did like Maddox Palmer. Liked the competent way he looked after things, kids and cars and her, without counting the cost to himself. Liked the not-a-dimple in his chin and the intense appreciation in his eyes. Liked his hands, big and square and gentle.

Except her child didn't need to hear that. Mitchell had just had his world shaken, and only she could set it firmly back on its foundation.

"He's all right," she said noncommittally.

Mitchell's shoulders relaxed slightly. "I like him. He does stuff with me. And he doesn't yell."

"Not yelling is good."

"Yeah." He gave her another of those sideways looks. "You don't yell."

Rob yelled. The knowledge trembled unspoken between them. She forced herself to smile. "Mothers aren't supposed to yell. Unless—I don't know—unless you run into the street or something."

"Dad says when boys start growing up, they need their fathers more. Especially if their mothers are working and can't take care of them."

Panic closed her throat. She swallowed. "I can take care of you fine. I want to take care of you."

After a moment, Mitchell reached over. She folded his thin hand in her clasped ones.

"I want to take care of you, too," her little boy said.

"I saw your light on," Maddox said, hoping he didn't sound like a trucker looking to get lucky at one of those places at the edge of town. "Is it okay if I come in?"

Ann stood in the doorway, pale and tense and so desirable his heart slammed in his chest. She threw one quick glance up the stairs and then stepped back to admit him.

"Of course. But keep your voice down. I put Mitchell to bed an hour ago."

Maddox frowned. She had "bad day" imprinted on her face like a slap. And he was about to make it worse.

"Everything all right?" he asked, following her into the living room.

She nodded. Right. Like telling him her troubles would make them go away. Although if Rob was bothering her, Maddox was fully prepared to take off his badge and his gun and tackle that problem with his bare hands.

But before he could frame the words to interrogate her, she turned suddenly into his body. He stopped, startled, his hands coming up automatically to catch her arms. She bowed her head against his chest. Her hair fell forward to hide her face. She shuddered in his arms.

"Annie. Darlin'. What—''

She was crying.

Shock dried his mouth. He wanted to explain to her she had the wrong guy. He was nobody's port in a storm. He was hard and rough and shot people, and he never stuck around for the weepy part of relationships.

Only he couldn't shift her.

Well, of course he *could,* Maddox corrected himself as he adjusted her head under his jaw. She was small and light in his arms. She weighed—what?—maybe a hundred-ten, hundred-fifteen pounds. He could move her easily.

Only he couldn't really bear to let her go.

She fit into his arms, under his chin, like she belonged. And where was he going to put her? Who did she have as backup when things went down? Who else would support her while she shook with the hard release of tears? Who else would hold her? Who else would love her like he did?

He clenched his jaw. He loved her. Not with the wondering body lust of adolescence, not with the rueful dissatisfaction of the past twelve years, though those were part of it, too. He wanted her, wanted to be with her, wanted to breathe in the scent of her hair and feel her just like this, warm and smooth against him. He could imagine making a life with her, only all his pictures of Annie had Cutler in the background, and that scared the hell out of him.

His arms tightened around her. "Damn."

She shivered. "S-sorry."

He stroked her hair. "Shh. It's okay."

She gulped. "I'm getting your shirt all wet."

"It's cotton. It'll dry."

She lifted her head, and her eyes, which had been sharp and shattered as a broken beer bottle, were fogged with tears. Her lashes were spiky and damp.

"Cotton wrinkles," she said, like that was somehow important. "I could iron it for you."

"Naw, I'll get it dry cleaned," he teased. And then, remembering how she was about him doing her favors, he added, "We can split the bill."

She studied him a moment, her green eyes searching and her mouth uncertain. She had such a pretty mouth. And then she smiled.

Tenderness twisted inside him. He kissed her forehead and she sighed, a soft puff of air across his jaw that shook him like a gale.

He lowered his head to find her lips. Just one kiss, he told himself. For comfort. But her lips were warm and moist and soft under his, and her arms tightened around him, and he lost his head for a minute, lost himself in her kiss.

She gave a little sob and opened for him all the way. He plunged in and she shuddered against him. He was drunk on her, her soft tongue, her slim body, her cheeks damp with tears... Tears. They scalded him.

She'd been crying and he'd taken advantage.

He sucked in his breath. Let it out real slow, while every red blood cell in his body hollered at him to stop being an idiot and take what he could while it was being offered.

Except he didn't want her offering sex as a trade-off for a little consideration.

Damn. He wanted sex. Wanted her, any way he could get her.

The hell of it was with Annie plastered up against his raging body, her thin cheeks flushed and her smooth hair tousled, he realized he wanted...more. Wanted her trust. Wanted her confidence. Wanted it all.

Did she want him? Or was this her way of saying thank you?

"Okay." He forced his arms to loosen, forced his body to calm. "What was that for?"

Chapter 14

Ann closed her eyes, looking defeated. "That was a kiss." Her mouth twisted as she looked back up at him. "Do women only kiss you when they want something?"

Anger licked through him. "Darlin', if you want what most of them want, I'm willing and able." He nudged against her to prove his point, meanly satisfied when her eyes widened. "But a woman as upset as you were generally isn't looking for love two minutes later."

Hot color stormed her face. *Way to be a pig, Palmer.*

"What is it?" he asked more gently. "What happened?"

She started to pull away from him, but he wasn't having it. Whatever had made her fall apart in his arms must be big enough that she felt she couldn't handle it alone. And his Annie could handle almost anything.

"Rob?" he guessed.

Her shrug admitted it.

Maddox swore. "Did he call you? Threaten you?"

"He stopped by. It's all right," she said quickly when he stiffened. "It's Mitchell's basketball night, I was expecting him. And I didn't call you because he didn't make a—what did the judge call it?—a specific threat.''

Rage roared through him. His hands fisted. He forced them open. Annie had seen enough fists.

''I'll give him a specific threat,'' he muttered. ''What did he want?''

She slipped out of his arms and sat on the couch, folding her own hands in her lap like a good girl. ''He said that if I went to court, then he would, too. That if I kept seeing you, he would seek custody of Mitchell.''

''He can't do that.''

She looked up, devastation in her eyes. ''His lawyer says he can.''

''He wouldn't win.''

''He might. Concerned father, local football hero, wants to rescue his son from white trash Annie Barclay.'' She didn't sound bitter, only resigned. ''Enough people in Cutler will support him. The judge could be one of them.''

Despite his anger, he was afraid she was right. He'd been a cop too long to believe the good guys always won in court. But she didn't need to hear that.

''You might be surprised,'' he said instead. ''No judge is going to buy that the angels presided at his birth. He's a convicted felon now.''

She met his eyes straight on. ''So am I,'' she said. ''And he'll argue that he can give Mitchell advantages I can't. The judge will believe him. For heaven's sake, I believed him. That's why I married him.''

''Yeah, and you divorced him. The guy's an abusive jerk.''

Her hands twisted in her lap. ''He's still Mitchell's father.''

He wanted to shout a denial. Like she needed him yelling at her on top of everything else. ''And you're his mother,'' he said as calmly as he could. ''His primary caregiver.

Judges pay attention to stuff like that. Rob is just jerking your chain."

"I can't take that chance."

His jaw hurt. He was clenching it too hard. "What's that supposed to mean?"

Her gaze slid away from his. "I think you investigating Val's case makes Rob nervous."

"Are you asking me to stop?"

"No. But—did you find a connection today between Rob and the motel?"

She wasn't going to like what he had to tell her. Hell, he didn't like it himself.

"Not yet." Frustration burned his gut. He wasn't in the habit of sharing with civilians. But this was Annie. It was her lead. Her friend. And at this point he couldn't let her hang false hopes on his police work. "Nobody could give me a positive ID. Maybe when I get a photo, it will jog somebody's memory. The manager doesn't remember if Rob was there last summer or not, the desk clerk wouldn't know him if he saw him, and the cleaning woman is new."

"What about records? You said there might be receipts—"

Maddox shook his head. "I got a subpoena for the motel's charge records from a year ago, but they'll take a while to wade through. My guess is he paid with cash he stole from the restaurant, anyway."

"I'm sorry you've had a wasted day."

He didn't want her sympathy. He didn't deserve it. Not when he had nothing to offer her in return.

"I wouldn't say wasted," he drawled. "So far I've pushed the lab for enough evidence to incriminate Con MacNeill and pressured your ex-husband into threatening you. Not bad for a day's work."

"You'll turn up something," she said with quiet faith. "There has to be something."

He didn't deserve her trust, either. He'd done nothing to

earn the warm feeling that caught his chest when she looked at him with those big green eyes like he was damn Dick Tracy. This investigation was a disaster. But telling her that wouldn't do a lot to help her peace of mind.

He rubbed the back of his neck. ''Yeah. Something.''

''You should get some sleep.''

Tenderhearted Annie. He didn't want sleep. He wanted her. He wanted to tail her to her room and see if she made up her bed with flowered sheets. He bet she did. He wanted to tuck her in and hold her close until the tension leaked from her shoulders. He wanted the stuff that came after that, too, wanted to feel her warm and wet and welcoming over him, around him, while he moved and she moved and her soft hair touched his face.

But he wasn't going to get what he wanted. Nothing new there. Not the sex and not the chance to come home at the end of the day and find himself in her smile. Though maybe… If he stayed in Cutler, did he have a shot at making it with her?

He frowned. Never mind that. Annie was exhausted. Her mouth drooped. Her eyes were shadowed. And there was no way in hell he could picture her inviting him up for an invigorating bounce on her bed while her boy slept down the hall.

So, it was the couch again.

Maddox sighed and looked around for the blankets he'd folded and stashed last night.

She pressed her lips together. Trouble?

''What?'' he demanded.

''I told you,'' she said with difficulty. ''People are talking. I can't risk talk. I can't risk anything that Rob can use against me, and he doesn't like it that we're…close.''

Not the couch, after all. The car.

''So, how far away do you figure will satisfy him?'' Maddox asked. ''The driveway? The curb? Across the street?''

Her silence reproached him.

Damn.

He tried to make a joke of it. "Maybe I'll knock on your neighbor's door, ask to use the bathroom. That should convince them I'm not sleeping over."

Her mouth was set. Her eyes were miserable. This was getting them nowhere.

He ran a hand through his hair in frustration. "Kiss me," he said.

That woke a flash of spirit. Her chin came back up. "What for?"

He made himself grin at her wickedly. "Do you only kiss me when you want something?"

Her answering smile started in her eyes. "I guess I want what all those other women want. But I'm not going to get it tonight."

Her frank regret stirred him more than the most practiced come-on.

"Kiss me good-night, then," he said hoarsely.

She did, wrapping her arms around him, pressing up tight against him, giving him a taste of her tears and her warmth and her sweetness. And he kissed her and hungered for her and cursed Rob Cross.

"Sleep well," she whispered.

"Sweet dreams," he replied.

He didn't sleep well. He hardly slept at all, and his dreams, when they came, were wild and heated. He woke up sweaty and stiff, and his condition had nothing to do with spending the night in his car and everything to do with Annie.

He'd parked across the street again.

The sight of his battered blue sedan keeping silent, stubborn vigil lured Ann to her window again and again. Peeking through the ruffled curtains the next morning, she felt like some boy-crazy sixth grader spying on a crush.

She bit her lip. Really, she ought to march out there and

tell Maddox that fifteen feet of asphalt was not likely to discourage the gossips.

But she didn't. Instead she stood and watched, her pulse loud in her ears, as he got slowly out of the car. He must be stiff. He rolled his shoulders beneath his wrinkled uniform shirt, and her breath jammed in a helpless confusion of lust and concern. He leaned against the hood of his car. Even from a distance she could see how his dark slacks pulled across his powerful thighs.

She thought of touching him there and everywhere and blushed alone in her bedroom. She would like that, she realized. Even he would like it. And she smiled with a delicious and unfamiliar confidence, hugging her arms as if to hold in a precious secret. Who would have guessed that plain, thin, awkward Annie Barclay would be dreaming of sex with Mad Dog Palmer?

It was as if by giving himself to her—his big square hands and hot solid body, his patience and whispered praise—he'd restored a part of herself. For that alone she was grateful to him.

Ann leaned against the cool wood of the window frame, watching as he ran a hand through his thick, short hair and resettled his hat on his head. Well, all right, more than grateful. Gratitude was too lukewarm to describe her feelings for Maddox. She admired his staunch acceptance of responsibility, his stubborn determination to protect and serve. She appreciated his strict control and dry humor. She liked the woman she saw reflected in his eyes, a strong woman, a competent woman...a woman who was dangerously close to falling in love with the man.

Panic formed a lump in her throat. She knew better. Really she did. She wasn't turning control of her heart, her future and her son over to another man ever again. Even a man like Maddox.

She swallowed hard, and the panic retreated halfway down her chest.

It was okay, she told herself. Maddox hadn't asked for control. He wasn't asking for more than her body. He wasn't asking for more than two weeks.

And she wanted those two weeks, wanted to be with him more than she wanted anything except to keep her son safe. For as long as she could have him, she wanted Maddox.

And to get him, she needed to do something to thwart Rob's threats.

She carried his coffee out to him in both hands like an offering. Which, Ann supposed, it was.

As she started down the short concrete walk, she saw Dorothy Hicks pause outside her one-story bungalow, her robe clutched closed and her mouth hanging open.

Maddox scooped up the woman's morning newspaper and handed it to her, saying something that sent the older lady scuttling back inside.

Ann crossed the street. "What was that all about?"

Maddox scowled, looking disgruntled and dear. "I told the old snoop I wasn't watching your house. I was staking out hers."

Ann fought a smile and lost. "Oh, that should stop the neighbors talking."

"Damn fools."

"It's this town," she said, handing him the mug. "If you parked twenty miles away and I wore a chastity belt, some-body would still swear I was stuck on you." She waited a beat before adding deliberately, "And they'd be right."

He gulped hot coffee. Grimaced. "You picked a hell of a time to mention it."

She sighed. "I picked a hell of a time to let it happen."

"Because of Mitchell," he said tightly.

"Because of the custody issue. Yes."

He nodded once. His eyes were bleak. She touched his arm.

"It's all right," she said softly. "I know you're doing everything you can."

"Yeah." His jaw worked. Whatever he did, she knew he wouldn't consider it enough. But he didn't say that, because he didn't want to worry her. His determined honesty, his dogged consideration, pressed on her tender heart like fingers on a bruise.

She propped next to him against the hood of the car, very conscious of the cold metal beneath her, and his hip warm beside her.

"Will you talk to Con today?" she asked.

He nodded. "I need to establish his alibi, so Rob's defense can't claim the police didn't do our job."

"I want to help," she said.

He gave her one of his dark, hooded looks. "Then take care of yourself. Stay at the restaurant with Val today."

She angled her chin. She was flattered, touched, seduced by his concern. But not to the point of putting herself under police surveillance. "It's my half day. Ten to two. But I'll be all right. Rob will be at his office."

"It could be dangerous."

"I don't think so. He's threatening me with a custody hearing now. He's not going to risk me calling the police."

"I don't like it," Maddox said flatly. "Why don't you put in a couple extra hours at the restaurant until I can bring you and Mitchell home?"

"Today? What about next week? What about every day between now and the trial?" She shook her head, frustrated by his inability to see and her own inability to act. "I can't live my life waiting for my ex-husband to jump out of the bushes. Rob spent years controlling me. I let him use my fear to control me. I'm not going to let him do it anymore."

"You need to be careful."

"I need to be *normal*." The words burst out. "I need to get on with my life. And that doesn't include you driving me everywhere like some kind of bodyguard."

"Doesn't include me, you mean."

She was shaken. "That's not what I said."

He was slapping his pockets, looking increasingly disgusted. With her? With himself? With the whole situation?

"I need a smoke," he said.

Perfect. He was turning back into a chain-smoker, and that was her fault, too. "Don't let me stop you."

He glowered. "You're not. I can't find a match."

"I'm sorry. I can't help you. I don't smoke."

"I know that," he said impatiently. "I just figured you might have matches for people who—" An arrested expression crossed his face.

"What is it?" she asked.

"I just thought of something I should do."

She frowned. He might as well have patted her on the head. "What?"

He bent his head to kiss her, a brief, hard kiss tasting of coffee. His stubble brushed her cheek. Despite her chagrin, something inside her softened and loosened.

"It's a long shot. I'll let you know if it works out," he promised.

Ann let herself into the house on Stonewall Drive with an old key and sweaty palms. Her heart beat so high in her throat she thought she might choke.

But Maddox Palmer wasn't the only one who thought of things to do.

Not that *he* would think of breaking and entering, she thought with a spurt of near-hysterical humor. Not that he would approve of what she was about to do. He was an officer of the law.

But Ann had broken the law already, at first unknowingly and then unwillingly and always for the wrong reasons. Maybe now she could bend it for the right ones, to protect the people she loved: Val and Mitchell and, God help her, Maddox, too.

She closed the front door behind her, and her past rushed in on her.

Nothing had changed. A row of gold-framed botanical prints she'd ordered from a catalogue still marched above the chair rail in the dining room. The custom-made drapes, stiff with starch, swooped over the front windows. A lamp shaped like a duck decoy angled its light over Rob's BarcaLounger. It was still her house, her pride, her prison, constructed bit by bit of matching paint chips and fabric samples. She had the creepy feeling she'd left this morning instead of twelve months ago.

She shivered.

Maybe when I get a photo, it will jog somebody's memory.

She had photos, albums and albums lining a living room shelf, all posed and preserved to support the illusion of the perfect family living a well-ordered life. Egg hunts, beach trips, trick-or-treating, with the focus on Mitchell and Rob scowling in the background.

Oh, yes, she had pictures. She hadn't had time to take them with her. And now, looking at them made her a little sick.

Kneeling on the living room carpet, she selected a recent snapshot—Rob's thirtieth birthday celebration at the club—and stuffed it in her purse and took a deep breath. What else?

I got a subpoena for the motel's charge records from a year ago, Maddox had said, *but they'll take a while to wade through.*

Maybe while she was here she could look at *Rob's* records? Maybe she could prove he had used the motel.

She hurried through the living room to Rob's home office, past Mitchell's baby portrait and the coffee table where she'd hit her head one night when Rob had knocked her down. The vacuumed carpet revealed a patch where she'd knelt and the track of her flat-soled shoes. He must use a cleaning service now.

She wondered how they did with bloodstains.

Receipts were filed in the corner cabinet of Rob's office. He settled the household bills. Settled them and sorted them and scrutinized them for extravagance. *Look at this water bill,* he'd complain, but she was the one who paid for the dripping faucet or watered lawn in tears and bruises and shame.

She wiped her sweaty palms on her skirt. She wasn't looking for utility bills, she reminded herself. She wanted credit card records, proof that would clear Val's husband and implicate her own. She reached for the metal handle, and the file drawer clattered in its frame.

It was locked.

She almost thought, *Oh, good. Now I can go home.* But that was the old Annie thinking, the old Annie acting. Or rather, not acting, just giving up again.

She could do better. She had the photo, didn't she? And she wasn't due at the restaurant for another forty-five minutes. She squared her shoulders. Plenty of time to find a key and open a file and save her friend and her own self-respect.

She approached the desk—Rob's desk—and gingerly slid open the top drawer. The file key was in plain sight, easily accessible.

So was the gun.

Her stomach jumped up to join her heart in her throat. She knew Rob kept a gun, of course, against her will and over her protests. But when had her will or her protests ever mattered in this house? At least he'd never threatened her with it.

Not while he could get at you with his fists. Maddox's reminder echoed in her head.

She slammed the drawer shut. Opened it again to take the key, ignoring the faint rattle that announced her hand was shaking.

Rob wasn't here. He was at his office. All she had to do—

she drew a deep breath—all she had to do was open the file and check the Visa and Mastercard statements from last year to see if he'd ever charged a room at Beyer's Motel.

He hadn't. With one eye on her watch and her attention on the door, she examined the contents of folder after folder, spreading the pages across Rob's desk. *The desk with the gun.*

She resisted the urge to look at it again, running her finger instead down printed lists of names and numbers. Charges for golf clubs and gas, for shoes and wine. No motels. No Beyer's, not in May or April or any month last year.

She shuffled the papers back together, fighting discouragement. At least she had the photo. Maybe Maddox would be able to get a positive ID from someone who worked at the motel. And now he wouldn't have to waste his time plodding through the motel's records. She tucked the folders away in hanging files, locked the cabinet and opened the desk to return the key.

The gun was there, dark and smooth as a snake coiled under the porch steps.

You never told me he was armed.

A man has a legal right to his guns.

Her heart pounded. Her head did, too. She didn't think Rob would take his gun after her, after Mitchell, but then, she'd never thought he would hit her, either.

The gun waited in the drawer. Accessible. Tempting. She almost picked it up herself, and she hated guns. Rob would have no hesitation reaching for it. She shivered.

She could take it. And add illegal possession of a firearm to breaking and entering? No.

She could hide it.

Now, there was an idea. If he couldn't find it, he couldn't use it. And it wouldn't be theft, since she wasn't removing it from the house.

But where? Not in the rose-and-cream bedroom she'd once shared with Rob. Not in the kitchen. Never in Mitchell's room. No place it could be stumbled over, nowhere Rob would go… The attic, she thought.

She grabbed the gun by the barrel so she couldn't accidentally touch the trigger, and hurried up the stairs, holding it away from her body at an awkward angle. Twenty-five minutes until she was due at Wild Thymes.

She was sweating. The attic was hot. The hanging bulb threw sharp shadows around the piled cartons, the out-of-season clothes and discarded toys.

Where did you hide a gun? She was a nice girl, not a career criminal, even if she was convicted of stealing twenty thousand dollars from her best friend. Somewhere Mitchell would never look by accident, someplace Rob would never find…

Her wildly searching gaze settled on a box by the water heater. Drapes, she thought. The old living room drapes, relegated to a carton after the new ones were hung. Perfect. Rob would never look there.

She tugged the flaps open, pushed the beige fabric aside and shoved the gun deep in the box.

She ran down the steps and stood a moment in the hall, her pulse thundering in her ears. Would Rob be able to tell she'd been here? She'd locked the file cabinet, closed the attic door.

Reaching for the front door, she gave one last glance over her shoulder, and saw her footprints marching over the carpet toward Rob's office.

Her heart stumbled. Not a problem, she thought. She would just vacuum before she left. She had—she checked her watch—seventeen minutes.

She pulled the upright from the hall closet and hastily erased her tracks from the living room, working back toward the hardwood floor of the hall. She yanked at the plug and wrapped the cord neatly before stowing the vacuum away. She pushed it under Rob's coats, where it bumped into something long and padded and propped in a corner.

She sucked in her breath in dismay. The rifle. Mitchell's rifle. She hadn't disarmed Rob at all.

Her mind darted back to the box in the attic. The tall gun wouldn't fit there. It wouldn't fit anywhere, really, which was why it was in the closet in the first place along with Rob's tennis racket and the dustpan and broom.

Dear Lord. Twelve minutes. She had to go. And the rifle would have to go with her. What was another charge against her compared to Mitchell's safety?

She held the padded case awkwardly in front of her as she hurried to the car. The zippered pocket that held the shells scraped against her legs. Besides, she wasn't really stealing, she argued with her conscience. It was Mitchell's gun, purchased for a deer hunting trip that thankfully never took place.

Mitchell. She clutched the thought of her precious son to her more tightly than any gun. She was only doing this to protect Mitchell. It wasn't like she was going to shoot the awful thing. She didn't even want to touch it. She was just taking it away from Rob.

She laid the rifle case carefully in the trunk of her car, as if it would explode, and drove to work.

Chapter 15

Ann's first thought when she saw Maddox standing on her front porch, eyes shaded by the brim of his uniform hat, was that he must be there about the gun. Visions of handcuffs danced briefly in her head.

And then reason returned. For one thing, Rob wouldn't even be home yet to notice and report the loss of his guns. Nobody on her street had been around half an hour ago to see her smuggle the rifle from the car trunk to her bedroom closet.

For another, if Maddox were there to arrest her, he would hardly be smiling.

She opened the door. His smile broadened into that wide, warm, you-and-me-babe grin that had flattened her in junior high. Her pulse spurted for reasons that didn't have anything to do with him locking her up.

"You look—" Relaxed. Satisfied. *Sexy.* "Pleased with yourself."

"Pleased with the investigation."

His cool cop routine didn't fool her for a minute. She searched his face. "It's good?"

"It's very good. I don't think Rob can take custody of Mitchell if he's serving fifteen to twenty for arson and attempted murder."

Hope fluttered in her stomach. "What happened? What did you find?"

"Something you said this morning set me off." He took off his hat. "How you didn't carry matches because you don't smoke?"

She nodded, distracted by the way the sunlight tipped his sandy hair with gold. But she remembered their conversation.

"See, Rob does. He told me he likes to be prepared for his clients who smoke. And then he tossed me a matchbook." Maddox paused significantly. "From his golf bag."

She blinked at him. "Motel matches?"

Maddox grinned. "Now that would have been *too* easy. But this morning I got a warrant to search the golf bag, and he's got like a dozen matchbooks stuffed in the pocket, and one of them's from Beyer's Motel. So we've got a nice little link to the arson there, and your friend's husband doesn't look so good for insurance fraud anymore."

"Well." It was hard to think with him smiling at her, his grimly handsome face relaxed and easy. She opened the door wider. "Wonderful. Come in. I found a photo for you. Of Rob." She led the way to the living room. Her purse was on the couch. She rifled through it. "Here."

He took the snapshot. Glancing at it, he put it away in the breast pocket of his uniform. "That's great. I'll try again for a supporting ID at the motel." But he made no move to go.

"Can I get you some tea?" she offered.

"No tea." He took a step toward her.

She felt her breath go at the look in his eyes. She started

to smile back, relief lightening the burden of guilt she'd carried for so long. "Then what can I possibly give you?"

"Got any cookies?"

She laughed. "It's Tuesday. I only bake on the weekends."

Which was nonsense, of course, but it was sweet nonsense. She hadn't known what it was like to laugh with a man she was in love—having sex with. She liked it.

He came closer. Close enough for her to feel his body heat. Close enough that, if she wanted, she could lay her head on his uniform shirt and absorb that strength and warmth into herself. He was so big, but she didn't feel threatened. Actually, she found his size reassuring, even…exciting.

He raised his eyebrows. Lowered his voice. "So, you don't have anything left over? From this weekend?"

This weekend. He meant Saturday night. Out on the river road, in the dark, with Maddox… Her heart began to pound in earnest.

"I maybe could find something," she said breathlessly.

"Let me help you look," he whispered, and bent to her.

His lips were firm and warm. He brushed them against hers with soft, light, teasing kisses that made her sigh and want. Want more. Want Maddox. She opened to him, inviting the slick, smooth entry of his tongue, standing on tiptoe to push her breasts into the solid wall of his chest.

"I think you, um, found it," she said, when at last he raised his head.

His full mouth quirked. "I'm a policeman. I'm supposed to find things."

And there it was, she realized, the reason for the difference she sensed in him. Since coming home, he'd worked his way toward a cautious peace with himself and with his job. She was glad of it, glad for him, even as his returning confidence emphasized the differences between them. She'd never been much good at anything.

"Well, you do it very well," she told him solemnly.

Color crept into his tanned cheeks. "You don't mind?"

"Mind what?"

Hesitation entered his eyes, attractive, beguiling. "That I've had—some experience."

Other women, he meant. He was worried about what she thought. He cared how she felt. Ann's heart swelled. So maybe she was good for something, after all. She took his hand and laid it on her breast.

"No," she said simply. "Why don't you see what else you can find?"

He went very still. And then his thumb brushed her nipple, already puckered with arousal.

"Well, there's this," he murmured.

"Evidence," she said.

He smiled faintly, his hooded gaze holding hers. "Yeah? What does it prove?"

"That I want you."

She'd surprised them both.

He drew a hard breath. His eyes were nearly black. "Annie. Darlin'. You're a good woman—"

Her mouth twisted. "Is that like being a nice girl?"

"No. Yes. I don't want your neighbors to think—"

"I'm tired of worrying what my neighbors will think. I've been worried about what people will think of me all my life."

"But my car's parked outside."

"We-e-e-ll... It's the middle of the afternoon. You could be interviewing me."

"That's not all I could be doing to you," he said with grim humor.

"Then why don't you?" she whispered.

It was as if her words broke the tight grip he kept on himself, on his body. He lunged, and she had what she wanted, Maddox holding her, Maddox kissing her, deeply, fiercely, possessively, his tongue driving into her mouth, his body hard and hot against hers.

She should have been panicked. She was thrilled. She was freed.

She wrapped her arms around him and took everything he could give. He pulled at her blouse. She tore at his shirt. He pressed his mouth to the tender area between her neck and shoulder, and she gasped and bit his ear. He was on his knees in front of her, his breath shockingly hot through her skirt. She sank to the floor, sliding against his aroused body, her hand seeking a hold in the short hair of his nape.

They devoured each other, pressed breast to chest and belly to thigh. He felt so good, so warm and firm and solid against her. Nothing had ever felt this good. Pushing his shirt off his shoulders, she stopped, stunned by the sight of her pink nipples brushing the rough bronze hair of his chest.

They were making love in the light. In the middle of the afternoon, she thought wonderingly. She could see him, his square muscled torso above the navy of his uniform pants. Touch him, if she wanted. She wanted to touch him everywhere.

"Let's move this to the bedroom," he rasped.

She jerked. The rifle was in her bedroom. Maddox had told her it was illegal for a felon to transport a gun. She wasn't going to break the law by driving around with one in her trunk. Not that she was crazy about hiding one in her bedroom, either. Maddox didn't seem set on conducting a search of her closets, but still...

"No," she said. "Here. Right here. Right now."

His eyes fired, but he shook his head. "Let's take it easy. I need to slow down."

She smiled at him, her insides humming. Her mouth felt sore. She felt wonderful. "No, you don't."

"I don't want to—"

"—shock me?" She lay back against the carpet, supporting herself on her elbows. "You could try," she suggested hopefully.

His breath hissed out. He dug in his slacks for his wallet and pulled out a foil packet. And then he was kissing her again, her breasts, her belly, lower, licking, hot, until she writhed and arched and cried out. He dragged up his head, his face hard and intense. He moved up and over her. His thighs pushed her legs apart.

"Right here." He gave her words back to her. "Right now."

She shivered as she reached for him. He was heavy on top of her. He was deep inside of her. He touched her everywhere, inside and out. He thrust hard, but it wasn't rough. It was raw and real and fast and sweaty, and every time it felt like too much, she looked up and saw Maddox's burning eyes and the planes of his face, hard and gleaming. He was losing himself in her, not holding back, not in control, reassuring and exciting her at once.

She had never felt so safe.

She had never felt so loved.

She had never felt so free.

This time she didn't wait for the wave to take her. This time she swam out for it. She could feel the muscles of his back flex under her palms, feel the muscles of his arms and the rigid wall of his abdomen as he came into her again and again. She gripped hard, gripped him, felt him pulse and pound inside her, and she pulsed, too, with his rhythm, pulsed and shuddered and cried out "Oh" as the wave crashed and her ears roared and Maddox held her steady with his eyes.

"Annie," he said, just her name, naming her. Seeing her. Loving her. And then his dark eyes squeezed shut, and his head reared back, and he gave himself all the way to her.

Ann lay under him, stroking his damp back, her breath uneven and her bottom raw against the carpet, and wondered how soon she could have this again.

His head dropped forward, and he exhaled, warm and gusty across her breasts. They puckered. He touched one nipple, very delicately, with his finger, and she shivered.

He lifted an eyebrow. "Okay?"

She moistened her lips and smiled. "Very okay. Can we do it again?"

"Okay." He let himself relax more fully against her, letting her take a portion of his weight. "Just give me a little time to recover. A year, maybe, and I'll be good as new."

Now that she'd found this, she didn't want to ever let it go. "I can't wait that long."

"I'll stick around," he promised, his eyes warm. "We could find something to do in the meantime. How long does it take to get a license in North Carolina?"

Her stomach caved, and it wasn't from the weight of him, hard and lovely above her.

"License?" she croaked.

"Yeah. Marriage license."

When she collected her thoughts, when she found her voice again, she said, as firmly as she could, "We are not getting married."

Panic flared in Maddox. She sounded so, so inflexible. Annie, who was soft and giving and tenderhearted and everything he needed in his life. He fought to keep from overreacting.

Do not screw this up, he ordered himself. You are not going to screw this up.

Unless he already had.

He pushed the thought away. "We're not?" he asked cautiously.

She shook her head. Her smooth hair brushed the inside of his forearm, distracting him. She was lying under him, pink and warm from his loving, telling him "no."

"Why not?"

She thrust out her chin. "I've been married. This is better."

He could feel his temper rising, feel the tension collecting in the back of his neck. He wanted a cigarette, and not because it was after sex. He fought to keep his face neutral. "So, what is 'this'?"

"Well…" Her lashes swept down as she considered. Then she looked straight at him with her gorgeous green eyes and said, "This is two adults who are free to make their own choices coming together without obligations."

She sounded more like a psychologist than the woman he'd just loved. "In other words, two uncommitted people having sex."

Her tongue moistened her lower lip. "That's not what I meant."

"Well, excuse me, but it sounded pretty damned uncommitted to me."

"And what about you? What about your job?"

He levered his weight off her. His body protested the separation. "What about it?"

She turned on her side away from him, reaching for her blouse. "You're the one leaving town. You can't expect me to just pack up and follow you to Atlanta."

"I don't," he protested.

But Annie was on a roll. "Aside from the fact that I'm on probation, I have a job, I have my son— What did you say?"

"I'd stay here," he explained as patiently as he could while his insides churned. "In Cutler." The idea had some appeal, now that he'd actually said it. "It wouldn't be so bad."

"Not…so bad," she said.

"No," he said, warming to the possibilities. "I'm getting along all right with the old man. The job—the whole community angle—has gone better than I expected. I could make a life here."

"And I'd fit into your new life," she said flatly.

What was she upset about? Of course she'd fit in. She was everything he'd ever wanted. "Well, sure."

She shook her head. "I'm only finally finding myself. I don't want to lose myself in another relationship."

Pure frustration tightened his chest. He sat up, too. How could they be arguing? He was still half naked. "What the hell does that mean? You think I want to change you?"

"I don't know what I think," Ann said. "That's part of the problem."

Maddox sucked in his breath. "So, how long is this little voyage of self-discovery going to take? Three months? One year? Five?"

"I don't know," she repeated, adding with a flash of spirit, "I don't 'do' recovery on a timetable."

"Yeah, well, I don't do relationships on a timetable, either." He was badgering her like a hostile witness. He made an effort to be calm, to be patient and understanding, but it was hard when everything inside him screamed to storm the barricades she'd raised against him. "I'm ready now. And I think you are, too. You were there just now. You were with me."

She colored. "This isn't about sex."

"I didn't say it was sex. I'm asking you to marry me."

"And I think we should wait."

"Wait for what?"

"Until we get to know each other better."

"We've known each other for twenty-three years."

"And you've been away for twelve."

"But you know me!" Unless, oh God, unless that was the problem. Unless she didn't want to tie her life to the sullen hood in Rob's shadow, a big, rough cop who'd left his last job after shooting somebody else's kid. "What more do you think we're going to find out by waiting?"

She put her little chin up, her blouse hanging open over

her small, perfect breasts. "I won't be rushed into making another mistake."

Her words hit with the force of a punch to the gut. "And you think marriage to me would be a mistake."

"Marriage to anyone could be a disaster."

"Not if you loved me. Not if you goddamn trusted me."

"I can't trust myself," she burst out.

He ached for her. Her face was white and strained, her eyes enormous and hurt. With his head, he understood that living with abuse had enormous emotional and psychological consequences. But in his heart, he needed her to love him enough to take a chance.

"So, what now?" he asked quietly. "You want to cool things, is that it?"

"I want…time."

"You figure maybe you should look around?"

Her hands twisted in her lap, but she looked him straight in the eye. "I'm not looking for anybody else. But it has to be my choice," she said.

"Yeah. You've got a right to your choices." He stood, jerking on his belt buckle, while everything inside him roared and crumbled like a building going down in flames. "My mistake for thinking you'd choose me."

A headache throbbed behind Ann's eyes. Her heart pulsed in miserable agreement. It had been a long, long day. Since Maddox left her, she'd gone through the motions, picking up Mitchell, making dinner, sorting the laundry and recycling. She couldn't wait for it to be over.

Why? a small voice jeered inside her. *So you can go to bed alone?*

Shut up, she told the voice, but even being rude didn't cheer her since Maddox had walked out of her house.

She was reaching for the front door chain to lock up for the night when a noise behind her made her jump and jerk around.

Her son stood on the stairs, still in dirty shorts and a camp T-shirt.

"Mitchell!" Her voice was sharp. Too sharp. She fought to moderate it. "Why aren't you in bed yet?"

He dragged his foot along the edge of one step. "I don't have any clean pajamas."

She raised her eyebrows. "And this is enough to keep you up forty minutes past your bedtime?"

He ducked his head and shrugged.

Ann sighed. She tried hard to provide Mitchell with discipline and routine. But he looked so endearing with his straight fair hair flopping into his face and his feet hanging over the edge of the step. He was growing. Maybe he was outgrowing the cocoon she wanted to keep him in? And it was good—wasn't it?—that her son felt confident enough now to act out sometimes.

Maybe she ought to be more like him.

"My room," she said. "The laundry basket is on the bed. Scoot."

He scooted, and she turned back to the door.

Locking up alone, jumping at noises. It was no kind of life.

She squared her shoulders. Think positive. The therapist in Chapel Hill was always telling her to count her accomplishments. After ten years of living under Rob's control, she was safe. She was free. Free from fear, free to make her own choices...

The memory of Maddox's deep voice shook the militant, upbeat cadence of her thoughts. *You've got a right to your choices. My mistake for thinking you'd choose me.*

Her heart squeezed. She wasn't free at all. She was still controlled by fear. Fear of the future. Fear of making a mistake. Fear that Maddox was offering her marriage as a prize for good behavior, because she fit some sort of picture he had of a new life in his old hometown.

He hadn't said he loved her.

Maybe that was her biggest fear of all.

Maybe she didn't deserve for him to love her.

But standing alone in the shadows of the hall, she thought of the way he'd said her name, his eyes burning into hers, his body joined with hers, his soul and his need naked in his eyes. *You are what I want. You've always been what I want.*

Why couldn't she believe him? Why should she make him wait and prove himself to her, the way he'd had to prove himself to everyone all his life?

She had never been any good at going after what she wanted. But she wanted Maddox.

Maybe it was time to confront her fear and tell him so.

Her heart was pounding, but that could be excitement. Her palms were sweating, but there was a hum in her blood now that might have been anticipation or the memory of Maddox naked and moving inside her.

She could call him. He was probably working, but she could dial 911. Let the dispatcher spread it all over town that Annie Barclay was tying up the police line chasing after Maddox Palmer.

She bit her lip. Silly. Maddox would worry if he got an emergency call to her house. She would leave a message. And if Wallace Palmer answered the phone, she would just tell him... Well, she didn't know what she would tell Maddox's father, but the older man probably knew perfectly well why she was calling his son at nine-thirty at night. The thought didn't bother her as much as it should have.

And anyway, when she called she got the machine.

Ann took a deep breath for courage and made her choice.

"Maddox, this is Annie. I've been thinking about what you said and—" Dear Lord. She couldn't answer a proposal of marriage over the phone. Especially if his father picked up his phone messages. "Can you call me when you get this? Or come over? Please come over," she said, surer now. "I love you."

She hung up, feeling suddenly certain. Both breathless and sure. Amazing how making one decision could percolate through your entire attitude. She could take on anything now. She wished Maddox would hurry. When did he get off duty? Ten?

It felt like an eternity, but really it was only about twenty minutes later that she heard the sounds of a car pulling into her driveway. Expectation bubbled through her.

A car door slammed. She heard footsteps coming up the walk and hurried to catch him before he could ring the bell and disturb Mitchell.

She tugged open the door. "I'm so glad you—"

Her voice died. Her heart died. The man waiting on her porch wasn't Maddox.

"Rob," she said flatly.

Maybe she should have dialed 911 after all.

Chapter 16

"You bitch," Rob said.

Alarm prickled up the backs of Ann's arms. He's not going to do anything, she rationalized. He's not going to risk an arrest for assault, not with his trial a few short weeks away. He'd threatened her with a custody battle, not his fists.

But as he swayed in the porch light, his head lowered, his jaw thrust forward, her hand tightened on the door.

Before she could make up her mind to slam it closed, Rob smacked it out of her grip and against the wall.

Fear ricocheted through her. Instinctively, she backed away as Rob followed the door in.

"Aren't you going to invite me in?" he mocked.

She drew a careful breath. She was not the old, cowed Annie. She could handle this. She would handle this. "It's late," she said. "Why don't you go home?"

"I don't have a home," he said, speaking with the precision of the very drunk. Dread curdled her stomach. He was bad on beer. Worse on bourbon. And not close enough—yet—for her to smell which was talking for him now. "I have a house. A very expensive house. An empty house, thanks to you." He took another step forward. This time she held her ground. "Why don't you ask me how my day was, dear?"

Her glance darted to the stairs. Dear Lord, please let Mitchell be in bed and asleep.

"All right," she said peaceably, her heart beating high in her throat. "How was your day?"

"It sucked. You wanna know why?"

She felt sure he was going to tell her. He was close enough now for her to smell his breath. Bourbon. She backed toward the living room, leading him away from her sleeping child. "If you want to share."

"Brent Wilks canceled our golf game. We've been friends for twenty years. He's a client. But after your little scene at the club Saturday night, he calls off a three o'clock tee time. What do you think about that?"

She didn't know what to think. At three o'clock she'd been getting rug burns on her fanny making love with Maddox. The memory gave her a moment's courage. But certainly she didn't believe that after all this time the town had decided to take her side against Rob's.

"Maybe something came up," she said.

Rob's face was red. "That's what I told myself, too. Only then I had dinner with my lawyer. Do you know what discovery is, Ann?"

"I—no." Should she try to reach the phone in the kitchen? No. She was supposed to stay out of the kitchen in an argument, because of the knives.

But Rob was still talking, still almost reasonable. "Discovery means the D.A. can't spring new evidence on my lawyer at trial."

She felt slow, her tongue thick, her mind frozen. He wanted something, he was getting at something, and she was too stupid to follow him. "If this is about my testimony—"

"Screw your testimony. I'm screwed. You screwed me."

She didn't stop being afraid, but she started to get angry. He would never accept responsibility, but she was sick of accepting blame. "Anything you've done, you've done to yourself. And I'd like you to leave now."

Immersed in his grievance, he didn't even hear her.

"He dug up evidence against me. Mad Dog. Went right into my golf bag at the club locker room. God knows who saw him. Who heard."

Rob sounded so bewildered. No wonder. He was seeing his life unravel before his eyes. His madras shirt and belted shorts were creased and sweaty. Ann fought an absurd urge to apologize for his spoiled game, his dirty laundry, his ruined life.

"Henry said they have a direct link to the arson now," he continued, pacing her living room. He turned. "It's all your fault. And I'll see you pay."

Her heart stumbled. *Don't panic. Stay calm.* "Pay for what?"

"You got him involved."

Maddox. He meant Maddox.

"I didn't." Her voice shook. The old Ann's voice. She bit her lip.

"You turned him against me. You turned everyone against me."

What did he want? Not her. To punish her. "Rob—"

He moved so fast that even though she was expecting it the blow was a shock. Pain exploded in her jaw, in her neck, in the back of her head as she flew off her feet and went down against the arm of the couch.

For a second she couldn't see anything but black with points of light, couldn't hear anything but the roaring in her ears. She started to curl—*In an attack, protect your head and stomach*—when something white moved on the floor into her line of vision. A sneaker.

Mitchell's sneakers.

Horrified, she dragged her gaze up to her nine-year-old

son, lurching forward with his rifle at the ready, sobbing, "Don't touch her. Don't you touch her. I'll shoot you."

I love you. She'd said it first. And he'd never said it at all. Maddox shook his head bemusedly as he sat at a stoplight. What a screw-up.

But it was hard to feel too upset with the memory of her lilting voice playing on his father's answering machine. And the second he got to Annie's house, he planned on telling her anything she wanted to hear. Now that he knew she loved him, he could wait for her another twelve years.

He grinned over the steering wheel. Of course, he hoped she had something sooner in mind.

He pulled onto her street. It was just after ten, and there were already two cars parked in Ann's driveway. That would give the lady in the bathrobe something to talk about.

Two cars. The observation stuck him like a prison knife.

Ann's rusting compact…and Rob's big blue Beemer.

The front door was open.

This was bad.

His heart stopped, but his brain didn't. And that was good, that at least some parts of him were working, taking over. Maddox accepted the numbing of his emotions, welcomed the cold settling in as he prepared to do his job. *Coordinate response, wait for cover, assess and stabilize the situation…*

If Rob hurt them, touched them, either one of them, he would kill the rat bastard.

"Request backup on a disturbance in progress, eight-two-five Hickory, that's eight-twenty-five Hickory—"

"Mad Dog?" Crystal sounded surprised. "You at Ann Cross's place?"

He was already sliding from the car, gun in hand. "That's affirm."

"Stand by."

"I'm going in."

The radio crackled with background noise, and then Crystal's voice came back, breathless with importance. "Chief requests that you wait for cover before making contact."

"Can't. I'm proceeding."

"The chief orders—"

He left the radio squawking behind him and glided up the walk, staying out of the path of the porch light.

Assess the situation. He could do that. The damn door was open. Light spilled from the living room window, but gauzy curtains obscured his view inside. No noise. No screams.

He crossed the porch low and quiet, feeling with his foot for the doormat, holding his gun at the ready. Edged to the door, and heard Rob say contemptuously, "What do you think you're doing, boy? Put down the damn gun."

Mitchell's voice answered, high, hysterical. "No! Get away from her."

Sweat ran on Maddox's forehead, although his lungs felt frozen. A child with a gun. His worst nightmare. And somewhere inside, Annie.

Pop. Pop. Pop. The memory shuddered through him. *A woman, a teacher, throwing herself down to shield the screaming child on the ground. And the boy, the shooter, weight back on his right leg, shoulder pointing toward his target...*

Maddox yanked himself back. Cold sweat collected above his belt. He could not see into the living room. He moved closer.

"I'm not going anywhere till you put down the gun," Rob said.

The sickening click of a rifle lever answered him.

Ann's soft voice played in Maddox's brain. *Rob has a gun. Two guns, if you count the hunting rifle he bought for Mitchell.*

Damn.

Maddox angled his body against the doorjamb. He could see Mitchell now through the living room arch. The rifle barrel trembled in the boy's hands, but his back was straight, his weight balanced correctly on his rear leg. At three yards, there wasn't much chance he'd miss. Hell, at that range, he'd blow a hole through his father the size of a basketball.

Maddox pushed the door open slightly with his foot, widening his view of the room to include Rob, swaying and sweating by the couch. No sign of Annie.

Stabilize the situation. Don't startle the kid into firing. Maddox flowed back down the steps, out of the line of fire. He was no good to anybody dead.

"Mitchell," he called softly. "It's Sergeant Palmer. Maddox. Everything okay?"

The rifle barrel wavered and then leveled at Rob's chest. "He hurt her. Mom's hurt."

His gut constricted. "All right. I'll take care of her. I'll call an ambulance, okay? You want to put down that gun."

"No!"

"Yeah, you do," he said gently, firmly, while everything inside him raged and shook. The kid couldn't live with his father's blood on his hands. Annie wouldn't be able to live… God, let her be alive. Maddox nudged the door open and came in, gun at the ready. "I'm coming in. You want to let me take care of it. I'm here now. Everything's okay."

The big lie.

"I want him to get away from her." Hysteria edged Mitchell's voice.

Her. Annie. He could see her now, lying on the floor, small and crumpled between the arm of the shabby couch and her ex-husband's feet. Her upraised arm shielded her face so that he couldn't see the damage Rob had done.

Cold rage steamed inside him. "Stand away," he ordered Rob in a low tone.

Rob looked from the .38 in Maddox's grip to the rifle wavering in his son's arms. "Get real."

Maddox clenched his jaw tight enough to send pain shooting through his skull. On the floor, Annie moaned and stirred. Alive, then. Thank God.

"Come on, Rob," he said. "We're the adults here. Move away from her, and Mitchell will put down the gun."

"Screw you. She's my wife, and he's my son."

Mitchell jerked.

Maddox cursed silently. "This is not what you'd call a stable situation. Let's not make things any worse."

"How can it get worse?" Rob demanded. "My life is ruined."

This moron could goad his kid into shooting him. That would make it worse. For Mitchell. And for Ann.

"You just let me handle things," Maddox said, dividing his words between Rob and Mitchell, trying not to focus on Ann on the floor. She'd raised her head and laid it down again. One quick glance showed him her split lip, her glazed eyes. Concussion? "It's going to be okay now."

He took another step into the room, Sergeant Cool, like he had an entire SWAT team at his back. Like he wasn't scared deep in his gut and his bones. Like he didn't see the ghosts of his failure, another woman's body, another child's face, swimming in front of his eyes.

"Come on, sport, put down the gun."

The barrel wavered. "I didn't want him to hurt her."

"Yeah. You were looking out for her. I know."

"Is she going to be all right?"

"Sure." God, he hoped so. "We'll get the paramedics to look at her in just a minute. Put the gun down now."

Mitchell's shoulders trembled with the weight of the rifle, with the consequences of his next choice. Maddox held his breath, willing the boy to do the right thing, praying that Rob had sense enough to keep his fat mouth shut.

Mitchell swallowed. His green eyes—Annie's eyes—turned to Maddox with a heartbreaking mix of trust and fear. And then slowly, slowly, he lowered the rifle. Maddox held the child's gaze, doing his best to broadcast confidence and reassurance while the tension inside him stretched to the screaming point.

The gun butt drifted to the floor. Relief swallowed Maddox's brief flare of satisfaction.

And then Rob lunged, ducking under the shelter of his son's body, and snatched the gun, and straightened with it on his shoulder before Maddox could squeeze off a shot that wouldn't hit Mitchell or Ann on the floor.

He grinned down the barrel at Maddox's frozen face of surprise. "Thanks, MD. I knew you'd always protect the quarterback."

Maddox died inside. Very quietly, he said, "Get out of the house, Mitchell. Now."

The boy started. Moved toward the door.

The rifle jerked in Rob's hand. "Uh-uh. You stay."

"Put down the gun, Rob."

"Oh, I will. Right after I blow a hole in you. And then I can do whatever I want to the two of them. Think about that while you're dying, buddy."

Sweat greased Maddox's grip on his gun. He was going to have to shoot. Despair hollowed his gut. With merciless precision, his mind replayed a slow-motion memory of a child falling in an Atlanta schoolyard.

"You don't want to kill a police officer, Rob. That's the death penalty for sure."

"What have I got to live for? You wrecked my life, you bastard. It'll be a pleasure to take you with me."

He was going to have to shoot, Ann thought.

The knowledge sank into her, drifting through the layers of pain and dizziness and nausea to strike some buried core of compassion. She didn't want to feel. It hurt too much. Her neck, her jaw, her head burned and throbbed. She wanted to close her eyes again and have it all be over.

But with her cheek pressed to the carpet, she watched Maddox waver in and out of focus through Rob's ankles. Tanned ankles, sockless in Italian shoes. Two Maddoxes, looming dark and perpendicular above her. He was wearing his granite cop face, but she could see the dreadful weight of decision in his eyes.

He would save them. At a terrible cost. The burden he'd spared Mitchell he would take on himself, shooting his old teammate to protect her.

Her heart tore. She couldn't help him. She couldn't lift her own head. How could she help him?

Rob was speaking, his voice goading. She shut him out, concentrating on dragging her arm in, inch by inch. Under the skirt of the couch, her spread fingers brushed something rough and cool and metallic. A Droid. One of Mitchell's Droids, with spear and claws. She closed her hand around it, ignoring the bite in her palm, and rolled her head to rest her brow on the rough carpet. Pain drove a thick spike through her skull. She ignored that, too. Another inch. Two. Hurry. Help.

She got her elbow under her and levered her weight onto her shoulder. Her stomach lurched into her throat. She could do this. She could. For Mitchell. For Maddox. For herself.

Trembling, she lifted her head. She raised her arm. She drew one shaky breath and drove the pointy metal toy as hard as she could into Rob's hairy, muscled calf.

He howled, and the living room exploded. His heel crashed back. Ann's head flew against the padded base of the couch. She heard a boom—the gun—oh, God, *Mitchell...* and then something heavy smashed into her legs and rolled away. She tasted blood. Dimly, she saw the two men struggling on the floor. Her ears ringing with the gunshot, she heard Maddox grunt and Mitchell sob and Rob swear. The acrid stink of powder burned her nostrils. The carpet vibrated under her cheek as arms and legs thudded against the floor.

And then warm, hard hands grasped her shoulders, supported her head.

''Annie.'' Maddox's voice, rough and urgent, called her

from the edge of oblivion. Maddox's face, tense and pale, swam in her vision. Sirens wailed at the border of consciousness.

She licked her lips, wincing at the tiny sting. "Mitchell?"

His grip tightened reassuringly. "He's fine. Rob's in cuffs."

Her chest eased. Safe. Her son and her love, both safe. The room smelled like the Fourth of July.

She smiled into his deep-set eyes. "I got him," she confided. "I stabbed him with the Avenger Droid."

Maddox laughed shakily. "Is that what you did?"

She nodded, well pleased with herself, and let the darkness take her.

Wallace Palmer hung up the phone. "The D.A.'s going for attempted murder, first degree," he announced with grim delight.

Maddox kept typing. God, he hated reports. "So now I should be thankful the gun went off when Annie stuck him in the ankle with a boy toy?"

The chief narrowed his eyes. "Don't get cute, MD. It was clearly stated intent with sufficient time for deliberation."

That was one way of looking at it. "How long?"

"With his priors, maybe twenty-five years. If the judge orders consecutive sentences, which Brailsford will, Rob Cross will go away for the rest of his natural life."

Maddox allowed himself a moment's bleak satisfaction. He'd failed to stop Rob from hurting Annie, but at least he could protect her with his testimony.

"What about Mitchell?" he asked.

"Your statement satisfied the D.A. that the boy was acting in defense of home."

"In defense of his mother," Maddox said.

"He only found the gun because he was looking for clean pajamas. He didn't want to shoot."

''Well, you persuaded the D.A. No charges against the child or his mother.''

Maddox grunted. He didn't want to talk about it. Muddied by emotion, distracted by Annie, focused on Mitchell, he'd screwed up. Again. He didn't wait for backup. He didn't secure the weapon. Rob should never have gotten his hands on the gun in the first place.

But the chief, unfortunately, was in a chatty mood. Propping his broad butt on the corner of Maddox's desk, he asked, ''How is she?''

Pointless to pretend he didn't know who his father was talking about. Maddox rolled another piece of paper into the typewriter. ''Better. I called the hospital. They released her Wednesday.''

''You haven't been to see her?''

Maddox gritted his teeth. ''I saw her when she was admitted.''

''Four days ago? Not since then?''

He fought the knife twist in his gut. ''No.''

''Why the hell not?''

''I'm giving her *time*.'' The word was a bad taste in his mouth.

''Time for what, for God's sake?''

Time to heal. Time to—what had she said?—finally find herself. Time to figure out if she wanted to spend the rest of her life with a man who'd failed to protect her.

I won't be rushed into making another mistake.

Maddox reached for the cigarettes on his desk. ''Time to recover. She's just been through a major trauma, Dad.''

His father regarded him with exasperation. ''All the more reason for you to be with her. Anyway, how much time do you think you have? You're going back to Atlanta in another week.''

''I'm not going back to Atlanta. I've resigned from the department.''

The chief was visibly shaken. "Look, MD, if this is about that shooting incident—"

Sudden affection for the old man swamped him. "No, I'm okay with that." And he was, he realized with gratitude. Annie and Mitchell had helped him to face and defeat that particular demon. "I just want to stay in Cutler."

"And do what?"

Maddox gave his father a level look. "There's an opening in the sheriff's department."

The chief bridled. "You called George Wilkerson?"

Maddox allowed himself a thin smile. The chief had always protected his jurisdiction fiercely. "He called me."

"Well, hell, boy, I know what the county pays. You might as well work for me."

Maddox raised his eyebrows. "Is that a job offer?"

"Yes, it is. You're a damn fine officer, MD."

Despite his worries over Annie, Maddox felt something ease inside him. "It's a good department."

"Then what do you say?"

"Yes. I say yes."

He stuck out his hand. His father gripped it tightly. Their hands clasped and tugged, sealing their awkward, strong connection.

The chief cleared his throat uncomfortably. "Good. Glad to have that settled. I'm not getting any younger, you know."

"Bull. You'll probably outlive us all."

"Still, the department can use somebody with your experience. And so can that nice woman."

Jeez. "I don't think so, Dad."

"Why don't you let her decide?"

"Damn it, that's what I'm trying to do."

Crystal stuck her beauty-queen mane through the door. "Somebody here to see you, Mad Dog."

"Tell 'em I went home," he growled.

But then he saw who trailed the dispatcher into the office,

and from somewhere he dragged his best Officer Friendly smile and pasted it on.

"Hey, sport," he said.

But Mitchell wasn't won over so easily. Fixing Maddox with accusing green eyes, he said, "I need to talk with you."

Hell. Everybody was chatty today. But this was Mitchell. Annie's boy. Maddox couldn't turn him away.

He stabbed out his cigarette in his overflowing ashtray. "Shoot."

Mitchell's gaze flickered to the chief. "It's kind of private."

Wallace Palmer coughed. "I'll be in my office if you, um—"

"Thanks, Dad," Maddox said dryly.

He waited until the door had closed behind the chief before he pushed out the chair opposite his with the sole of his shoe, silently inviting the boy to sit.

"Okay," he said. "Let's have it."

Mitchell sat, a thin, intense boy with his mother's courage and his mother's eyes. Maddox's chest squeezed with sudden longing for all the things he couldn't lay claim to. Time, he reminded himself. Annie needed time.

"Are you mad at me?" Mitchell asked.

Maddox straightened, making his inadequate desk chair creak under him. "Hell, no."

"Because I know what I did was wrong. If I didn't get, you know, the rifle, then—"

"Hey." Maddox stopped him with one broad hand. "You were trying to protect your mother. That wasn't a bad thing. It's just there are better ways to do it. You don't pick up a gun. You—"

"—call a policeman." Mitchell's head bobbed. "Mom told me."

His chagrined tone suggested Annie had told him more than once in the past few days. Maddox cleared his throat. "That's right."

"I'm just trying to look out for her."

"Sometimes that's not so easy."

The boy scowled. "You said you wouldn't hurt her."

Maddox thought he couldn't feel any worse. He was wrong. "I know," he said painfully. "I'm sorry. I should have been there. I should have reacted faster."

But Mitchell only shook his head, fierce and unforgiving. "You said you wouldn't hurt her, but you don't come see us anymore. If you're not mad at me, why don't you come see us?"

Hell. Maddox stared at the boy.

"She cried last night," Mitchell confided.

That did it. Maddox's chair shrieked as he pushed back from his desk. "Chief!"

His father appeared in the door. "What is it?"

Maddox peeled a couple of dollars out of his pocket and tossed them on top of the pile of reports. "Mitchell's going to stay with you awhile. Buy him candy, buy him Coke, but don't take him home for at least an hour, okay?"

"Where are you going?"

"I've got something to take care of."

"About time," the chief said with satisfaction.

Maddox couldn't have agreed with him more.

But when he pulled to the curb in front of Annie's house, he turned off the engine and sat for a moment observing the quiet, sunlit street. In the tree above him, a bird with more feathers than brains was chirping its little heart out.

He would have felt more at ease going into a crack house without backup.

He got out of the car.

The gate to the backyard stood open. Through the chain link fence, he could see Annie stooping in front of a bed of pink and yellow flowers. He paused on the walk to admire the graceful set of her shoulders, the delicate line of her neck, her pretty hair pulled back in some sort of clasp thingy....

He frowned. Didn't she know better than to work in this heat without a hat? She had a concussion, for God's sake.

He reached the gate in three quick strides. She looked up at the sound of his footsteps, and the wary expression in her eyes, the sight of her jaw gone from purple to yellow and the stitches in her bottom lip, made something inside him twist and bleed.

"Hello, Annie," he said quietly.

Dear Lord, he'd come back.

Ann sat back on her heels, with the grass tickling her knees and the sun in her eyes, and stared up at Maddox. He looked good, tall and broad against the light, with a cellophane-wrapped pot in his hands and a hooded, hungry look that did funny things to her stomach.

She put her hands to her hair. "Of course, you would show up now," she said resignedly.

She thought he winced. He laid a hand on the gate and came in. "Sorry. I know you didn't want to see me yet."

What was he talking about? "No. It's just for the past four days I've showered and dressed and made up my face and waited in my living room like a nice girl for you to come see me. And you never did. So when I've finally given up on you, and I'm covered in dirt and bug spray, here you are."

He was too tall, and she was at too much of a disadvantage. She climbed to her feet. Swayed.

He stepped forward quickly, cupping her elbow with his free hand. His palm was warm and callused. "You shouldn't stand up so fast."

She wasn't about to tell him it wasn't standing that made her flushed and dizzy. Or the heat. It was him. "Thank you, Dr. Palmer. I can take care of myself."

He released her arm. "Sure, you can."

He couldn't even bear to touch her, she thought miserably. "What are you doing here, anyway?"

"I came to see you."

"Well, that makes a nice change. Pretty bad, aren't I?"

"Annie, don't. You look—" His fingers touched her jaw tenderly. Gently, he turned her face to the light. His look was a caress. "Beautiful," he whispered.

Regret burned at the back of her eyes. She wanted to fall into him, into his strong, hard chest and his warm, rough voice and the promise of his eyes. But of course she couldn't do that. He didn't want that.

He cleared his throat, proffering the little pot. "I brought you these."

Flowers.

She fought a shiver of aversion. Rob used to buy her flowers, at least in the beginning. Red roses when they were dating and on all the morning-afters, showy apologies without scent or meaning. Blood bouquets.

Maddox brought her pentas growing in a pot, pink star-shaped clusters. "I didn't know what else to bring," he said roughly. "I figured your jaw was still sore, so candy was out. Wine...I didn't know if you could take alcohol with painkillers. Flowers seemed safe. Besides, the color made me think of you."

They weren't safe. But they would be. Flowers from Maddox meant something. She just didn't know what. She looked again from the delicate pink flowers to his frustrated face, and tried not to mind so much that he was only doing his duty.

"They're lovely." She accepted the pot. Forced a smile. "Well, now that you've made your delivery, I guess you can go."

His mouth compressed. "In a hurry to get rid of me?"

She felt her chin tremble and stuck it out. "I don't want you coming around just because you feel guilty."

"I do feel guilty. Annie—"

Quickly, she added, "It's all right. I'm responsible for my own feelings." She moved toward the porch, away from the temptation of his hot, solid body. "Things are pretty complicated now with Mitchell. And the trial. Cops can't consort with felons. I understand if under the circumstances you don't feel the same anymore."

He glared at her. "You can't think that."

"What am I supposed to think?" she asked crossly. Her jaw hurt. Her head ached. And her heart was breaking. "I tell you I love you, and you take a hike."

"You told me you needed time, damn it. My staying away has nothing to do with my feelings for you."

She set the pot down on the porch and faced him, crossing her arms. "Then why did you say you feel guilty?"

"Because I let you get hurt," he snapped.

Dear Lord, he meant it. The knot in her chest loosened. Dear, responsible Maddox. His granite cop face was set and unhappy. His back was stiff with stress.

She frowned. And his determination to assume blame was going to ruin everything.

"I don't need you to protect me," she said softly, deliberately. "I need you to love me."

His hooded eyes blazed. He took a stride toward her, quickly checked, and her brief flare of hope died. "I haven't earned the right yet. I wasn't there when you needed me."

Goodness, he was stubborn. Well, Annie had learned that she could be stubborn, too.

"Close enough," she said.

"You're the one who saved my sorry butt." Wry humor curved his mouth. Touched her heart. "You and that toy robot."

"It was the Avenger Droid." He had a lot to learn. She only prayed she would be the one to teach him.

"Whatever. The point is, I let you and Mitchell down."

"Why? Because you didn't come in with guns blazing? You saved me, Maddox. You saved my son when you talked him into laying down that rifle. Mitchell needs to see that a strong man doesn't have to be violent. And I can't think of a better role model for him than you."

He shook his head, but she could see the desperate longing in his eyes. "Maybe you should think some more. I'm a screw-up, Annie."

"Once upon a time, maybe. Neither of us is the same person we were twelve years ago. I'm not a teenager with a crush on the town bad boy. I don't need to be protected for my own good. I know what I want."

He stuck his fists in his pockets. "And is that what you want?" he asked steadily. "A role model for Mitchell?"

Emotion clogged her throat. Didn't he see? Didn't he know? "If that's all I can have. What do *you* want?"

His need was naked in his eyes. "You know what I want. I want you, Annie. I've always wanted you."

All her doubts disappeared, and joy rose up to take their place.

"Come and get me, then," she whispered.

He swooped fast enough to make her dizzy. But his big, square hands, cupping her face, were tender enough to break a girl's heart.

"I want marriage, too," he warned her. "But I can wait until you're sure. I love you, Annie."

She smiled with all the love and trust in her heart and quoted back at him. "How long can you wait? Three months? One year? Five?"

His brows drew together. "Well, I—"

"Because I'll need a week to buy my wedding dress, and Val can't organize a reception in less than three."

His answering smile started deep in his eyes, a lazy, sexy smile that made her blood pound. "I think maybe I can hold out for three weeks," he said, and kissed her.

With concentrated gentleness, he touched his lips to her unbroken upper lip and then the corners of her mouth. His breath flowed warm across her sensitive stitched skin, making her shiver with surprise and need. His big hands framing her face, he feathered comfort kisses along her aching jaw, butterfly kisses on her cheek. He worked around her bruised and battered face with exquisite tenderness.

Ann sighed and arched into him, into his hot, hard, powerful body. She was melting. He was rigid with restraint and desire. Oh, my, she thought dizzily.

He lifted his head, breathing hard. "Three weeks," he growled.

She pressed her lips together to hold the bubbling joy inside, to keep the taste of him on her mouth.

"Two," she suggested. "I'll be better by then."

And Maddox laughed.

Epilogue

Fourth of July, one year later

The parade was over. The Cutler Cougars marching band had packed up their instruments. From the trumpet-shaped loudspeakers atop the picnic shelter "I'm Proud To Be an American" drifted over the park, a patriotic accompaniment to shouts from the field races and squeals from the dunking booth.

Ann's blouse clung to her in the ninety-degree heat. Her feet were swollen in their neat, flat sandals, but her heart was as light as the blue balloon floating over the tops of the trees. Pressed in a corridor of sweating, whooping parents, she clapped as a sturdy seven-year-old pelted over the finish line under the steady regard of her father's camcorder.

Ann glanced back to the start a hundred yards away, where the older children milled around, waiting for their race. There was Mitchell, his fair hair plastered to his head, his thin face anxious as he scanned the assembled parents.

A tiny pang pierced Ann's happiness. Did her son even see her? Or was he looking for somebody else?

His therapist had advised that Mitchell have no more contact with his father than he wanted—and so far, he hadn't wanted any. But with Rob in prison for what would probably be the rest of his life, Ann figured Mitchell had plenty of time to come to terms with his father's guilt. After Rob was convicted of arson and attempted murder, Mitchell had soldiered on. His grades remained steady. At home, he was quiet and obedient. Too quiet, Ann thought.

But recently, he seemed to be coming out of his shell. Stretching at the starting line, his friend Sam leaned over and whispered in his ear. Mitchell nodded, giving her a quick thumbs-up.

"Sorry I'm late." Maddox's big arms came around Ann from behind. His rough voice was warm and amused. "Got caught up with some teenagers who decided to see how far the hose on the fire truck extended."

"Oh, my." She leaned back against her husband, loving the feel of his broad, hard chest against her shoulder blades, enjoying his solid support. "Everyone all right?"

"You bet. And that truck's gonna be real shiny by the time they're done waxing."

Ann laughed, reveling in the heat at her back, the strength of the arms around her. And then she straightened as the president of the Rotary Club stepped to the line with his tiny pistol. "They're starting."

"Looks like it." Maddox's voice was still lazy and amused. But the arms holding her tightened.

Mitchell took his place in the lineup, eyes on the ground, face pale with excitement. Ann tensed in sympathy, remembering past athletic humiliations.

"It's only a race," Maddox said reassuringly over her head.

"I know that."

"Yeah, but did you know that when I hold you like this I can see down your blouse?"

Ann went warm with pleasure. "Stop it," she scolded. But she didn't want him to stop. She didn't want ever to lose the suggestive, tender, private conversations bad boy Maddox Palmer carried on with her in public—or the way he made good on his teasing when they got home.

The starting pistol cracked. The line surged raggedly as twenty-seven nine-and ten-year-olds bolted over the withered grass and their parents shrieked encouragement.

"Come on, Taylor!"

"Run, Brittany!"

"Mitchell," Ann whispered under her breath.

And there he was, at the front of the pack, his long legs stretching, his wiry arms pumping, a look of absolute determination on his face.

"Go, sport!" Maddox roared, and the boy threw himself forward and over the finish line.

First.

Ann jumped up and down in surprised delight. "He won!"

"Damn straight," Maddox said.

She turned to look at him, but he only grinned down at her with such obvious pride and pleasure that her heart eased. And then her boy was pushing toward them through the crowd of parents and children, his face red, his hair rumpled.

The words tumbled out before he could even reach her.

"Oh, Mitchell! I'm so pr—"

He beamed, but his eyes went past her to Maddox. "Did you see me? I put my head up at the end just like you told me, and I won. I *won,* Dad."

Joy seized Ann by the throat. Tears started to her eyes. Maddox stepped forward, extending his powerful arm to pull Mitchell to him and hold him tightly against his shoulder. His own eyes were glistening.

''You sure did, son,'' he said gruffly. ''You sure did.''

Mitchell flung his arms around Maddox's broad torso. As she stared at the two fair heads so close together, Ann's heart was so full she thought it might burst.

Sam came up to them, her dark ponytail bouncing on her neck. ''Nice race, Mitch. Guess I owe you an ice cream.''

Mitchell lifted his head and grinned. ''Nice race, Sam. And you owe me an ice cream.''

Maddox's shoulders shook with suppressed laughter. He straightened, reaching for his wallet. ''How about you let it be my treat.''

Pulling out a five, he handed it to the girl.

''Gee, thanks, Sergeant Palmer.''

''Thanks, Dad.''

They ran off.

Ann smiled. ''Nice job, *Dad*.''

Maddox colored with equal pleasure and embarrassment. ''He never called me that before.''

''I know.'' She touched his cheek, ignoring the indulgent glances of the people around them. He slid his arms around her, turning his lips into her palm.

''Better get used to it,'' she said. ''I'd say you've got seven months.''

He went very still. ''Annie...are you sure?''

Anticipation brimmed inside her. ''As sure as I can be. I'm not very far along. Six weeks? Eight?''

''Oh, God.'' He closed his eyes and rested his forehead on hers.

''Maddox?''

He opened his eyes, and his hooded gaze was so deep and loving her heart wept with joy. ''I'm just happy, Annie. You make me incredibly happy.''

She smiled with tender understanding. ''It takes me that way sometimes, too. I have everything I ever wanted with you. I'm still not used to it.''

His slow, rare grin ignited as he quoted back at her. "Better get used to it, Annie Palmer."

"Oh, I think I will," she said. "After all, we've got—"

"—all the time in the world," he promised her.

* * * * *

Silhouette

INTIMATE MOMENTS™

presents a riveting 12-book continuity series:

a Year of loving dangerously

Where passion rules and nothing is what it seems...

When dishonor threatens a top-secret agency, the brave
men and women of SPEAR are prepared to risk it all as they
put their lives—and their hearts—on the line.

Available January 2001:

THE SPY WHO LOVED HIM
by Merline Lovelace

Although headstrong Margarita Alfonsa de las Fuentes was
mesmerized by Carlos Caballero's fearless courage, she wasn't
about to bow to *any* man. But now that a murderous traitor was hot
on their trail deep in the Central American jungle, the beautiful
secret spy struggled with the raw emotions Carlos's fierce
protectiveness stirred in her!

*Available only from Silhouette Intimate Moments
at your favorite retail outlet.*

Silhouette®

Where love comes alive™

Spines will tingle...mysteries await...
and dangerous passion lurks in the night
as *Reader's Choice* presents

DREAM SCAPES!

Thrills and chills abound in these four romances
welcoming readers to the dark side of love.
Available January 2001 at your
favorite retail outlet:

THUNDER MOUNTAIN
by Rachel Lee

NIGHT MIST
by Helen R. Myers

DARK OBSESSION
by Amanda Stevens

HANGAR 13
by Lindsay McKenna

Visit Silhouette at www.eHarlequin.com   RCDREAM01

If you enjoyed what you just read,
then we've got an offer you can't resist!

Take 2 bestselling love stories FREE!

Plus get a FREE surprise gift!

Don't miss this
great offer to save
on *New York Times*
bestselling author
Linda Howard's
touching love story

SARAH'S CHILD,

a must have for any
romance reader.

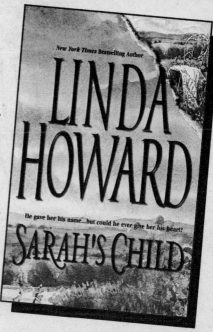

New York Times Bestselling Author

LINDA HOWARD

He gave her his name...but could he ever give her his heart?

SARAH'S CHILD

Available December 2000 wherever hardcovers are sold.

Don't miss this great offer to save on *New York Times* bestselling author Linda Howard's touching love story

SARAH'S CHILD,

a must have for any romance reader.

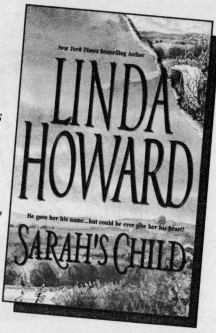

New York Times Bestselling Author

LINDA HOWARD

He gave her his name...but could he ever give her his heart?

SARAH'S CHILD

Available December 2000 wherever hardcovers are sold.

#1 *New York Times* bestselling author

NORA ROBERTS

brings you more of the loyal and loving,
tempestuous and tantalizing Stanislaski family.

Coming in February 2001

The Stanislaski Sisters

Natasha and Rachel

Though raised in the Old World traditions of their
family, fiery Natasha Stanislaski and cool, classy
Rachel Stanislaski are ready for a *new* world of love....

*And also available in February 2001 from
Silhouette Special Edition, the newest book in the
heartwarming Stanislaski saga*

CONSIDERING KATE

Natasha and Spencer Kimball's daughter Kate turns her
back on old dreams and returns to her hometown, where
she finds the *man* of her dreams.

Available at your favorite retail outlet.

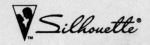

COMING NEXT MONTH

CMN1200